THE LEOPARD

ALSO BY GIUSEPPE DI LAMPEDUSA

Two Stories and a Memory

THE LEOPARD

Giuseppe di Lampedusa

Translated from the Italian
by Archibald Colquhoun

PANTHEON BOOKS, NEW YORK

Grateful acknowledgment is made
to Principessa Alessandra di Lampedusa
for her help in the translation.

A.C.

The Library of Congress Cataloged the First Printing
of this Title as Follows:

Tomasi di Lampedusa, Giuseppe, 1896–1957.

The leopard [by] Giuseppe di Lampedusa. Translated
from the Italian by Archibald Colquhoun.   [New York]
Pantheon [1960]
319p.   22 cm.
I. Title.
PZ4.T655Le   853.912   60–6794 rev ‡

ISBN 0-394-75668-1
[r62f1]

Manufactured in the United States of America

T HIS book opens when the Bourbon state of Naples and Sicily, called the Kingdom of the Two Sicilies, was about to end. King Ferdinand II ("Bomba") had just died; and the whole Italian peninsula would soon be one state for the first time since the fall of the Roman Empire.

The Risorgimento, as this movement for unification came to be known, had been gathering strength since the occupation of the North by the Austrians after the Napoleonic Wars, and had already come to a head once, in 1848. Leadership had now fallen mainly to Piedmont, the so-called Kingdom of Sardinia, ruled from Turin by Victor Emmanuel of Savoy, with Cavour as his Prime Minister.

Early in May, 1860, the popular hero Garibaldi, acting against Cavour's wishes, sailed from near Genoa with a thousand volunteers for Sicily, to win the island from the

Bourbons. The Redshirts, or "Garibaldini," landed at Marsala, defeated the Bourbon troops at Calatafimi, and within three weeks had occupied the capital, Palermo. Garibaldi, hailed as "Dictator" of Sicily, gathered more volunteers, crossed to the mainland, swept up the coast, and entered Naples in triumph. That autumn the Bourbon armies were defeated on the Volturno, the Piedmontese besieged the last Bourbon King, Francis II, in Gaeta, and Garibaldi handed over southern Italy to King Victor Emmanuel; he then withdrew to private life.

Plebiscites were held; every state in the peninsula agreed to join the new united Kingdom, except the Papal States, which were occupied, for reasons of internal French politics, by troops of Napoleon III. In 1862 Garibaldi tried to force this issue and march on Rome. But on the slopes of Aspromonte in Calabria his men were routed and he himself was wounded by Piedmontese troops.

This action by Italian government forces ended the revolutionary phase of the Risorgimento, which culminated officially in the declaration of Rome as capital of Italy in 1870.

A. C.

CONTENTS

1

Rosary and introduction to the Prince · The garden and the dead soldier · Royal audiences · Dinner · A carriage to Palermo · Going to Mariannina's · Conversation with Tancredi · In the office; estates and politics · In the observatory with Father Pirrone · Relaxation at luncheon · Don Fabrizio and the peasants · Don Fabrizio and his son Paolo · News of the landing, and Rosary again

NUNC ET IN HORA MORTIS NOSTRAE. AMEN.
The daily recital of the Rosary was over. For half an
hour the steady voice of the Prince had recalled the Glorious and the Sorrowful Mysteries; for half an hour other
voices had interwoven a lilting hum from which, now and
again, would chime some unlikely word: love, virginity,
death; and during that hum the whole aspect of the rococo
drawing room seemed to change; even the parrots spreading iridescent wings over the silken walls appeared abashed;
even the Magdalen between the two windows looked a
penitent and not just a handsome blonde lost in some dubi-
ous daydream, as she usually was.

Now, as the voices fell silent, everything dropped back
into its usual order or disorder. Bendicò, the great Dane,
vexed at having been shut out, came barking through the

door by which the servants had left. The women rose slowly to their feet, their oscillating skirts as they withdrew baring bit by bit the naked figures from mythology painted all over the milky depths of the tiles. Only an Andromeda remained covered by the soutane of Father Pirrone, still deep in extra prayer, and it was some time before she could sight the silvery Perseus swooping down to her aid and her kiss.

The divinities frescoed on the ceiling awoke. The troops of Tritons and Dryads, hurtling across from hill and sea amid clouds of cyclamen pink toward a transfigured Conca d'Oro,* and bent on glorifying the House of Salina, seemed suddenly so overwhelmed with exaltation as to discard the most elementary rules of perspective; meanwhile the major Gods and Goddesses, the Princes among Gods, thunderous Jove and frowning Mars and languid Venus, had already preceded the mob of minor deities and were amiably supporting the blue armorial shield of the Leopard. They knew that for the next twenty-three and a half hours they would be lords of the villa once again. On the walls the monkeys went back to pulling faces at the cockatoos.

Beneath this Palermitan Olympus the mortals of the House of Salina were also dropping speedily from mystic spheres. The girls resettled the folds in their dresses, exchanged blue-eyed glances and snatches of schoolgirl slang; for over a month, ever since the "riots" of the Fourth of April, they had been home for safety's sake from their

* Conca d'Oro, literally "Golden Shell," is the name of the hills encircling Palermo.

convent, and regretting the canopied dormitories and collective coziness of the Holy Redeemer. The boys were already scuffling with each other for possession of a medal of San Francesco di Paola; the eldest, the heir, the young Duke Paolo, was longing to smoke and, afraid of doing so in his parents' presence, was fondling the outside of his pocket in which lurked a braided-straw cigar case. His gaunt face was veiled in brooding melancholy; it had been a bad day: Guiscard, his Irish sorrel, had seemed off form, and Fanny had apparently been unable (or unwilling) to send him her usual lilac-tinted billet-doux. Of what avail then, to him, was the Incarnation of his Saviour?

Restless and domineering, the Princess dropped her rosary brusquely into her jet-fringed bag, while her fine crazy eyes glanced around at her slaves of children and her tyrant of a husband, over whom her diminutive body vainly yearned for loving dominion.

Meanwhile he himself, the Prince, had risen to his feet; the sudden movement of his huge frame made the floor tremble, and a glint of pride flashed in his light blue eyes at this fleeting confirmation of his lordship over both human beings and their works.

Now he was settling the huge scarlet missal on the chair which had been in front of him during his recitation of the Rosary, putting back the handkerchief on which he had been kneeling, and a touch of irritation clouded his brow as his eye fell on a tiny coffee stain which had had the presumption, since that morning, to fleck the vast white expanse of his waistcoat.

Not that he was fat; just very large and very strong; in houses inhabited by common mortals his head would touch the lowest rosette on the chandeliers; his fingers could twist a ducat coin as if it were mere paper; and there was constant coming and going between Villa Salina and a silversmith's for the mending of forks and spoons which, in some fit of controlled rage at table, he had coiled into a hoop. But those fingers could also stroke and handle with the most exquisite delicacy, as his wife Maria Stella knew only too well; and up in his private observatory at the top of the house the gleaming screws, caps, and studs of the telescopes, lenses, and "comet-finders" would answer to his lightest touch.

The rays of the westering sun, still high on that May afternoon, lit up the Prince's rosy skin and honey-colored hair; these betrayed the German origin of his mother, the Princess Carolina, whose haughtiness had frozen the easy-going Court of the Two Sicilies thirty years before. But in his blood also fermented other German strains particularly disturbing to a Sicilian aristocrat in the year 1860, however attractive his fair skin and hair amid all that olive and black: an authoritarian temperament, a certain rigidity in morals, and a propensity for abstract ideas; these, in the relaxing atmosphere of Palermo society, had changed respectively into capricious arrogance, recurring moral scruples, and contempt for his own relatives and friends, all of whom seemed to him mere driftwood in the languid meandering stream of Sicilian pragmatism.

In a family which for centuries had been incapable even

of adding up their own expenditures and subtracting their own debts he was the first (and last) to have a genuine bent for mathematics; this he had applied to astronomy, and by his work gained a certain official recognition and a great deal of personal pleasure. In his mind, now, pride and mathematical analysis were so linked as to give him an illusion that the stars obeyed his calculations too (as, in fact, they seemed to be doing) and that the two small planets which he had discovered ("Salina" and "Speedy" he had called them, after his main estate and a shooting dog he had been particularly fond of) would spread the fame of his family through the empty spaces between Mars and Jupiter, thus transforming the frescoes in the villa from the adulatory to the prophetic.

Between the pride and intellectuality of his mother and the sensuality and irresponsibility of his father, poor Prince Fabrizio lived in perpetual discontent under his Jovelike frown, watching the ruin of his own class and his own inheritance without ever making, still less wanting to make, any move toward saving it.

That half-hour between Rosary and dinner was one of the least irritating moments of his day, and for hours beforehand he would savor its rather uncertain calm.

With a wildly excited Bendicò bounding ahead of him he went down the short flight of steps into the garden. Enclosed between three walls and a side of the house, its seclusion gave it the air of a cemetery, accentuated by the parallel little mounds bounding the irrigation canals and looking like the graves of very tall, very thin giants. Plants were growing in thick disorder on the reddish clay; flowers sprouted in all directions, and the myrtle hedges seemed put there to prevent movement rather than guide it. At the end a statue of Flora speckled with yellow-black lichen exhibited her centuries-old charms with an air of resignation; on each side were benches holding quilted cushions, also of gray marble; and in a corner the gold of an acacia tree introduced a sudden note of gaiety. Every sod seemed to exude a yearning for beauty soon muted by languor.

But the garden, hemmed and almost squashed between these barriers, was exhaling scents that were cloying, fleshy, and slightly putrid, like the aromatic liquids distilled from the relics of certain saints; the carnations superimposed their pungence on the formal fragrance of roses and the oily emanations of magnolias drooping in corners; and somewhere beneath it all was a faint smell of mint mingling with a nursery whiff of acacia and the jammy one of myrtle; from a grove beyond the wall came an erotic waft of early orange blossom.

It was a garden for the blind: a constant offense to the eyes, a pleasure strong if somewhat crude to the nose. The Paul Neyron roses, whose cuttings he had himself bought in Paris, had degenerated; first stimulated and then enfeebled by the strong if languid pull of Sicilian earth, burned by apocalyptic Julies, they had changed into things like flesh-colored cabbages, obscene and distilling a dense, almost indecent, scent which no French horticulturist would have dared hope for. The Prince put one under his nose and seemed to be sniffing the thigh of a dancer from the Opera. Bendicò, to whom it was also proffered, drew back in disgust and hurried off in search of healthier sensations amid dead lizards and manure.

But the heavy scents of the garden brought on a gloomy train of thought for the Prince: "It smells all right here now; but a month ago . . ."

He remembered the nausea diffused throughout the entire villa by certain sweetish odors before their cause was traced: the corpse of a young soldier of the Fifth Regiment of Sharpshooters who had been wounded in the skirmish with the rebels at San Lorenzo and come up there to die, all alone, under a lemon tree. They had found him lying face downward in the thick clover, his face covered in blood and vomit, his nails dug into the soil, crawling with ants; a pile of purplish intestines had formed a puddle under his bandoleer. Russo, the agent, had discovered this object, turned it over, covered its face with his red kerchief, thrust the guts back into the gaping stomach with some twigs, and then covered the wound with the blue flaps of the cloak; spitting continuously with disgust, meanwhile, not right on, but very near the body. And all this with meticulous care. "Those swine stink even when they're dead." It had been the only epitaph to that derelict death.

After other soldiers, looking bemused, had taken the body away (and yes, dragged it along by the shoulders to the cart so that the puppet's stuffing fell out again), a *De Profundis* for the soul of the unknown youth was added to the evening Rosary; and now that the conscience of the ladies in the house seemed placated, the subject was never mentioned again.

The Prince went and scratched a little lichen off the feet of the Flora and then began to stroll up and down; the lowering sun threw an immense shadow of him over the gravelike flower beds.

No, the dead man had not been mentioned again; and anyway soldiers presumably become soldiers for exactly that, to die in defense of their King. But the image of that gutted corpse often recurred, as if asking to be given peace in the only possible way the Prince could give it: by justifying that last agony on grounds of general necessity. And then, around, would rise other even less attractive ghosts. Dying for somebody or for something, that was perfectly normal, of course; but the person dying should know, or at least feel sure, that someone knows for whom or for what he is dying; the disfigured face was asking just that; and that was where the haze began.

"He died for the King, of course, my dear Fabrizio, obviously," would have been the answer of his brother-in-law Màlvica, had the Prince asked him, and Màlvica was always the chosen spokesman of most of their friends. "For the King, who stands for order, continuity, decency, honor, right; for the King, who is sole defender of the Church, sole bulwark against the dispersal of property, 'The Sect's' ultimate aim." * Fine words, these, pointing to all that lay dearest and deepest in the Prince's heart. But there was something that didn't quite ring true, even so. The King,

* "The Sect" refers to liberals and Freemasons.

all right. He knew the King well, or rather the one who had just died; the present one was only a seminarian dressed up as a General. And the old King had really not been worth much. "But you're not reasoning, my dear Fabrizio," Màlvica would reply; "one particular sovereign may not be up to it, yet the idea of monarchy is still the same."

That was true too; but kings who personify an idea should not, cannot, fall below a certain level for generations; if they do, my dear brother-in-law, the idea suffers too.

He was sitting on a bench, inertly watching the devastation wrought by Bendicò in the flower beds; every now and again the dog would turn innocent eyes toward him as if asking for praise at labor done: fourteen carnations broken off, half a hedge torn apart, an irrigation canal blocked. How human! "Good! Bendicò, come here." And the animal hurried up and put its earthy nostrils into his hand, anxious to show that it had forgiven this silly interruption of a fine job of work.

Those audiences! All those audiences granted him by King Ferdinand at Caserta, at Capodimonte, at Portici, Naples, anywhere at all.

Walking beside the chamberlain on duty, chatting as he guided with a cocked hat under an arm and the latest Neapolitan slang on his lips, they would move through innumerable rooms of superb architecture and revolting décor (just like the Bourbon monarchy itself), plunge into dirty passages and up ill-kept stairs, and finally emerge into an antechamber filled with waiting people: closed faces of police spies, avid faces of petitioners. The chamberlain apologized, pushed through this mob, and led him toward another antechamber reserved for members of the Court; a little blue and silver room of the period of Charles III. After a short wait a lackey tapped at thè door and they were admitted into the August Presence.

The private study was small and consciously simple; on the white-painted walls hung a portrait of King Francis I and one with an acid, ill-tempered expression of the reigning Queen; above the mantelpiece was a Madonna by Andrea del Sarto looking astounded at finding herself in the company of colored lithographs representing obscure Neapolitan saints and sanctuaries; on a side table stood a wax statuette of the Child Jesus with a votive light before it; and the modest desk was heaped with papers white, yellow, and blue; the whole administration of the Kingdom here attained its final phase, that of signature by His Majesty (D. G.).

Behind this paper barricade was the King. He was already standing so as not to be seen getting up; the King with his pallid, heavy face between fairish side whiskers, with his rough cloth military jacket under which burst a purple cataract of falling trousers. He gave a step forward with his right hand out and bent for the hand-kiss which he would then refuse.

"Well, Salina, blessings on you!" His Neapolitan accent was far stronger than the chamberlain's.

"I must beg Your Majesty to excuse me for not wearing Court dress; I am only just passing through Naples; but I did not wish to forgo paying my respects to Your Revered Person."

"Nonsense, Salina, nonsense; you know that you're always at home here at Caserta."

"At home, of course," he repeated, sitting down behind the desk and waiting a second before motioning to his guest to sit down too.

"And how are the little girls?"

The Prince realized that now was the moment to produce a play on words both salacious and edifying. "The little girls, Your Majesty? At my age and under the sacred bonds of matrimony?"

The King's mouth laughed as his hands primly settled the papers before him. "Those I'd never let myself refer to, Salina. I was asking about your little daughters, your little Princesses. Concetta, now, that dear godchild of ours, she must be getting quite big, isn't she, almost grown up?"

From family he passed to science. "Salina, you're an honor not only to yourself but to the whole Kingdom! A fine thing, science, unless it takes to attacking religion!" After this, however, the mask of the Friend was put aside and its place assumed by that of the Severe Sovereign. "Tell me, Salina, what do they think of Castelcicala down in Sicily?"

Salina had never heard a good word for the Viceroy of Sicily from either Royalists or liberals, but not wanting to let a friend down he parried and kept to generalities. "A great gentleman, a true hero, maybe a little old for the fatigues of viceroyalty. . . ."

The King's face darkened: Salina was refusing to act the spy. So Salina was no use to him. Leaning both hands on his desk, he prepared the dismissal: "I've so much work! The whole Kingdom rests on these shoulders of mine." Now for a bit of sweetening: out of the drawer came the friendly mask again. "When you pass through Naples next, Salina, come and show your Concetta to the Queen. She's too young to be presented, I know, but there's nothing against our arranging a little dinner for her, is there? Sweets to the sweet, as they say. Well, Salina, 'bye, and be good!"

On one occasion, though, the dismissal had not been so amiable. The Prince had made his second bow while backing out when the King called after him, "Hey, Salina, listen. They tell me you've some old friends in Palermo. That nephew of yours, Falconeri . . . Why don't you knock some sense into him?"

"But, Your Majesty, Tancredi thinks of nothing but women and cards."

The King lost patience: "Take care, Salina, take care. You're responsible, remember, you're his guardian. Tell him to look after that neck of his. You may withdraw."

Repassing now through the sumptuously second-rate rooms on his way to sign the Queen's book, he felt suddenly discouraged. That plebeian cordiality had depressed him as much as the police sneers. Lucky those who could interpret such familiarity as friendship, such threats as royal might. He could not. And as he exchanged gossip with the impeccable chamberlain, he was asking himself what was destined to succeed this monarchy which bore the marks of death upon its face. The Piedmontese, the so-called *Galantuomo* * who was getting himself so talked of from that little out-of-the-way capital of his? Wouldn't things be just the same? Just Torinese instead of Neapolitan dialect; that's all.

He had reached the book. He signed: Fabrizio Corbera, Prince of Salina.

Or maybe the Republic of Don Peppino Mazzini? "No, thanks. I'd just be plain Signor Corbera."

And the long jog back to Naples did not calm him. Nor even the thought of an appointment with Cora Danolo.

This being the case, then, what should he do? Just cling to the status quo and avoid leaps in the dark? That would mean more shooting, like that which had resounded a short time before through a squalid square in Palermo; and what use was shooting anyway? "One never achieves anything by going bang! bang! Does one, Bendicò?"

"Ding! Ding! Ding!" rang the bell for dinner. Bendicò rushed ahead with mouth watering in anticipation. "Just like a Piedmontese!" thought Salina as he moved back up the steps.

Dinner at Villa Salina was served with the slightly

* Victor Emmanuel II, of Piedmont, northern Italian province with Turin as its capital. In 1861 he became the first King of the United Kingdom of Italy.

shabby grandeur then customary in the Kingdom of the Two Sicilies. The number of those taking part (fourteen in all, with the master and mistress of the house, children, governesses, and tutors) was itself enough to give the dining table an imposing air. Covered with a fine but mended lace cloth, it glittered beneath a powerful oil lamp hung precariously under the Murano chandelier. Daylight was still streaming through the windows, but the white figures in painted bas-relief against the dark backgrounds of the door mantels were already lost in shadow. The silver was massive and the glass splendid, bearing on smooth medallions amid cut Bohemian ware the initials F. D. (*Ferdinandus dedit*) in memory of royal munificence; but the plates, each signed by an illustrious artist, were mere survivors of many a scullion's massacre and originated from different services. The biggest, from Capodimonte, with a wide almond-green border, engraved with little gilt anchors, were reserved for the Prince, who liked everything around him, except his wife, to be on his own scale.

When he entered the dining room the whole party was already assembled, only the Princess sitting, the rest standing behind their chairs. Opposite his own chair, flanked by a pile of plates, swelled the silver flanks of the enormous soup tureen with its cover surmounted by a prancing Leopard. The Prince ladled out the *minestra* himself, a pleasant chore, symbol of his proud duties as paterfamilias. That evening, though, there came a sound that had not been heard for some time, a threatening tinkle of the ladle against a side of the tureen: a sign of great though still controlled anger, one of the most terrifying sounds in the world, as one of his sons used to call it even forty years later. The Prince had noticed that the sixteen-year-old Francesco Paolo was not in his place. The lad entered at once ("Excuse me, Papa") and sat down. He was not reproved, but Father Pirrone, whose duties were more or less those of sheep dog, bent his head and muttered a prayer. The bomb did not explode, but the gust from its passage had swept the table and ruined the dinner all the same. As they ate in silence the Prince's blue eyes, narrowed behind half-closed lids, stared at his children one by one and numbed them with fear.

But, "A fine family," he was thinking. The girls plump, glowing, with gay little dimples, and between forehead and nose that frown which was the hereditary mark of the Salinas; the males slim but wiry, wearing an expression of fashionable melancholy as they wielded knives and forks with subdued violence. One of these had been away for two years: Giovanni, the second son, the most loved, the most difficult. One fine day he had vanished from home and there had been no news of him for two months. Then a cold but respectful letter arrived from London with apologies for any anxiety he had caused, reassurances about his health, and the strange statement that he preferred a modest life as clerk in a coal depot to a pampered (read: "fettered") existence in the ease of Palermo. Often a twinge of anxiety for the errant youth in that foggy and heretical city would prick the Prince's heart and torture him. His face grew darker than ever.

It grew so dark that the Princess, sitting next to him, put out her childlike hand and stroked the powerful paw reposing on the tablecloth. A thoughtless gesture, which loosed a whole chain of reactions in him: irritation at being pitied, then a surge of sensuality, not, however, directed toward her who had aroused it. Into the Prince's mind flashed a picture of Mariannina with her head deep in a pillow. He raised a dry voice: "Domenico," he said to a lackey, "go and tell Don Antonio to harness the bays to the brougham; I'll be going down to Palermo immediately after dinner." A glance into his wife's eyes, which had gone glassy, made him regret his order; but as it was quite out of the question to withdraw instructions already given, he persevered and even added a jeer to his cruelty: "Father Pirrone, you will come with me; we'll be back by eleven; you can spend a couple of hours with your Jesuit friends."

There could obviously be no valid reason for visiting Palermo at night in those disordered times except for some low love-adventure; and taking the family chaplain as companion was sheer offensive arrogance. So at least Father Pirrone felt, and he was offended, though of course he acquiesced.

The last medlar had scarcely been eaten when the carriage wheels were heard crunching under the porch; in the hall, as a lackey handed the Prince his top hat and the Jesuit his tricorne, the Princess, now on the verge of tears, made a last attempt to hold him—vain as ever: "But, Fabrizio, in times like these . . . with the streets full of soldiers, of hooligans . . . why, anything might happen."

"Nonsense," he snapped, "nonsense, Stella; what could happen? Everyone knows me; there aren't many men as tall in Palermo. See you later." And he placed a hurried kiss on her still unfurrowed brow, which was level with his chin. But, whether the smell of the Princess's skin had called up tender memories, or whether the penitential steps of Father Pirrone behind him evoked pious warnings, on reaching the carriage door he very nearly did countermand the trip. At that moment, just as he was opening his mouth to order the carriage back to the stables, a loud shriek of "Fabrizio, my Fabrizio!" followed by a scream, reached him from the window above. The Princess was having one of her fits of hysteria. "Drive on," he said to the coachman on the box holding a whip diagonally across his paunch. "Drive on, down to Palermo, and leave Father at the Jesuit house," and he banged the carriage door before the lackey could shut it.

It was not dark yet and the road meandered on, very white, deep between high walls. As they came out of the Salina property they passed on the left the half-ruined Falconeri villa, owned by Tancredi, his nephew and ward. A spendthrift father, married to the Prince's sister, had squandered his whole fortune and then died. It had been one of those total ruins which included even the gold braid on the lackeys' liveries, and when the widow died the King had conferred the guardianship of her son, then aged four-teen, on his uncle Salina. The lad, scarcely known before, had become very dear to the irascible Prince, who perceived in him a riotous zest for life and a frivolous temperament contradicted by sudden serious moods. Though the Prince never admitted it to himself, he would have preferred the lad as his heir to that booby Paolo. Now, at twenty-one, Tancredi was enjoying life on the money which his uncle never grudged him, even from his own pocket. "I wonder what the silly boy is up to now," thought the Prince as they drove past Villa Falconeri, whose huge bougainvillaeas cascaded over the gates like swags of episcopal silk, lending a deceptive air of gaiety to the dark.

"What is he up to now?" For King Ferdinand, in speak-ing of the young man's undesirable acquaintances, had been wrong to mention the matter but right in his facts. Swept up in a circle of gamblers and ladies called "light," as the euphemism went, all dominated by his slim charm, Tan-credi had actually got to the point of sympathizing with the Sect and getting in touch with the secret National Com-mittee; maybe he drew money from them as well as from the Royal coffers. It had taken the Prince a great deal of labor and trouble, visits to a skeptical Castelcicala and an overpolite Maniscalco, to prevent the youth from getting into real trouble after the Fourth of April "riots." That hadn't been too good; on the other hand, Tancredi could never do wrong in his uncle's eyes; so the real fault lay with the times, these confused times in which a young man of good family wasn't even free to play a game of faro

without involving himself with compromising acquaintanceships. Bad times.

"Bad times, Your Excellency." The voice of Father Pirrone sounded like an echo of his thoughts. Squeezed into a
corner of the brougham, hemmed in by the massive Prince,
subject to that same Prince's bullying, the Jesuit was suffering in body and conscience and, being a man of parts himself, was now transposing his own ephemeral discomfort
into the perennial realms of history. "Look, Excellency,"
and he pointed to the mountain heights of the Conca
d'Oro still visible in the last dusk. On their slopes and
peaks glimmered dozens of flickering lights, bonfires lit
every night by the rebel bands, silent threats to the city
of palaces and convents. They looked like the lights that
burn in sickrooms during the last nights.

"I can see, Father, I can see," and it occurred to him
that perhaps Tancredi was beside one of those ill-omened
fires, his aristocratic hands throwing on sticks being burned
to damage just such hands as his. "A fine guardian I am,
with my ward up to any nonsense that passes through his
head."

The road was now beginning to slope gently downhill,
and Palermo could be seen very close, plunged in complete
darkness, its low shuttered houses weighted down by the
huge edifices of convents and monasteries. There were
dozens of these, all vast, often grouped in twos or threes,
for women and for men, for rich and poor, nobles and
plebeians, for Jesuits, Benedictines, Franciscans, Capuchins,
Carmelites, Redemptorists, Augustinians. . . . Above them

rose squat domes in flabby curves like breasts emptied of milk; but it was the religious houses which gave the city its grimness and its character, its sedateness and also the sense of death which not even the vibrant Sicilian light could ever manage to disperse. And at that hour, at night, they were despots of the scene. It was against them really that the bonfires were lit on the hills, stoked by men who were themselves very like those living in the monasteries below, as fanatical, as self-absorbed, as avid for power or rather for the idleness which was, for them, the purpose of power.

This was what the Prince was thinking as the bays trotted down the slope; thoughts in contrast to his real self, caused by anxiety about Tancredi and by the sensual urge which made him turn against the restrictions embodied by the religious houses.

Now the road was crossing orange groves in flower, and the nuptial scent of the blossoms absorbed all the rest as a full moon absorbs a landscape; the smell of sweating horses, the smell of leather from the carriage upholstery, the smell of Prince and the smell of Jesuit, were all cancelled out by that Islamic perfume evoking houris and fleshly joys beyond the grave.

It even touched Father Pirrone. "How lovely this would be, Excellency, if . . ."

"If there weren't so many Jesuits," thought the Prince, his delicious anticipations interrupted by the priest's voice. At once he regretted this rudeness of thought, and his big hand tapped his old friend's tricorne.

Where the suburbs began, at Villa Airoldi, the carriage

was stopped by a patrol. Voices from Apulia, voices from Naples, called a halt, bayonets glittered under a wavering lantern; but a sergeant soon recognized the Prince sitting there with his top hat on his knees. "Excuse us, Excellency, pass on." And a soldier was even told to get up onto the box so that the carriage would have no more trouble at other block posts. The loaded carriage moved on more slowly, around Villa Ranchibile, through Torrerosse and the truck gardens of Villafranca, and into the city by Porta Maqueda. Outside the Caffè Romeres at the Quattro Canti di Campagna officers from units on guard were sitting laughing and eating huge ices. But that was the only sign of life in the entire city; the deserted streets echoed only to the rhythmic march of pickets on their rounds, passing with white bandoleers crossed over their chests. On each side monastery walls were continuous, the Monastery of the Mountain, of the Stigmata, of the Crusaders, of the Theatines, massive, black as pitch, immersed in a sleep that seemed like the end of all things.

"I'll fetch you in a couple of hours, Father. Pray well."

And poor Pirrone knocked confusedly at the door of the Jesuit house as the brougham wheeled off down a side street.

Leaving the carriage at his palace, the Prince set off for his destination on foot. It was a short walk, but through a quarter of ill repute. Soldiers in full equipment, who had obviously just slipped away from the patrols bivouacked in the squares, were issuing with shining eyes from little houses on whose balconies pots of basil explained the ease of entry. Sinister-looking youths in wide trousers were quarrelling in the guttural grunts Sicilians use in anger. In the distance echoed shots from nervous sentries. Once past this district, his route skirted the Cala; in the old fishing port decaying boats bobbed up and down, desolate as mangy dogs.

"I'm a sinner, I know, doubly a sinner, by Divine Law and by Stella's human love. There's no doubt of that, and tomorrow I'll go and confess to Father Pirrone." He smiled to himself at the thought that it might be superfluous, so certain must the Jesuit be of his sins of today. And then a spirit of quibble came over him again. "I'm sinning, it's true, but I'm sinning so as not to sin worse, to stop this sensual nagging, to tear this thorn out of my flesh and avoid worse trouble. That the Lord knows." Suddenly he was swept by a gust of tenderness toward himself. "I'm just a poor, weak creature," he thought as his heavy steps crunched the dirty gravel. "I'm weak and without support. Stella! Oh well, the Lord knows how much I've loved her; but I was married at twenty. And now she's too bossy, as well as too old." His moment of weakness passed. "But I've still got my vigor; and how can I find satisfaction with a woman who makes the sign of the Cross in bed before every embrace and then at the crucial moment just cries, *'Gesummaria!'* When we married and she was sixteen I found that rather exalting; but now . . . seven children I've had with her, seven; and never once have I seen her navel. Is that right?" Now, whipped by this odd anguish, he was almost shouting, "Is it right? I ask you all!" And he turned to the portico of the Catena. "Why, she's the real sinner!"

Comforted by this reassuring discovery, he gave a firm knock at Mariannina's door.

Two hours later he was in his brougham on the way home with Father Pirrone beside him. The latter was worried: his colleagues had been telling him about the political situation, which was, it seemed, much tenser than it looked from the detached calm of Villa Salina. There was fear of a landing by the Piedmontese in the south of the island, near Sciacca; the authorities had noticed a silent ferment among the people; at the first sign of weakening control, the city rabble would take to looting and rape. The Jesuit Fathers were thoroughly alarmed and three of them, the oldest, had left for Naples by the afternoon packet boat, taking their archives with them. "May the Lord protect us, and spare this holy Kingdom!"

The Prince scarcely listened. He was immersed in sated ease tinged with disgust. Mariannina had looked at him with her big opaque peasant's eyes, had refused him nothing, and had been humble and compliant in every way. A kind of Bendicò in a silk petticoat. In a moment of particularly intense pleasure he had heard her exclaim, "My Prince!" He smiled again with satisfaction at the thought. Much better than *"mon chat"* or *"mon singe blond"* produced in equivalent moments by Sarah, the Parisian slut he had frequented three years ago, when the Astronomical Congress gave him a gold medal at the Sorbonne. Better than *"mon chat,"* no doubt of that; much better than

"Gesummaria!" No sacrilege, at least. A good girl, Marian-nina; next time he visited her he'd take her three lengths of crimson silk.

But how sad, too: that manhandled, youthful flesh, that resigned lubricity; and what about him, what was he? A pig, just a pig! Suddenly there occurred to him a verse read by chance in a Paris bookshop, while glancing at a vol-ume by someone whose name he had forgotten, one of those poets the French incubate and forget next week. He could see once more the lemon-yellow pile of unsold copies, the page, an uneven page, and hear again the verses ending a jumble of a poem:

> *. . . donnez-moi la force et le courage*
> *de contempler mon coeur et mon corps sans dégoût.*

And as Father Pirrone went worrying on about a person called La Farina and another called Crispi, the Prince dozed off into a kind of tense euphoria, lulled by the trot-ting of the bays, on whose plump flanks quivered the light from the carriage lamps. He woke up at the turning by Villa Falconeri. "Oh, he's a fine one too, tending bonfires that'll destroy him!"

In the matrimonial bedroom, glancing at poor Stella with her hair well tucked into her nightcap, sighing as she slept in the huge, high brass bed, he felt touched. "Seven children she's given me, and she's been mine alone." A faint whiff of valerian drifted through the room, last vestige of her crisis of hysterics. "Poor little Stella," he murmured pityingly as he climbed into bed. The hours passed and he could not sleep; some powerful hand was stirring three fires smoldering in his mind: of Mariannina's caresses, of those French verses, of the autos-da-fé on the hills.

Toward dawn, however, the Princess had occasion to make the sign of the Cross.

Next morning the sun lit on a refreshed Prince. He had taken his coffee and was shaving in front of the mirror in a red and black flowered dressing gown. Bendicò was leaning a heavy head on one of his slippers. As he shaved his right cheek he noticed in the mirror a face behind his own, the face of a young man, thin and elegant, with a shy, quizzical look. He did not turn around and went on shaving. "Well, Tancredi, where were you last night?"

"Good morning, Uncle. Where was I? Oh, just out with friends. An innocent night. Not like a certain person I know who went down to Palermo for some fun!"

The Prince concentrated on shaving the difficult bit between lips and chin. His nephew's slightly nasal voice had such youthful zest that it was impossible to be angry; but he might allow himself a touch of surprise. He turned and with his towel under his chin looked his nephew up and down. The young man was in shooting kit, a long tight jacket, high leggings. "And who was this person, may I ask?"

"Yourself, Uncle, yourself. I saw you with my own eyes, at the Villa Airoldi block post, as you were talking to the sergeant. A fine thing at your age! And a priest with you too! You old playboy!"

Really, this was a little too insolent. Tancredi thought he could allow himself anything. Dark blue eyes, the eyes of his mother, his own eyes, gazed laughingly at him through half-closed lids. The Prince was offended: the boy didn't know where to stop; but he could not bring himself to reprove him; and anyway he was quite right. "Why are you dressed like that, though? What's going on? A fancy-dress ball in the morning?"

The youth became serious; his triangular face assumed an unexpectedly manly look. "I'm leaving, Uncle, leaving in an hour. I came to say goodbye."

Poor Salina felt his heart tighten. "A duel?"

"A big duel, Uncle. A duel with little King Francis. I'm going into the hills at Ficuzza; don't tell a soul, particularly not Paolo. Great things are in the offing, and I don't want to stay at home. And anyway I'd be arrested at once if I did."

The Prince had one of his visions: a savage guerrilla skirmish, shots in the woods, and Tancredi, his Tancredi, lying on the ground with his guts hanging out like that poor soldier. "You're mad, my boy, to go with those people! They're all in the *maffia*, all troublemakers. A Falconeri should be with us, for the King."

The eyes began smiling again. "For the King, yes, of course. But which King?" The lad had one of those sudden serious moods which made him so mysterious and so endearing. "Unless we ourselves take a hand now, they'll foist a republic on us. If we want things to stay as they are, things will have to change. D'you understand?" Rather moved, he embraced his uncle. "Well, goodbye, for now. I'll be back with the tricolor." The rhetoric of those friends of his had touched Tancredi a little too; and yet, no, there was a tone in that nasal voice which undercut the emphasis.

What a boy! Talking rubbish and contradicting it at the same time. And all that Paolo of his was probably thinking of at that moment was Guiscard's digestion! This was his real son! The Prince jumped up, pulled the towel from his neck, and rummaged in a drawer. "Tancredi, Tancredi, wait!" He ran after his nephew, slipped a roll of gold pieces into his pocket, and squeezed his shoulder.

The other laughed. "You're subsidizing the Revolution now! Thank you, Uncle, see you soon; and my respects to my aunt." And off he rushed down the stairs.

Bendicò was called from following his friend with joyous barks through the villa, the Prince's shave was over, his face washed. The valet came to help him into shoes and clothes. "The tricolor! Tricolor indeed! They fill their mouths with these words, the rascals. What does that ugly geometric sign, that aping of the French mean, compared to our white banner with its golden lily in the middle? What hope can those clashing colors bring them?" It was now the moment for the monumental black satin cravat to be wound around his neck: a difficult operation during which political worries were best suspended. One turn, two turns, three turns. The big delicate hands smoothed out the folds, settled the overlaps, pinned into the silk the little head of Medusa with ruby eyes. "A clean waistcoat.

Can't you see this one's dirty?" The valet stood on tiptoe
to help him slip on a frock coat of brown cloth; he proffered a handkerchief with three drops of bergamot. Keys,
watch and chain, money, the Prince put in a pocket himself.
Then he glanced in a mirror; no doubt about it, he was
still a fine-looking man. "Old playboy indeed! A bad joke,
that one of Tancredi's! I'd like to see him at my age, all
skin and bone that he is!"

His vigorous steps made the windows tinkle in the
rooms he crossed. The house was calm, luminous, ornate;
above all it was his own. On his way downstairs he suddenly understood that remark of Tancredi's, "If we want
things to stay as they are . . ." Tancredi would go a long
way: he had always thought so.

The estate office was still empty, lit silently by the sun
through closed shutters. Although the scene of more fri-
volity than anywhere else in the villa, its appearance was
of calm austerity. On whitewashed walls, reflected in wax-
polished tiles, hung enormous pictures representing the
various Salina estates: there, in bright colors contrasting
with the gold and black frame, was Salina, the island of
the twin mountains, surrounded by a sea of white-flecked
waves on which pranced beflagged galleons; Querceta, its
low houses grouped around the rustic church on which
were converging groups of bluish-colored pilgrims; Ragattisi, tucked under mountain gorges; Argivocale, tiny in
contrast to the vast plains of corn dotted with hard-work-
ing peasants; Donnafugata, with its baroque palace, goal of

coaches in scarlet and green and gilt, loaded with women, wine, and violins; and many others, all protected by a taut reassuring sky and by the Leopard grinning between long whiskers. Each picture was festive—each trying to show the enlightened empire, like wine, of the House of Salina. Ingenuous masterpieces of rustic art from the previous century; useless, though, at showing boundaries, or detailing areas or tenancies; such things remained obscure. The wealth of many centuries had been transmitted into ornament, luxury, pleasure; no more; the abolition of feudal rights had swept away duties as well as privileges; wealth, like an old wine, had let the dregs of greed, even of care and prudence, fall to the bottom of the barrel, leaving only verve and color. And thus eventually it cancelled itself out; this wealth which had achieved its object was composed now only of essential oils—and, like essential oils, it soon evaporated. Already some of the estates which looked so gay in those pictures had taken wing, leaving behind only bright-colored paintings and names. Others seemed, like those September swallows which though still present are grouped stridently on trees, ready for departure. But there were so many; it seemed they could never end.

In spite of this the sensation felt by the Prince on entering his own office was, as always, an unpleasant one. In the center of the room towered a huge desk, with dozens of drawers, niches, recesses, hollows, and folding shelves; its mass of yellow wood and black inlay was carved and decorated like a stage set, full of unexpected, uneven surfaces, secret drawers which no one now knew how to work except thieves. It was covered with papers, and, although the Prince had taken care that most of these referred to the starry regions of astronomy, there were quite enough others to fill his princely heart with dismay. Suddenly he was reminded of King Ferdinand's desk at Caserta, also covered with papers needing decisions which could claim to influence the course of fate, that was actually flowing along on its own in another valley.

Salina thought of a medicine recently discovered in the United States of America which could prevent suffering even during the most serious operations and produce serenity amid disaster. "Morphia" was the name given to this crude substitute for the stoicism of the ancients and for Christian fortitude. With the late King, poor man, phantom administration had taken the place of morphia; he, Salina, had a more refined recipe: astronomy. And thrusting away the memory of lost Ragattisi and precarious Argivocale, he plunged into reading the latest number of the *Journal des Savants*. "*Les dernières observations de l'Observatoire de Greenwich présentent un intérêt tout particulier. . . .*"

But he was soon exiled from these stellar realms. In came Don Ciccio Ferrara, the accountant. He was a scraggy little man who hid the deluded and rapacious mind of a "liberal" behind reassuring spectacles and immaculate cravats. That morning he looked brisker than usual; obviously, the same news which had depressed Father Pirrone had acted as a tonic on him. "Sad times, Your Excellency," he said after the usual ritual greetings. "Big troubles ahead, but after a bit of bother and a shot or two things will turn out for the best; then glorious new days will dawn for this Sicily of ours; if it weren't that so many fine lads are sure to get killed, we should be really pleased."

The Prince grunted and expressed no opinion. "Don Ciccio," he said then, "the Querceta rents need looking into; we haven't had a thing from them for two years."

"The books are all in order, Excellency." It was the magic phrase. "I only have to write to Don Angelo Mazza to send out collectors; I will prepare the letter for your signature this very day."

He went to turn over the huge registers. In them, with two years' delay, were inscribed in minute writing all the Salina accounts, except for the really important ones. When he was alone again the Prince waited a little before soaring back through the clouds. He felt irritated not so much by the events themselves as by the stupidity of Don Ciccio, whom he sensed at once to represent the class which would now be gaining power. "What the fellow says is the very contrary of the truth. Regretting the fine lads who're sure to die! There'll be very few of those, if I'm any judge of the two adversaries; not a single casualty more than is strictly necessary for a victory bulletin, whether compiled at Naples or Turin. But he does believe in 'glorious new days for this Sicily of ours,' as he puts it; these have been promised us on every single one of the thousand invasions we've had from Nicias onward, and they've never come. And why should they come, anyway? What will happen then? Oh, well. Just negotiations punctuated by a little harmless shooting, then all will be the same though all will be changed." Into his mind had come Tancredi's ambiguous words, which he now found himself really understanding. Reassured, he ceased turning over the pages of the scientific review and looked up at the scorched slopes of Monte Pellegrino, scarred like the face of misery by eternal ravines.

Soon afterward appeared Russo, to the Prince the most significant of his dependents. Clever, dressed rather smartly in a striped velvet jacket, with greedy eyes below a remorseless forehead, the Prince found him a perfect specimen of a class on its way up. He was obsequious too, and even sincerely friendly in a way, for his cheating was done in the certainty of exercising a right. "I can imagine how Your Excellency must be worried by Signorino Tancredi's departure; but he won't be away long, I'm sure, and all will end well." Again the Prince found himself facing one of the enigmas of Sicily; in this secret island, where houses are barred and peasants refuse to admit they even know the way to their own village in clear view on a hillock within a few minutes' walk from here, in spite of the ostentatious show of mystery, reserve is a myth.

He signed to Russo to sit down and stared him in the eyes. "Pietro, let's talk to each other man to man. You're involved in all this too, aren't you?" No, was the answer, not actually; he had a family and such risks were for young men like Signorino Tancredi. "I'd never hide anything from Your Excellency, who's like a father to me." (Yet three years before he had hidden in his cellar three hundred baskets of lemons belonging to the Prince, and he knew that the Prince knew.) "But I must say that my heart is with them, those bold lads." He got up to let in Bendicò, who was making the door shake under his friendly impetus. Then he sat down again. "Your Excellency knows we can't stand any more: searches, questions, nagging about every little thing, a police spy at every street corner; an honest man can't even look after his own affairs. Afterward, though, we'll have liberty, security, lighter taxes, ease, trade. Everything will be better; the only ones to lose will be the priests. But the Lord protects poor folk like me, not them."

The Prince smiled. He knew that he, Russo, was at that moment trying through intermediaries to buy the estate of Argivocale. "There will be a day or two of shooting and trouble, but Villa Salina will be safe as a rock; Your Excellency is our father, I have many friends here. The Piedmontese will come cap in hand to pay Your Excellencies their respects. And then, you are also the uncle, the guardian of Don Tancredi!"

The Prince felt humiliated, reduced to the rank of one protected by Russo's friends; his only merit, as far as he could see, was being uncle to that urchin Tancredi. "In a week's time I'll find my life's safe only because I keep Bendicò." He squeezed one of the dog's ears so hard that the poor creature whined, honored doubtless, but in pain.

Shortly afterward a remark of Russo's relieved the Prince. "Everything will be better, believe me, Excellency. Honest and able men will have a chance to get ahead, that's

all. The rest will be as it was before." All that these people, these petty little local "liberals," wanted was to find
ways of making more money themselves. No more. The
swallows would take wing a little sooner, that was all. Anyway, there were still plenty in the nest.

"You may be right. Who knows?" Now he had penetrated all the hidden meanings: the enigmatic words of
Tancredi, the rhetorical ones of Ferrara, the false but revealing ones of Russo, had yielded their reassuring secret.
Much would happen, but all would be play-acting; a noisy,
romantic play with a few spots of blood on the comic cos-
tumes. This was a country of arrangements, with none of
that frenzy of the French; and anyway, had anything
really serious happened in France, except for that June of
'48? He felt like saying to Russo, but his innate courtesy
held him back, "I understand now; you don't want to destroy us, who are your 'fathers.' You just want to take our
places. Gently, nicely, putting a few thousand ducats in
your pockets meanwhile. And what then? Your nephew,
my dear Russo, will sincerely believe himself a baron;
maybe you will become, because of your name, descendant
of a grand duke of Muscovy instead of some red-skinned
peasant, which is what that name of yours means. And long
before that your daughter will have married one of us,
perhaps Tancredi himself, with his blue eyes and his wil-
lowy hands. She's good-looking, anyway, and once she's
learned to wash . . . For all will be the same. Just as it
is now: except for an imperceptible shifting about of classes.
My Court Chamberlain's gilt keys, my cherry-colored

ribbon of St. Januarius will stay in a drawer and end up in some glass case of Paolo's. But the Salinas will remain the Salinas; they may even get some compensation or other: a seat in the Sardinian Senate, that pink ribbon of the Order of St. Maurice. Both have tassels, after all."

He got up. "Pietro, talk to your friends, will you? There are a lot of girls here. They mustn't be alarmed."

"I thought so, Excellency, and have already spoken of it: Villa Salina will be quiet as a convent," and he smiled with amiable irony.

Don Fabrizio went out, followed by Bendicò; he wanted to go up and see Father Pirrone, but the dog's yearning look forced him out into the garden; for Bendicò had thrilling memories of the fine work he'd put in the night before and wanted to finish it off like a good artist. The garden was even more odorous than the day before, and under the morning sun the gold of the acacia tree clashed less. "What about our King and Queen, though, what about them? And what about the principle of legitimacy?" The thought disturbed him a moment, he could not avoid it. For a second he felt like Màlvica. Those Ferdinands, those Francises that had been so despised, seemed for a moment like elder brothers, trusting, just, affectionate, true kings. But the defense forces of his inner calm, always on the alert in the Prince, were already hurrying to his aid, with the musketry of law, the artillery of history. "What about France? Isn't Napoleon III illegitimate? And aren't the French quite happy under that enlightened Emperor, who will surely lead them to the highest of destinies? Any-

way, let's face it. Was our Charles III so definitely within
his rights? Was his Battle of Bitonto so unlike that of
Bisacquino or Corleone or any of these battles in which the
Piedmontese are now sweeping our troops before them?
One of those battles fought so that all should remain as it
was? And anyway, even Jupiter wasn't the legitimate King
of Olympus."

At this, of course, Jupiter's *coup d'état* against Saturn
was bound to bring his mind back to the stars.

Leaving Bendicò panting from his own dynamism, he
climbed the stairs again, crossed rooms in which his daughters sat chatting with friends from the Holy Redeemer (at
his passage the silken skirts rustled as the girls rose), went
up a long ladder, and came into the bright blue light of the
observatory. Father Pirrone, with the serene air of a priest
who has said Mass and drunk black coffee with Monreale
biscuits, was sitting immersed in algebraic formulas. The
two telescopes and three lenses were lying there quietly,
dazed by the sun, with black pads over the eyepieces, like
well-trained animals who knew their meal was given them
only at night.

The sight of the Prince drew the priest from his calculations and reminded him of his humiliation of the night
before. He got up, and then, as he bowed politely, found
himself saying, "Is Your Excellency coming to confession?"
The Prince, whose sleep that night and conversations that
morning had driven the episode of the previous night from
his mind, looked amazed. "Confession? It's not Saturday."

Then he remembered and smiled. "Really, Father, there wouldn't even be need, would there? You know it all already."

This insistence on his enforced complicity irritated the Jesuit. "Excellency, the efficacy of confession consists not only in telling our sins but in being sorry for them. And until you do so and show me you do so, you will remain in mortal sin, whether I know what your sins are or not." He blew a meticulous puff at a bit of fluff on his sleeve and plunged back into his abstractions.

Such was the calm produced in the Prince's mind by the political discoveries of that morning that he did nothing but smile at what would at other times have seemed to him a gross impertinence. He opened one of the windows of the little tower. The countryside spread below in all its beauty. Under the leaven of the strong sun everything seemed weightless: the sea in the background was a dash of pure color, the mountains which had seemed so alarmingly full of hidden men during the night now looked like masses of vapor on the point of dissolving, and grim Palermo itself lay crouching quietly around its convents like a flock of sheep around their shepherds. Even the foreign warships anchored in the harbor in case of trouble spread no sense of fear in the majestic calm. The sun, which was still far from its blazing zenith on that morning of the thirteenth of May, showed itself to be the true ruler of Sicily; the crude brash sun, the drugging sun, which annulled every will, kept all things in servile immobility, cradled in violence as arbitrary as dreams.

"It'll take any number of Victor Emmanuels to change this magic potion forever being poured out for us."

Father Pirrone had got up, adjusted his sash, and moved toward the Prince with a hand out. "Excellency, I was too brusque. Let me not trespass on your kindness, but do please listen and come to confession."

The ice was broken. And the Prince could tell Father Pirrone of his own political intuitions. But the Jesuit was far from sharing his relief, and even became acid again. "Briefly, then, you nobles will come to an agreement with the 'liberals,' and even with the Masons, at our expense, at the expense of the Church. Then, of course, our property, which is the patrimony of the poor, will be seized and carved up among the most brazen of their leaders; who will then feed all the destitute who are sustained and guided by the Church today?" The Prince was silent. "How will those desperate masses be placated? I'll tell you at once, Excellency. They will be flung first a portion, then another portion, and eventually all the rest of your estates. And so God will have done His justice, even by means of the Masons. Our Lord healed the blind in body; but what will be the fate of the blind in spirit?"

The unhappy priest was breathing hard; sincere horror at the foreseen dispersal of Church property was linked with regret at his having lost control of himself again, with fear of offending the Prince, whom he genuinely liked and whose blustering rages as well as disinterested kindness he knew well. So he sat down warily, glancing every now and again at Don Fabrizio, who had taken up a little brush and was cleaning the knobs of a telescope, apparently absorbed. A little later he got up and cleaned his hands thoroughly with a rag; his face was quite expressionless, his light eyes seemed intent only on finding any remaining stain of oil in the cuticles of his nails. Down below, around the villa, all was luminous and grandiose silence, emphasized rather than disturbed by the distant barking of Bendicò baiting the gardener's dog on the manure heap, and by the dull rhythmic beat of a cook's knife chopping meat in the kitchen for the next meal. The sun had absorbed the turbulence of men as well as the harshness of earth. The Prince moved toward the priest's table, sat down, and began drawing pointed little Bourbon lilies with a carefully sharpened pencil which the Jesuit had left behind in his anger. He looked serious but so serene that Father Pirrone no longer felt on tenterhooks.

"We're not blind, my dear Father, we're just human. We live in a changing reality to which we try to adapt ourselves like seaweed bending under the pressure of water. Holy Church has been granted an explicit promise of immortality; we, as a social class, have not. Any palliative which may give us another hundred years of life is like eternity to us. We may worry about our children and perhaps our grandchildren; but beyond what we can hope to stroke with these hands of ours we have no obligations. I cannot worry myself about what will happen to any possible descendants in the year 1960. The Church, yes, she must worry for she is destined not to die. Solace is implicit in her desperation. Don't you think that if now or in the future she could save herself by sacrificing us she wouldn't do so? Of course she would, and she would do right!"

Father Pironne was so pleased at not having offended the Prince that he did not take offense either. Of course that word "desperation" applied to the Church was quite inadmissible, but long habit as confessor had made him capable of appreciating Don Fabrizio's disillusioned mood. He must not let the other triumph, though. "Now, Excellency, you have a couple of sins to confess to me on Saturday, remember: one of the flesh yesterday, one of the spirit today. Remember!"

Both soothed, they began discussing a report which they would soon be sending to a foreign observatory, the one at Arcetri. Supported, guided, it seemed, by calculations which were invisible at that hour yet ever present, the stars cleft the ether in those exact trajectories of theirs. The comets would be appearing as usual, punctual to the minute, in sight of whoever was observing them. They were not messengers of catastrophe as Stella thought; on the contrary, their appearance at the time foreseen was a triumph of the human mind's capacity to project itself and to participate in the sublime routine of the skies. "Let's leave the Bendicòs down there running after rustic prey, and the cooks' knives chopping the flesh of innocent beasts. Above this observatory the bluster of the one and the blood on the other merge into tranquil harmony. The real problem is how to go on living this life of the spirit in its most sublimated moments, those moments that are most like death."

So reasoned the Prince, forgetting his own recurrent whims, his own cavortings of the night before. During those moments of abstraction he seemed more intimately absolved, in the sense of being linked anew with the universe, than by any blessing of Father Pirrone. For half an hour that morning the gods of the ceilings and the monkeys on the walls were again put to silence. But in the drawing room no one noticed.

When the bell for luncheon called them downstairs, both had regained their serenity, owing to understanding the political scene and to setting the understanding aside. An atmosphere of unusual relaxation had spread over the house. The midday meal was the chief one of the day, and went, God be thanked, quite smoothly. This in spite of one of the ringlets framing the face of the twenty-year-old Carolina, the eldest daughter, dropping into her soup plate because, apparently, of an ill-secured pin. Another day the incident might have had dreadful consequences, but now it only heightened the gaiety; and when her brother, sitting next to her, took the lock of hair and pinned it on his neckerchief, where it hung like a scapular, even the Prince allowed himself a smile. Tancredi's departure, destination, and reasons were now known to all, and everyone talked of them, except Paolo, who went on eating in silence. No one was really worrying about him, in fact, but the Prince, who showed no signs of the anxiety he still felt deep down, and Concetta, who was the only one with a shadow on her pretty forehead. "The girl must have her eye on the young rascal. They'd make a fine couple. But I fear Tancredi will have to aim higher, by which of course I mean lower."

Today, as political calm had cleared the mists generally veiling it, the Prince's fundamental good nature showed on the surface. To reassure his daughter he began explaining what useless muskets the Royal Army had; the barrels of those enormous pieces had no rifling, he said, so bullets coming from them would have very little penetration: technical comments thought up on the spur of the moment, understood by few and convincing none but consoling all, including Concetta, as they managed to transform war into a neat little diagram of fire-trajectories from the very squalid and very positive chaos that it really was.

At the end of the meal appeared a rum jelly. This was the Prince's favorite pudding, and the Princess had been careful to order it early that morning in gratitude for favors granted. It was rather threatening at first sight, shaped like a tower with bastions and battlements and smooth slippery walls impossible to scale, garrisoned by red and green cherries and pistachio nuts; but into its transparent and quivering flanks a spoon plunged with astounding ease. By the time the amber-colored fortress reached Francesco Paolo, the sixteen-year-old son, who was served last, it consisted only of shattered walls and hunks of wobbly rubble. Exhilarated by the aroma of rum and the delicate flavor of the multicolored garrison, the Prince enjoyed watching the rapid demolishing of the fortress beneath the assault of his family's appetites. One of his glasses was still half full of Marsala. He raised it, glanced around the family, gazed for a second into Concetta's blue eyes, then said, "To the health of our Tancredi." He drained his wine in a single gulp. The initials F. D. which before had stood out clearly on the golden color of the full glass were no longer visible.

In the estate office, to which he returned after luncheon, the sunlight was oblique, and the pictures of his estates, now shadowed, sent no messages of reproof. "Blessings on Your Excellency," muttered Pastorello and Lo Nigro, the two tenants of Ragattisi who had brought the portion of their rent they paid in kind. They were standing very straight with stunned-looking eyes in faces carefully shaven and burned dark by sun. They gave out a smell of flocks and herds. The Prince talked to them cordially in his very stylized dialect, inquired about their families, the state of their livestock, the outlook for the crops. Then he asked, "Have you brought anything?" And when the two answered yes, that it was in the room next door, the Prince felt a twinge of shame as he realized that the interview was a repetition of his own audiences with King Ferdinand. "Wait five minutes, and Ferrara will give you the receipts." He put into their hands a couple of ducats each, worth more, probably, than what they had brought. "Drink my health, will you?" and then he went and looked at their produce: on the ground were four *caciocavallo* cheeses, each weighing approximately ten kilos; he gave them a careless glance; he loathed that particular cheese; there were six baby lambs, the last of the year's litter, with their heads lolling pathetically above the big gash through which their lifeblood had flowed a few hours before. Their bellies had been slashed open too, and iridescent intestines hung out. "May God receive his soul," he thought, remembering the gutted soldier of a month before. Four pairs of chickens tied by the claws were twisting in terror under the poking snout of Bendicò. "Another example of pointless alarm," he thought; "the dog is no danger to them at all; he wouldn't even touch one of their bones, as it would give him a bellyache."

All this blood and panic revolted him, however. "Pastorello, take the chickens into the coop, will you, as there's no need of them in the larder; and another time take the baby lambs straight into the kitchen, will you; they make a mess here. And you, Lo Nigro, go and tell Salvatore to come and clean up and take away the cheese. And open the window to let the smell out."

Then Ferrara came and made out the receipts.

When the Prince went upstairs again, he found Paolo, his heir, the Duke of Querceta, waiting for him in his study on the red sofa where he proposed to take his siesta. The youth had screwed up all his courage to talk to him. Short, slim, olive-skinned, he seemed older than the Prince himself. "I wanted to ask you, Papa, how we're to behave with Tancredi when we next meet him."

The Prince understood at once and felt a twinge of annoyance. "What d'you mean? Has anything changed?"

"But, Papa, you can't possibly approve; he's gone to join those swine who're making trouble all over Sicily; things like that just aren't done."

Personal jealousy, a bigot's resentment at his agnostic cousin, a dullard's at the other's zest, had taken political guise. The Prince was so indignant that he did not even ask his son to sit down. "Better to make a fool of oneself than spend all day staring at horses' dung! I'm even fonder of Tancredi than I was before. And anyway what he's doing isn't as silly as all that. If in the future you're able to go on putting 'Duke of Querceta' on your cards, and if you inherit any money when I'm gone, you will owe it to Tancredi and others like him. Out with you now, and don't mention the subject to me again! I'm the only one who gives orders here." Then he became kindlier and substituted irony for anger. "Be off now, son, as I want to have a snooze. Go and talk politics with Guiscard, you'll understand each other."

And as a shaken Paolo closed the door behind him, the Prince took off his frock coat and boots, made the sofa creak under his weight, and slid calmly off to sleep.

When he awoke, his valet came in with a newspaper and a letter on a tray. They had been sent up from Palermo by his brother-in-law Màlvica, brought by a mounted groom a short while before. Still a little dazed from his afternoon nap, the Prince opened the letter. "My dear Fabrizio, I am writing to you in a state of utter collapse. Such dreadful news in the paper. The Piedmontese have landed. We are all lost. Tonight I and my whole family will take refuge on a British man-o'-war. You will want to do the same, I am sure; if you wish I can reserve a berth or two for you. May God save our beloved King! As always, Ciccio."

He folded up the letter, put it in his pocket, and began laughing out loud. That fool Màlvica! He'd always been a rabbit. Not understanding a thing, and now panic-stricken. Abandoning his palace to the mercy of his servants; this time he'd certainly find it empty on his return. "That reminds me, Paolo must go and stay down at Palermo; a house empty at a moment like this means a house lost. I'll tell him at dinner."

He opened the newspaper. "On the 11th of May an act of flagrant piracy culminated in the landing of armed men at Marsala. The latest reports say that the band numbers about eight hundred, and is commanded by Garibaldi. When these brigands set foot on land they were very careful to avoid any encounter with the Royal troops and moved off, as far as can be ascertained, in the direction of Castelvetrano, threatening peaceful citizens and spreading rapine and devastation, etc., etc. . . ."

The name of Garibaldi disturbed him a little. That adventurer, all hair and beard, was a pure Mazzinian. He had caused a lot of trouble already. "But if that *Galantuomo* King of his has let him come down here it means they're sure of him. They'll curb him!"

Reassured, he combed his hair and had his shoes and frock coat put on again. He thrust the newspaper into a drawer. It was almost time for Rosary, but the drawing room was still empty. He sat down on a sofa, and as he waited noticed how the Vulcan on the ceiling was rather like the lithographs of Garibaldi he had seen in Turin. He smiled. "A cuckold!"

The family was gathering. Silken skirts rustled. The youngest were still joking together. Behind the door could be heard the usual echo of controversy between servants and Bendicò, determined to take part.

A ray of sunshine full of dust specks lit up the malicious monkeys.

He knelt down. *"Salve Regina, Mater misericordiae."*

2

"THE trees! The trees!"

This shout from the leading carriage could just be heard along the row of four behind, almost invisible in clouds of white dust; and at every window perspiring faces expressed tired satisfaction.

The trees were only three, in truth, and eucalyptus at that, scruffiest of Mother Nature's children. But they were also the first seen by the Salina family since leaving Bisacquino at six that morning. It was now eleven, and for the last five hours all they had set eyes on were bare hillsides flaming yellow under the sun. Trots over level ground had alternated briefly with long, slow trudges uphill and then careful shuffles down; both trudge and trot merging, anyway, into the constant jingle of harness bells, imperceptible, now, to the dazed senses, except as sound equivalent of the blazing landscape. They had passed through crazed-look-ing villages washed in palest blue; crossed dry river beds over fantastic bridges; skirted sheer precipices which no sage and broom could temper. Never a tree, never a drop of water; just sun and dust. Inside the carriages, tightly shut against that sun and dust, the temperature must have been well over 120 degrees Fahrenheit. Those desiccated trees yearning away under bleached sky bore many a mes-sage: that they were now within a couple of hours of their journey's end; that they were coming into the family estates; that they could lunch, and perhaps even wash their faces in the verminous waters of the well.

Ten minutes later they reached the farm buildings of Rampinzèri: a huge pile, used only one month in the year by laborers, mules, and cattle gathered there for the har-vest. Over the great solid but sagging door, a stone Leopard pranced, in spite of legs broken off by flung stones; next to the main farm building a deep well, watched over by those eucalyptuses, mutely offered various services: as swimming pool, drinking trough, prison, or cemetery. It slaked thirst, spread typhus, guarded the kidnapped, and hid the corpses of both animals and men till they were reduced to the smoothest of anonymous skeletons.

The whole Salina family alighted from their various car-riages. The Prince, cheered by the thought of soon reach-ing his beloved Donnafugata; the Princess irritated and yet inert, in part restored, however, by her husband's serenity; tired girls; boys excited by novelty and untamed by the heat; Mademoiselle Dombreuil, the French governess, utterly exhausted, remembering years spent in Algeria with the family of Marshal Bugeaud, moaning, *"Mon Dieu, mon Dieu, c'est pire qu'en Afrique!"* and mopping at her turned-up nose. Father Pirrone, whose breviary reading had lulled him into a sleep which had shortened the whole trip and made him the spryest of the party; a maid and two lackeys, city folk worried by the unusual aspect of the countryside; and Bendicò, who had rushed out of the last carriage and was baying at the funereal suggestions of rooks swirling low in the light.

All were white with dust to the eyebrows, lips, or pigtails; whitish puffs arose around those who had reached the stopping place and were dusting each other off.

Amid all the dirt Tancredi's elegant spruceness stood out. He had travelled on horseback and, reaching the farm half an hour before the carriages, had had time to shake off dust, brush up, and change his white cravat. While drawing some water from that well of many uses he had glanced for a second into the mirror of the bucket and found himself in good order, with the black patch over his right eye now more reminiscent than protective of a wound received three months before in the fighting at Palermo; with that other dark blue eye which seemed to have assumed the task of expressing enough shy gaiety for its mate in temporary eclipse; and with, above his cravat, a scarlet thread alluding discreetly to the red shirt he had once worn. He helped the Princess to alight, dusted the Prince's top hat with his sleeve, distributed sweets to his girl cousins and quips to the boys, nearly genuflected to the Jesuit, returned the passionate caress of Bendicò, consoled Mademoiselle Dombreuil, laughed at all, enchanted all.

The coachmen were walking the horses slowly around to freshen them up before watering, the lackeys laying tablecloths out on straw left over from the threshing in the oblong of shade from the building. Luncheon began near the accommodating well. All around quivered the funereal countryside, yellow with stubble, black with burned patches; the lament of cicadas filled the sky. It was like a death rattle of parched Sicily at the end of August vainly awaiting rain.

An hour later they were all on the road again, refreshed. Although the horses were tired and going more slowly than ever, the last part of the journey seemed short; the landscape, no longer unknown, had lost its more sinister aspects. They began recognizing places they knew well, arid goals of past excursions and picnics in other years —the Dragonara ravine, the Misilbesi crossroads; soon they would reach the Shrine of Our Lady of All Graces, end of their longest walks from Donnafugata. The Princess had dozed off; the Prince, alone with her in the wide carriage, was beaming.

Never had he been so glad to be going to spend three months at Donnafugata as he was now, in that late August of 1860. Not only because he loved the house at Donnafugata, the people, the sense of feudal ownership surviving there, but also because, unlike other times, he felt no regret for his peaceful evenings in the observatory, his occasional visits to Mariannina. The truth was he had found the spectacle of Palermo in the last three months rather nauseating. He would have liked to have the fun of being the only one to understand the situation and accept that red-shirted "bogeyman" Garibaldi; but he had to admit that second sight was not a Salina monopoly. Everyone in Palermo seemed pleased; everyone except a mere handful of grumblers: his brother-in-law Màlvica, who had got himself arrested by Garibaldi's police and spent ten days in prison; his son Paolo, just as discontented but slightly more prudent, and now left behind at Palermo deep in some silly plot or other. Everyone else was making a great show of joy: wearing tricolor cockades on lapels, marching about in processions from morning till night, and above all talking, haranguing, declaiming; and if in the very first days of the occupation all this was given some sense of purpose by the acclamations greeting the few wounded passing through the main streets and by the shrieks of Bourbon police "rats" being tortured in the side alleys, now that the wounded had recovered and the surviving "rats" were enrolled in the new police, this hubbub, inevitable though he realized it to be, began to seem pointless and petty.

But he had to admit that all this was mere surface manifestation of ill breeding; the fundamentals of the situation, economic and social, were satisfactory, just as he had foreseen. Don Pietro Russo had kept his promises and not a shot had been heard near Villa Salina; and though a whole service of Chinese porcelain had been stolen from the palace in Palermo, that was merely due to the idiocy of Paolo, who had had it packed into a couple of cases which he had then left out in the palace courtyard during the shelling— a positive invitation for the packers themselves to cart it away.

The "Piedmontese" (as the Prince continued to call them for reassurance, just as others called them "Garibaldini" in exaltation or "Garibaldeschi" in vilification) had paid a call at the house, if not precisely cap in hand as the Prince had been told, at least with a hand at the visors of those red caps of theirs, as floppy and faded as those of any Bourbon officer.

About the twentieth of June, announced twenty-four hours beforehand by Tancredi, appeared a General in a red tunic with black froggings. He was followed by an aide-de-camp and asked most politely for admission in order to admire the frescoes on the ceilings. In he was ushered without ado, as there had been sufficient warning to clear from one of the drawing rooms a portrait of King Ferdinand II in full Court dress and substitute for it a neutral *Pool of Bethesda*, an operation combining advantages both political and aesthetic.

The General was a quick-witted Tuscan of about thirty, talkative and inclined to show off, though perfectly well behaved and agreeable; he had treated the Prince with all proper respect and even called him "Excellency," in com-

plete contradiction to one of the Dictator's first decrees.
The aide-de-camp, a new recruit of nineteen, was a Milanese Count, who fascinated the girls with his glittering
boots and his slurred *r*'s. With them came Tancredi, promoted, or rather created, Captain on the field of battle; a
little drawn from the pain of his wound, he stood there
red-shirted and irresistible, showing an easy intimacy with
the victors, an intimacy demonstrated by a lavish use of the
familiar *tu* and of "my dear fellow" with childish fervor
by the two officers from the mainland and returned in kind
by Tancredi, though with a faint nasal twang that to the
Prince seemed full of muted irony. While greeting them
from heights of imperturbable courtesy, the Prince had in
fact been much amused and quite reassured. So much so
that three days later the two "Piedmontese" had been invited to dinner; it was a fine sight then to see Carolina at
the piano accompanying the singing of the General, who,
in homage to Sicily, had risked "I see you again, oh lovely
land," with Tancredi gravely turning the pages of the
score as if false notes didn't exist. The young Milanese
Count, meanwhile, was leaning over a sofa, chatting away
about orange blossoms to Concetta and revealing to her the
existence of a writer she had never heard of, Aleardo
Aleardi; she was pretending to listen to him, though worrying about the gaunt looks of her cousin, whom the light
of the candle on the piano made appear even more languid
than he was in reality.

It had been an idyllic evening and was followed by

others equally cordial. During one of these the General was asked to try to obtain an exemption from the order expelling Jesuits for Father Pirrone, described as very aged and very ill; the General, who had taken a liking to the good priest, pretended to believe in his wretched state and agreed; he talked to political friends, pulled a string or two, and Father Pirrone stayed. Which went to confirm the Prince more than ever in the accuracy of his predictions.

The General was also most helpful about the complicated permits necessary in those troubled times for anyone wanting to move from place to place; and it was largely due to him that the Salina family was able to enjoy its annual sojourn in the country in that year of revolution. The young Captain asked for a month's leave and set off with his uncle and aunt. Even apart from permits, preparations for the Salinas' journey had been lengthy and complicated. Cryptic negotiations had to be conducted in the agent's office with "persons of influence" from Girgenti, negotiations ending in smiles, handclasps, and the tinkle of coin. Thus a second and more useful permit had been obtained; though this was no novelty. Piles of luggage and food had to be collected too, and cooks and servants sent on three days ahead; then there was one of the smaller telescopes to be packed and Paolo persuaded to stay behind in Palermo. After this they were able to move off; the General and the little Lieutenant came to wish them Godspeed and bring them flowers; and as the carriages moved off from Villa Salina two scarlet-covered arms continued to wave for a long time; at a carriage window appeared the Prince's black top hat, but the little hand in black lace mittens which the young Count had hoped to see remained in Concetta's lap.

The journey had lasted more than three days and had been appalling. The roads, the famous Sicilian roads because of which the Prince of Satriano had lost the Viceregency, were no more than tracks, all ruts and dust. The first night at Marineo, at the home of a notary and friend, had been more or less bearable, but the second at a little inn at Prizzi had been torture, with three of them to a bed, besieged by repellent local fauna. The third was at Bisacquino; no bugs there, but to make up for that the Prince had found thirteen flies in his glass of fruit juice, while a strong smell of excrement wafted in from the street and the privy next door, and all this had caused him most unpleasant dreams; waking at very early dawn amid all that sweat and stink, he had found himself comparing this ghastly journey with his own life, which had first moved over smiling level ground, then clambered up rocky mountains, slid over threatening passes, to emerge eventually into a landscape of interminable undulations, all of the same color, all bare as despair. These early morning fantasies were the very worst that could happen to a man of middle age; and although the Prince knew that they would vanish with the day's activities, he suffered acutely all the same, as he was used enough to them by now to realize that deep inside him they left a sediment of grief which, accumulating day by day, would in the end be the real cause of his death.

With the rising of the sun those monsters had gone back

to their lairs in his unconscious; near by now were Donnafugata and his palace, with its many-jetted fountains, its memories of saintly forebears, the sense it gave him of everlasting childhood. Even the people there were pleasant, simple, and devoted. At this point a thought occurred: Would they, after recent events, be just as devoted as before? "We'll soon see."

Now at last they were nearly there. Tancredi's mischievous face appeared at the carriage window sill. "Uncle, Aunt, get ready, in five minutes we'll be there." Tancredi was too tactful to precede the Prince into the town. He put his horse to a walk and proceeded in silence beside the leading carriage.

Beyond the short bridge leading into the town the authorities, surrounded by a few dozen peasants, were waiting. As the carriages moved onto the bridge the municipal band struck up with frenzied enthusiasm "Gypsy girls we," from *La Traviata*, the first odd and endearing greeting by Donnafugata to its Prince in recent years; after this, at a warning by some urchin on the lookout, the bells of the Mother Church and of the Convent of the Holy Spirit filled the air with festive sound.

"Thanks be to God, everything seems as usual," thought the Prince as he climbed out of his carriage. There was Don Calogero Sedàra, the Mayor, with a tricolor sash bright and new as his job tight around his waist; Monsignor Trottolino, the Archpriest, with his big red face; Don Ciccio Ginestra, the notary, all braid and feathers, as

Captain of the National Guard; there was Don Toto Giam-
bono, the doctor, and there was little Nunzia Giarritta, who
offered the Princess a rather messy bunch of flowers, gathered half an hour before in the palace gardens. There was
Ciccio Tumeo, the cathedral organist, who was not strictly
speaking of sufficient standing to be there with the authorities but had come along all the same as friend and hunting
companion of the Prince, and had had the excellent notion
of bringing along with him, for the Prince's pleasure, his
pointer bitch Teresina, with two little brown spots above
her eyes; daring rewarded with a special smile from Don
Fabrizio.

The latter was in high good humor and sincerely amiable; he and his wife got out of the carriage to express their
thanks, and against the tempestuous music of Verdi and the
crashing of bells embraced the Mayor and shook hands with
all the others. The crowd of peasants stood there silent, but
their motionless eyes emitted a curiosity in no way hostile,
for the poor of Donnafugata really did have a certain affection for their tolerant lord, who so often forgot to demand
their little rents of kind or money; also, used as they were
to seeing the bewhiskered Leopard on the palace façade, on
the church front, above the fountains, on the majolica tiles
in their houses, they were glad to set eyes now on the real
animal, in nankeen trousers, distributing friendly shakes of
the paw to all, his features amiably wreathed in feline
smiles. "Yes indeed; everything is the same as before, better, in fact, than before." Tancredi, too, was the object of
great curiosity; though everybody had known him for a

long time, now he seemed to them transfigured; no longer
did they see him as a mere unconventional youth, but as an
aristocratic liberal, companion of Rosolino Pilo, wounded
hero of the battle of Palermo. Amid this open admiration
he was swimming about like a fish in water; these rustic
admirers he found really rather fun; he talked to them
in dialect, joked, laughed at himself and his own wounds;
but when he said "General Garibaldi," his voice dropped
an octave and he put on the rapt look of a choirboy before
the Monstrance; then to Don Calogero Sedàra, of whom
he had vaguely heard as being very active during the period
of the liberation, he said in booming tones, "Ah, Don
Calogero, Crispi said lots of nice things to me about you."
After which he gave his arm to his cousin Concetta and
moved off, leaving everyone in raptures.

The carriages, with servants, children, and Bendicò,
went on to the palace; but according to ancient usage, before the others set foot in their home they had to hear a
Te Deum in the cathedral. This was, anyway, only a few
paces off, and they moved there in procession, the new
arrivals dusty but imposing, the authorities gleaming but
humble. Ahead walked Don Ciccio Ginestra, the prestige
of his uniform cleaving a path; he was followed by the
Prince, giving an arm to the Princess, and looking like a
sated and pacified lion; behind them came Tancredi with,
on his right, Concetta, who found this walk toward a
church beside her cousin most upsetting and conducive to
gentle weeping: a state of mind in no way alleviated by the

dutiful young man's strong pressure on her arm, though its only purpose was to save her from potholes and ruts. The others followed in disorder. The organist had rushed off so as to have time to deposit Teresina at home and be back at his resonant post at the moment of entry into church. The bells were clanging away ceaselessly, and on the walls of the houses the slogans "Viva Garibaldi," "Viva King Vittorio," "Death to the Bourbon King," scrawled by an inexpert brush two months before, were fading away as if they wanted to merge back into the walls. Firecrackers were exploding all around as they moved up the steps, and as the little procession entered the church Don Ciccio Tumeo, who had arrived panting but in time, broke impetuously into the strains of Verdi's "Love me, Alfredo."

The nave was packed with curious idlers between its squat columns of red marble; the Salina family sat in the choir, and during the short ceremony Don Fabrizio got up and made an impressive bow to the crowd; meanwhile the Princess was on the verge of swooning from heat and exhaustion; Tancredi, pretending to brush away flies, more than once grazed Concetta's blonde head. All was in order and, after a short address by Monsignor Trottolino, they all genuflected to the altar, turned toward the doors, and issued into the sun-dazed square.

At the bottom of the steps the authorities took their leave, and the Princess, acting under instructions whispered to her during the ceremony, invited the Mayor, the Archpriest, and the notary to dine that same evening. The Archpriest was a bachelor by profession and the notary one by vocation, so that for them the question of consorts did not arise; the invitation to the Mayor was rather languidly extended to his wife; she was some peasant woman, of great beauty, but considered by her own husband as quite unpresentable in public for a number of reasons; thus no one was surprised at his saying that she was indisposed; but great was the amazement when he added, "If Your Excellencies will allow I'll bring along my daughter Angelica, who's been talking for the past month of nothing but her longing to be presented to you now that she's grown up." Consent was, of course, given; and the Prince, who had seen Tumeo peering at him from behind the others' shoulders, called out to him, "You come too, of course, Don Ciccio, and bring Teresina." And he added, turning to the others, "And after dinner, at nine o'clock, we shall be happy to see all our friends." For a long time Donnafugata commented on these last words. And the Prince, who had found Donnafugata unchanged, was found very much changed himself, for never before would he have issued so cordial an invitation; and from that moment, invisibly, began the decline of his prestige.

The Salina palace was next door to the Mother Church. Its short façade with seven windows on the square gave no hint of its vast size, which extended three hundred yards back; the buildings were of different styles, but all harmoniously grouped around three great courtyards ending in a large garden. At the main entrance in the square the travellers were subjected to new demonstrations of welcome. Don Onofrio Rotolo, the family's local steward, took no part in the official greetings at the entry of the town. Educated under the rigid rule of the Princess Carolina, he considered the *"vulgus"* as nonexistent and the Prince as resident abroad until the moment when he crossed the threshold of his own palace. So there he stood, exactly two steps outside the gates, very small, very old, very bearded, with a much younger and plumper wife standing beside him, flanked by lackeys and eight keepers with golden Leopards on their caps and in their hands eight shotguns of uncertain damaging power. "I am happy to welcome Your Excellencies to your home. And I beg to hand back the palace in the exact state in which it was left to me."

Don Onofrio Rotolo was one of the rare persons held in esteem by the Prince, and perhaps the only one who had never cheated him. His honesty was on the verge of mania, and spectacular tales were told of it, such as the glass of rosolio once left half full by the Princess at the moment of departure, and found a year later in exactly the same place with its contents evaporated and reduced to a state of sugary rubber, but untouched. "For it is an infinitesimal part of the Prince's patrimony and must not be dispersed."

After a proper exchange of greetings with Don Onofrio and Donna Maria, the Princess, who was still on her feet only by sheer strength of will, went straight to bed, the girls and Tancredi hurried off to the tepid shade of the gardens, while the Prince and his steward went on a tour of the main apartments. Everything was in perfect order: the pictures were clear of dust in their heavy frames, the

old gilt bindings emitted discreet gleams, the high sun
made the gray marble glitter around the doorposts. Everything was in the state it had been in for the last fifty years.
Away from the noisy whirlwind of civil dissent Don Fabrizio felt refreshed, full of serene confidence, and glanced
almost tenderly at Don Onofrio trotting along beside him.
"Don Nofrio, you're like one of those djinns standing
guard over treasure, really you are; we owe you a great
debt of gratitude." In another year the sentiment might
have been the same but the words themselves would never
have come to his lips; Don Nofrio looked at him in gratitude and surprise. "My duty, Your Excellency, it's just
my duty," and to hide his emotion he scratched the back of
his ear with the long nail on the little finger of his left
hand.

After this the steward was put to the torture of tea. Don
Fabrizio had two cups brought, and with death in his heart
Don Nofrio had to swallow one. After this he began to
recount the chronicles of Donnafugata: he had renewed the
lease for the Aquila estate two weeks before, on rather
worse terms; he had had to meet heavy expenses for the
repairs of the roof in the guest wing; but in the safe, at His
Excellency's disposal, was the sum of three thousand, two
hundred and seventy-five ounces of gold, after paying all
expenses, taxes, and his own salary.

Then came the private news, all of which turned around
the great novelty of the year: the rapid rise to fortune of
Don Calogero Sedàra; six months ago a mortgage arranged
by the latter with Baron Tumino had been foreclosed, and

he had gained possession of the estate; thus by the loan of a thousand ounces of gold he now owned a property which yielded five hundred ounces a year; in April Don Calogero had also been able to buy for practically nothing a certain piece of land which contained a vein of much sought-after stone that he intended to exploit; he had also made some very profitable sales of grain in the period of confusion and famine after the landings. The voice of Don Nofrio filled with rancor. "I've totted it up roughly on my fingers: Don Calogero's income will very shortly be equal to that of Your Excellency here at Donnafugata." With riches had also grown political influence. He had become head of the liberals in the town and also in the surrounding districts; when the elections were held he was sure to be returned as Deputy to Turin. "And what airs they give themselves; not he, who's far too shrewd to do that, but his daughter, who's just got back from school in Florence and goes around town in a crinoline and with velvet ribbons hanging from her hat."

The Prince was silent; the daughter, yes, that must be the Angelica who would be coming to dinner tonight; he was curious to see this dressed-up shepherdess; it was not true that nothing had changed: Don Calogero was as rich as he was! But deep down he had foreseen such things; they were the price to be paid.

Don Nofrio was disturbed by his master's silence, and imagined he had put the Prince out by telling him petty local gossip. "Excellency, I ordered a bath to be prepared for you, it should be ready by now." Don Fabrizio sud-

denly realized that he was tired; it was almost three
o'clock, and he had been up and about for nine hours under
that torrid sun, and after that ghastly night. He felt his
body covered in dust to the remotest creases. "Thank you,
Don Nofrio, for thinking of it; and for everything else.
We shall meet tonight at dinner."

He went up the inner staircase; passed through the Tapestry Hall, through the Blue Salon, the Yellow Salon;
lowered blinds filtered the light; in his study the Boulle
clock ticked away discreetly. "What peace, my God, what
peace!" He entered the bathroom: small, whitewashed,
with a rough tiled floor and a hole in the middle to let the
water out. The bath itself was a kind of oval trough, vast,
of enamelled iron, yellow outside and gray in, propped on
four heavy wooden feet. Hanging on a nail was a dressing
gown; fresh linen was laid out on a rush chair; it still
showed creases from the packing. Beside the bath lay a big
piece of pink soap, a brush, a knotted handkerchief containing salts which would emit a sweet scent when soaked,
and a huge sponge, one sent by the Salina agent. Through
the unshaded window beat the savage sun.

He clapped his hands; two lackeys entered, each carrying
a pair of pails filled to the brim, one with cold, the other
with boiling water; they went to and fro a number of times;
the trough filled up; he tried the temperature with a hand;
it was all right. He ordered the servants out, undressed, got
in. Under his huge bulk the water brimmed over a little.
He soaped himself, rubbed himself; the warmth did him

good, relaxed him. He was almost dozing off when he heard a knock at the door; Mimí, his valet, entered timidly. "Father Pirrone is asking to see Your Excellency at once. He is waiting outside for Your Excellency to leave the bathroom." The Prince was surprised; if there'd been some accident he had better know at once. "No, no, let him come in now."

Don Fabrizio was alarmed by this haste of Father Pirrone; and partly from this and partly from respect for the priestly habit, he hurried to leave the bath, expecting to get into his dressing gown before the Jesuit entered, but he did not succeed; and Father Pirrone came in at the very moment when, no longer veiled by soapy water, he was emerging quite naked, like the Farnese Hercules, and steaming as well, while the water flowed in streams from neck, arms, stomach, and legs like the Rhone, the Rhine, the Danube, and the Adige crossing and watering Alpine ranges. The sight of the Prince in a state of nature was quite new to Father Pirrone; the sacrament of penance had accustomed him to naked souls, but he was far less used to naked bodies; and he, who would not have blinked an eyelid at hearing the confession, say, of an incestuous intrigue, found himself flustered by this innocent but vast expanse of naked flesh. He stuttered an excuse and made to back out; but Don Fabrizio, annoyed at not having had time to cover himself, naturally turned his irritation against the priest: "Now, Father, don't be silly; hand me that towel, will you, and help me to dry, if you don't mind." Then suddenly he remembered a discussion they had once had and went on: "And take my advice, Father, have a bath your-self." Satisfied at being able to give advice on hygiene to one who so often gave it to him on morals, he felt soothed. With the upper part of the towel in his hands at last he began drying his hair, whiskers, and neck, while with the lower end the humiliated Father Pirrone rubbed his feet.

When the peak and slopes of the mountain were dry, the Prince said, "Now sit down, Father, and tell me why you're in such a hurry to talk to me." And as the Jesuit sat down he began some more intimate moppings on his own.

"Well, Excellency, I've been given a most delicate com-mission. One who is very dear to you indeed has opened her heart to me and charged me to tell you of her feelings, trusting, perhaps wrongly, that the consideration with which I am honored . . ." Father Pirrone hesitated and hovered from phrase to phrase.

Don Fabrizio lost patience. "Well, come on, Father, who is it? The Princess?" And his raised arm seemed to be threatening: in fact he was drying an armpit.

"The Princess is tired; she's asleep and I have not seen her. No, it is the Signorina Concetta." Pause. "She is in love." A man of forty-five can consider himself still young till the moment comes when he realizes that he has chil-dren old enough to fall in love. The Prince felt old age come over him in one blow; he forgot the huge distances still tramped out shooting, the "*Gesummaria*" he could still evoke from his wife, how fresh he now was at the end of a long and arduous journey. Suddenly he saw himself as a white-haired old man walking beside herds of grandchildren on billy goats in the public gardens of Villa Giulia.

"Why ever did the silly girl go and tell you such a thing? Why not come to me?" He did not even ask who the man was; there was no need to.

"Your Excellency hides his fatherly heart almost too well under the mask of authority. It's quite understandable that the poor girl should be frightened of you, and so fall back on the family chaplain."

Don Fabrizio slipped on his long drawers and snorted; he foresaw long interviews, tears, endless bother. The silly girl was spoiling his first day at Donnafugata with her fancies. "I know, Father, I know. Here no one really understands me. It's my misfortune." He was sitting now on a stool with the fuzz of fair hair on his chest dotted with pearly drops of water. Rivulets were snaking over the tiles, and the room was full of the milky smell of bran and the almond smell of soap. "Well, what should I say, in your opinion?"

The Jesuit was sweating in the heat of the little room, and now that his message had been delivered would have liked to go, but he was held back by a feeling of responsibility. "The wish to found a Christian family is most agreeable to the eyes of the Church. The presence of Our Lord at the marriage in Cana . . ."

"Let's keep to the point, shall we? I wish to talk about this marriage, not about marriage in general. Has Don Tancredi made any definite proposal, by any chance, and if so, when?"

For five years Father Pirrone had tried to teach the boy Latin; for seven years he had put up with his quips and pranks; like everyone else, he had felt his charm. But Tancredi's recent political attitudes had offended him; his old affection was struggling now with a new rancor. He did not know what to say. "Well, not a real proposal, exactly, no. But the Signorina Concetta is quite certain: his attentions, his glances, his remarks, have all become more and more open and frequent and quite convinced the dear creature; she is sure that she is loved; but, being an obedient and respectful daughter, she wants me to find out from you what her answer is to be if a proposal does come. She thinks it imminent."

The Prince felt a little reassured; however, did a chit of a girl like that think she had acquired enough experience to be able to judge so surely the behavior of a young man, and particularly of a young man like Tancredi? Perhaps it was just imagination, one of those "golden dreams" which convulse the pillows of schoolgirls. The danger might not be so near.

Danger. The word resounded so clearly in his mind that he gave a start of surprise. Danger. But danger for whom? He had a great affection for Concetta; he liked her perpetual submission, the placidity with which she yielded to the slightest hint of a paternal wish: a submission and placidity, incidentally, which he rather overvalued. His natural tendency to avoid any threat to his own calm had made him miss the steely glint which crossed her eyes when the whims she was obeying were really too vexing. Yes, the

Prince was very fond of this daughter of his. But he was even fonder of his nephew. Conquered for ever by the youth's affectionate banter, he had begun during the last few months to admire his intelligence too: that quick adaptability, that worldly penetration, that innate artistic subtlety with which he could use the demagogic terms then in fashion while hinting to initiates that for him, the Prince of Falconeri, this was only a momentary pastime; all this amused Don Fabrizio, and in people of his character and standing the faculty for being amused makes up four fifths of affection. Tancredi, he considered, had a great future; he would be the standard-bearer of a counterattack which the nobility, under new trappings, could launch against the new social State. To do this he lacked only one thing: money; this Tancredi did not have; none at all. And to get on in politics, now that a name counted less, would require a lot of money: money to buy votes, money to do the electors favors, money for a dazzling style of living. Style of living . . . And would Concetta, with all those passive virtues of hers, be capable of helping an ambitious and brilliant husband to climb the slippery slopes of the new society? Timid, reserved, bashful as she was? Wouldn't she always remain just the pretty schoolgirl she was now, a leaden weight on her husband's feet?

"Can you see Concetta, Father, as ambassadress in Vienna or Petersburg?"

The question astounded Father Pirrone. "What has that to do with it? I don't understand."

Don Fabrizio did not bother to explain; he plunged back

into his silent thoughts. Money? Concetta would have a dowry, of course. But the Salina fortune would have to be divided into seven parts, unequal parts at that, of which the girls' would be the smallest. Well, then? Tancredi needed much more: Maria Santa Pau, for instance, with four estates already hers and all those uncles priests and misers; or one of the Sutèra girls, so ugly but so rich. Love. Of course, love. Flames for a year, ashes for thirty. He knew what love was. . . . Anyway, Tancredi would always find women falling for him like ripe pears.

Suddenly he felt cold. The water on him had evaporated, and the skin of his arms was icy. The ends of his fingers were crinkling. Oh dear, what a lot of bothersome talk it would all mean. That must be avoided. . . . "Now I have to go and dress, Father. Tell Concetta, will you, that I'm not in the least annoyed, but that we'll talk about all this later when we're quite sure it's not all just the fancy of a romantic girl. *Au revoir*, Father."

He got up and passed into the dressing room. From the Mother Church next door rang a lugubrious funeral knell. Someone had died at Donnafugata, some tired body unable to withstand the deep gloom of Sicilian summer had lacked the stamina to await the rains. "Lucky person," thought the Prince, as he rubbed lotion on his whiskers. "Lucky person, with no worries now about daughters, dowries, and political careers." This ephemeral identification with an unknown corpse was enough to calm him. "While there's death there's hope," he thought; then he saw the absurd side of letting himself get into such a state of depression because one of his daughters wanted to marry. *"Ce sont leurs affaires, après tout,"* he thought in French, as he did when his cogitations were becoming embarrassing. He settled in an armchair and dropped off into a doze.

An hour later he awoke refreshed and went down into the garden. The sun was already low, and its rays, no longer overwhelming, were lighting amiably on the araucarias, the pines, the lusty plane trees which were the glory of the place. From the end of the main alley, sloping gently down between high laurel hedges framing anonymous busts of broken-nosed goddesses, could be heard the gentle drizzle of spray falling into the fountain of Amphitrite. He moved swiftly toward it, eager to see it again. The waters came spurting in minute jets, blown from shells of Tritons and Naiads, from noses of marine monsters, spluttering and pattering on greenish verges, bouncing and bubbling, wavering and quivering, dissolving into laughing little gurgles; from the whole fountain, the tepid water, the stones covered with velvety moss, emanated a promise of pleasure that would never turn to pain. Perched on an islet in the middle of the round basin, modelled by a crude but sensual sculptor, a vigorous smiling Neptune was embracing a willing Amphitrite; her navel, wet with spray and gleaming in the sun, would be the nest, shortly, for hidden kisses in subaqueous shade. Don Fabrizio paused, gazed, remembered, regretted. He stood there a long while.

"Uncle, come and look at the foreign peaches. They've turned out fine. And leave these indecencies, which are not for men of your age."

Tancredi's affectionate mocking voice called him from his voluptuous torpor. He had not heard the boy come; he was like a cat. For the first time he felt a touch of rancor prick him at sight of Tancredi; this fop with the pinched-in waist under his dark blue suit had been the cause of those sour thoughts of his about death two hours ago. Then he realized that it was not rancor, just disguised alarm: he was afraid the other would talk to him about Concetta. But his nephew's approach and tone was not that of one preparing to make amorous confidences to a man like himself. Don Fabrizio grew calm again; his nephew was looking at him with the affectionate irony which youth accords to age. "They can allow themselves to be a bit nice to us, as they're so sure to be free of us the day of our funerals." He went with Tancredi to look at the "foreign peaches." The graft with German cuttings, made two years ago, had succeeded perfectly; there was not much fruit, a dozen or so, on the two grafted trees, but it was big, velvety, luscious-looking; yellowish, with a faint flush of rosy pink on the cheeks, like those of Chinese girls. The Prince gave them a gentle squeeze with his delicate fleshy fingers. "They seem quite ripe. A pity there are too few for tonight. But we'll get them picked tomorrow and see what they're like."

"There! That's how I like you, Uncle; like this, in the part of *agricola pius*—appreciating in anticipation the fruits of your own labors, and not as I found you a moment ago, gazing at all that shameless naked flesh."

"And yet, Tancredi, these peaches are also products of love, of coupling."

"Of course, but legal love, blessed by you as their master, and by Nino the gardener as notary. Considered, fruitful love. As for those," he went on, pointing at the fountain whose shimmer could just be discerned through a veil of plane trees, "d'you really think they've been before a priest?"

The conversation was taking a dangerous turn and Don Fabrizio hastily changed its direction. As they moved back up toward the house Tancredi began telling what he had heard of the love-life of Donnafugata: Menica, the daughter of Saverio the keeper, had let herself be put with child by her young man; the marriage would be rushed now. Calicchio had just avoided being shot by an angry husband.

"But how d'you know such things?"

"I know, Uncle, I know. They tell me everything; they know I'll sympathize."

When they reached the top of the steps, which rose from the garden to the palace with gentle turns and long landings, they could see the dusky horizon beyond the trees; over toward the sea huge, inky clouds were climbing up the sky. Perhaps the anger of God was satiated and the annual curse on Sicily nearly over? At that moment those clouds loaded with relief were being stared at by thousands of other eyes, sensed in the womb of the earth by billions of seeds.

"Let's hope the summer is over, and that the rains are finally here," said Don Fabrizio; and with these words the haughty noble to whom the rain would only be a personal nuisance showed himself a brother to his roughest peasants.

The Prince had always taken care that the first dinner at Donnafugata should bear the stamp of solemnity: children under fifteen were excluded from table, French wines were served, there was punch *alla Romana* before the roast; and the flunkeys were in powder and knee-breeches. There was only one unusual detail: he did not put on evening dress, so as not to embarrass his guests who would, obviously, not possess any. That evening, in the "Leopold" drawing room, as it was called, the Salina family were awaiting the last of their guests. From under lace-covered shades the oil lamps spread circles of yellow light; the vast equestrian portraits of past Salinas seemed but imposing symbols, vague as their memories. Don Onofrio, with his wife, had already arrived, and so had the Archpriest, who, with his light mantle folded back on his shoulders in sign of gala, was telling the Princess about tiffs at the College of Mary. Don Ciccio, the organist, had also arrived (Teresina had already been tied to the leg of a table in the scullery) and was recalling with the Prince their fantastic bags in the ravines of Dragonara. All was placid and normal when Francesco Paolo, the six-teen-year-old son, burst into the room and announced, "Papa, Don Calogero is just coming up the stairs. In *tails*!"

Tancredi, intent on fascinating the wife of Don Onofrio, had realized the importance of the news a second before the others. But when he heard that last fatal word he could not contain himself and burst into convulsive laughter. No laugh, though, came from the Prince, on whom, one might almost say, this news had more effect than the bulletin about the landing at Marsala. That had been an event not only foreseen but also distant and invisible. Now, with his sensibility to presages and symbols, he saw revolution in that white tie and two black tails moving at this moment up the stairs of his own home. Not only was he, the Prince, no longer the major landowner in Donnafugata, but he now found himself forced to receive, when in afternoon dress himself, a guest appearing in evening clothes.

His distress was great; it still lasted as he moved mechanically toward the door to receive his guest. When he saw him, however, his agonies were somewhat eased. Though perfectly adequate as a political demonstration, it was obvious that, as tailoring, Don Calogero's tail coat was a disastrous failure. The material was excellent, the style modern, but the cut quite appalling. The Word from London had been most inadequately made flesh by a tailor from Girgenti to whom Don Calogero had gone in his tenacious avarice. The tails of his coat pointed straight to heaven in mute supplication, his huge collar was shapeless, and, what is more, the Mayor's feet were shod in buttoned boots.

Don Calogero advanced toward the Princess with a hand outstretched and gloved. "My daughter begs you to excuse her; she was not quite ready. Your Excellency knows how females are on these occasions," he added, expressing in his near-dialect terms a touch of Parisian levity, "but she'll be here in a second; it's only a step from our place, as you know."

The second lasted five minutes; then the door opened

and in came Angelica. The first impression was of dazed surprise. The Salina family all stood there with breath taken away; Tancredi could even feel the veins pulsing in his temples. Under the first shock from her beauty the men were incapable of noticing or analyzing its defects, which were numerous; there were to be many forever incapable of this critical appraisal. She was tall and well made, on an ample scale; her skin looked as if it had the flavor of fresh cream, which it resembled; her childlike mouth, that of strawberries. Under a mass of raven hair, curling in gentle waves, her green eyes gleamed motionless as those of statues, and like them a little cruel. She was moving slowly, making her wide white skirt rotate around her, and emanating from her whole person was the invincible calm of a woman sure of her beauty. Only many months later was it known that at the moment of that victorious entry she had been on the point of fainting from anxiety.

She took no notice of the Prince hurrying toward her; she passed by Tancredi grinning at her in a daydream; before the Princess's armchair she bent her superb waist in a slight bow, and this form of homage, unusual in Sicily, gave her for an instant the fascination of the exotic as well as that of local beauty.

"Angelica my dear, it's so long since I've seen you. You've changed a lot; not for the worse!" The Princess could not believe her own eyes; she remembered the rather ugly and uncared-for thirteen-year-old girl of four years before and could not make her tally with this voluptuous maiden here before her. The Prince had no memories to reorganize; he only had forecasts to overturn; the blow to his pride dealt by the father's tail coat was now repeated by the daughter's looks; but this time it was not a matter of black stuff, but of milky white skin, and well cut, yes, very well indeed! Old war horse that he was, the bugle call of feminine beauty found him ready, and he turned to the girl with the tone of gracious respect which he would have used with the Duchess of Bovino or the Princess of Lampedusa: "How fortunate we are, Signorina Angelica, to have gathered such a lovely flower in our home; and I hope that we shall have the pleasure of seeing you here often."

"Thank you, Prince; I see that you are as kind to me as you have always been to my dear father." The voice was pretty, low-pitched, a little too careful perhaps; Florentine schooling had cancelled the sagging Girgenti accent; the only Sicilian characteristic still in her speech was the harsh consonants, which anyway toned in well with her clear but emphatic type of beauty. In Florence she had also been taught to drop the "Excellency."

About Tancredi there seems little to be said; after being introduced by Don Calogero, after maneuvering the searchlight of his blue eyes, after just managing to resist implanting a kiss on Angelica's hand, he had resumed his chat with the Signora Rotolo without taking in a word that the good lady said. Father Pirrone, in a dark corner, was deep in meditation over Holy Scripture, which that night appeared only in the guise of Delilahs, Judiths, and Esthers.

The central doors of the drawing room were flung open and the butler declaimed mysterious sounds announcing that dinner was ready. *"Prann' pronn'."* The heterogeneous group moved toward the dining room.

The Prince was too experienced to offer Sicilian guests, in a town of the interior, a dinner beginning with soup, and he infringed the rules of *haute cuisine* all the more readily as he disliked it himself. But rumors of the barbaric foreign usage of serving insipid liquid as first course had reached the major citizens of Donnafugata too insistently for them not to quiver with a slight residue of alarm at the start of a solemn dinner like this. So when three lackeys in green, gold, and powder entered, each holding a great silver dish containing a towering mound of macaroni, only four of the twenty at table avoided showing their pleased surprise: the Prince and Princess from foreknowledge, Angelica from affectation, and Concetta from lack of appetite. All the others, including Tancredi, showed their relief in varying ways, from the fluty and ecstatic grunts of the notary to the sharp squeak of Francesco Paolo. But a threatening circular stare from the host soon stifled these improper demonstrations.

Good manners apart, though, the appearance of those monumental dishes of macaroni was worthy of the quivers of admiration they evoked. The burnished gold of the crusts, the fragrance of sugar and cinnamon they exuded, were but preludes to the delights released from the interior when the knife broke the crust; first came a mist laden with aromas, then chicken livers, hard-boiled eggs, sliced ham, chicken, and truffles in masses of piping-hot, glistening macaroni, to which the meat juice gave an exquisite hue of suède.

The beginning of the meal, as happens in the provinces, was quiet. The Archpriest made the sign of the Cross, and plunged in head-first without a word. The organist absorbed the succulent dish with closed eyes; he was grateful to the Creator that his ability to shoot hare and woodcock could bring him ecstatic pleasures like this, and the thought came to him that he and Teresina could exist for a month on the cost of one of these dishes. Angelica, the lovely Angelica, forgot her Tuscan affectations and part of her good manners and devoured her food with the appetite of her seventeen years and the vigor derived from grasping her fork halfway up the handle. Tancredi, in an attempt to link gallantry and greed, tried to imagine himself tasting, in the aromatic forkfuls, the kisses of his neighbor Angelica, but he realized at once that the experiment was disgusting and suspended it, with a mental reservation about reviving this fantasy with the pudding. The Prince, although rapt in the contemplation of Angelica sitting opposite him, was the only one able to note that the *demi-glace* was too rich, and made a mental note to tell the cook so next day; the others ate without thinking of anything, and without realizing that the food seemed so delicious because a whiff of sensuality had wafted into the house.

All were calm and contented. All except Concetta. She had of course embraced and kissed Angelica, told her not

to use the formal third person and insisted on the familiar
"*tu*" of their infancy, but under her pale blue bodice her
heart was being torn to shreds; the violent Salina blood
came surging up in her, and under a smooth forehead she
found herself brooding over daydreams of poisoning. Tancredi was sitting between her and Angelica and distributing,
with the slightly forced air of one who feels in the wrong,
his glances, compliments, and jokes equally between both
neighbors; but Concetta had an intuition, an animal intuition, of the current of desire flowing from her cousin toward the intruder, and the little frown between her nose
and forehead deepened; she wanted to kill as much as she
wanted to die. But being a woman she snatched at details:
Angelica's little finger in the air when her hand held her
glass; a reddish mole on the skin of her neck; an attempt,
half repressed, to remove with a finger a bit of food stuck in
her very white teeth. She noticed even more sharply a certain coarseness of spirit; and to these details, which were
really quite insignificant as they were cauterized by sensual
fascination, she clung as trustingly and desperately as a falling carpenter's apprentice snatches at a leaden gutter; she
hoped that Tancredi would notice too and be revolted by
these obvious traces of ill breeding. But Tancredi had already noticed them and, alas! with no result. He was letting
himself be drawn along by the physical stimulus that a
beautiful woman was to his fiery youth, and also by the (as
it were) measurable excitement aroused by a rich girl in the
mind of a man both ambitious and poor.

At the end of dinner the conversation became general:

Don Calogero told in bad Italian but with knowing insight some inside stories about the conquest of the province by Garibaldi; the notary told the Princess of a little house he was having built "out of town"; Angelica, excited by lights, food, Chablis, and the obvious admiration she was arousing in every man around the table, asked Tancredi to describe some episodes of the "glorious battle" for Palermo. She had put an elbow on the table and was leaning her cheek on her hand. Her face was flushed and she was perilously attractive to behold; the arabesque made by her forearm, elbow, finger, and hanging white glove seemed exquisite to Tancredi and repulsive to Concetta. The young man, while continuing to admire, was describing the campaign as if it had all been quite light and unimportant: the night march on Gibilrossa, the scene between Bixio and La Masa, the assault on Porta di Termini. "It was the greatest fun, Signorina. Our biggest laugh was on the night of the twenty-eighth of May. The General needed a lookout post at the top of the convent at Origlione; we knocked, banged, cursed, knocked again: no one opened; it was an enclosed community. Then Tassoni, Aldrighetti, I, and one or two others tried to break down the door with our rifle butts. Nothing doing. We ran to fetch a beam from a shelled house near by and finally, with a hellish din, the door gave way. We went in; not a soul in sight; but from a corner of the passage we heard desperate screams; a group of nuns had taken refuge in the chapel and were all crouching around the altar; I wonder *what* they feared at the hands of those dozen excited young men! They looked absurd, old and ugly in their black habits, with starting eyes, ready and prepared for . . . martyrdom. They were whining like bitches. Tassoni, who's a card, shouted, 'Nothing doing, sisters, we've other things to think of; but we'll be back when you've got some novices.' And we all laughed fit to burst. Then we left them there, their tongues hanging out, to go and shoot at Royalists from the terraces above. Ten minutes later I was wounded."

Angelica laughed, still leaning on her elbow, and showed all her pointed teeth. The joke seemed most piquant to her; that hint of rape perturbed her; her lovely throat quivered. "What fine lads you have been! How I wish I'd been with you!" Tancredi seemed transformed; the excitement of the story, the thrill of memory, mingling with the agitation produced by the girl's air of sensuality, changed him for an instant from the gentle youth he was in reality into a brutal and licentious soldier.

"Had you been there, Signorina, we'd have had no need to wait for novices."

Angelica had heard a lot of coarse talk at home; but this was the first time (and not the last) when she found herself the object of a sexual innuendo; the novelty of it pleased her, her laughter went up a tone, became strident.

At that moment everyone rose from table; Tancredi bent to gather up the feather fan dropped by Angelica; as he rose to his feet he saw Concetta with face aflame and two little tears in the corners of her lids. "Tancredi, one tells nasty tales like that to a confessor, not to young ladies at table; or at least not when I'm there." And she turned her back on him.

Before going to bed Don Fabrizio paused a moment on the little balcony of his dressing room. The shadowed garden lay sunk in sleep, below; in the inert air the trees seemed like fused lead; from the overhanging bell tower came an elfin hoot of owls. The sky was clear of clouds; those which had greeted the dusk had moved away, maybe toward places less sinful, condemned by divine wrath to lesser penalties. The stars looked turbid and their rays scarcely penetrated the pall of sultry air.

The soul of the Prince reached out toward them, toward the intangible, the unattainable, which gave joy without laying claim to anything in return; as many other times, he tried to imagine himself in those icy tracts, a pure intellect armed with a notebook for calculations: difficult calculations, but ones which would always work out. "They're the only really genuine, the only really decent beings," thought he, in his worldly formulae. "Who worries about dowries for the Pleiades, a political career for Sirius, matrimonial joy for Vega?" It had been a bad day; he realized it now, not only from a pressure at the pit of his stomach but from the stars too; instead of seeing them disposed in their usual groupings, every time he raised his eyes he noticed a single diagram up there: two stars above, the eyes; one beneath, the tip of a chin; a mocking symbol of a triangular face which his mind projected into the constellations when it was disturbed. Don Calogero's tail coat, Concetta's love, Tancredi's blatant infatuation, his own cowardice; even the threatening beauty of that girl Angelica: bad things; rubble preceding an avalanche. And Tancredi! The lad was right, agreed, and he would help him too; but Don Fabrizio could not deny that he found it all slightly ignoble. And he himself was like Tancredi. "Enough of that now, let's sleep on it."

Bendicò in the shadow rubbed a big head against his knee. "You see, you, Bendicò, are a bit like them, like the stars; happily incomprehensible, incapable of producing anxiety." He raised the dog's head, which was almost invisible in the darkness. "And then with those eyes of yours at the same level as your nose, with your lack of chin, that head of yours can't possibly evoke malignant specters in the sky."

Centuries-old tradition required that the day following their arrival the Salina family should visit the Convent of the Holy Spirit to pray at the tomb of Blessed Corbèra, forebear of the Prince and foundress of the convent, who had endowed it, there lived a holy life, and there died a holy death.

The Convent of the Holy Spirit had a rigid rule of enclosure, and entry was severely forbidden to men. That was why the Prince particularly enjoyed visiting it, for he, as direct descendant of the foundress, was not excluded; and of this privilege, shared only with the King of Naples, he was both jealous and childishly proud.

This faculty of canonical arrogance was the chief but not the only reason for his liking the Convent of the Holy Spirit. Everything about the place pleased him, beginning with the humble simplicity of the parlor, with its raftered ceiling centered on the Leopard, its double gratings for interviews, a little wooden wheel for passing messages in and out, and a heavy door whose threshold he and the King were the only men in the whole world allowed to cross. He liked the look of the nuns with their wide wimples of purest white linen in tiny pleats, gleaming against the rough black robes; he was edified at hearing for the hundredth time the Mother Abbess describe Blessed Corbèra's ingenuous miracles, at her showing the corner of the dank garden where the saintly nun had suspended in the air a huge stone which the Devil, irritated by her austerity, had flung at her; he was astounded at the sight of the two famous and indecipherable letters framed on the wall of a cell, one to the Devil from Blessed Corbèra to convert him to virtue, and the other the Devil's reply, expressing, it seems, his regret at not being able to comply with her request; the Prince liked the almond cakes the nuns made from an ancient recipe, he liked listening to the Office chanted in choir, and he was even quite happy to pay over to the community a not inconsiderable portion of his own income, in accordance with the act of foundation.

So that morning there were only happy people in the two carriages moving toward the convent just outside the town. In the first were the Prince, the Princess, and their daughters Carolina and Concetta; in the second, his daughter

Caterina, with Tancredi and Father Pirrone; the two men, of course, would stay *extra muros* and wait in the parlor during the visit, consoled by macaroons from the wooden wheel. Concetta looked serene, though a little absent-minded, and the Prince did his best to hope that yesterday's nonsense had all blown over.

Entry into an enclosed community is never a quick matter, even for one possessing the most sacred of rights. Nuns like to show a certain reluctance, formal maybe but prolonged, which gives a greater flavor to however certain an admission; and, although the visit had been announced beforehand, there was a considerable wait in the parlor. Toward the end of this Tancredi unexpectedly asked the Prince, "Uncle, can't you get me in too? After all, I'm half a Salina, and I've never been here before."

Though pleased at heart by the request, the Prince shook his head decisively. "But, my boy, you know only I can enter here, and no other man." It was not easy, however, to put Tancredi off. "Excuse me, Uncle; the rule says, *The Prince of Salina may enter together with two gentlemen of his suite if the Abbess so permits.* I read it again yesterday. I'll be the gentleman in your suite, I'll be your squire, I'll be whatever you like. Do ask the Abbess, please." He was speaking with unusual warmth; perhaps he wanted a certain person there to forget his ill-considered chatter of the night before. The Prince was flattered. "If you're so keen on it, dear boy, I'll see . . ." But Concetta turned to her cousin with her sweetest smile: "Tancredi, as we passed we saw a wooden beam on the ground in front of Ginestra's house. Go and fetch it, it'll get you in all the quicker." Tancredi's blue eyes clouded over and his face went red as a poppy, either from shame or from anger. He tried to say something to the surprised Prince, but Concetta interrupted again, acidly now, and without a smile: "Let him be, Father, he's only joking; he's been in one convent already, that ought to be enough for him; it's not right for him to enter one of ours." With a grinding of drawn bolts, the door opened. Into the stuffy parlor entered the freshness of the cloister together with the murmur of assembled nuns. It was too late to ask questions, and Tancredi was left behind to walk up and down in front of the convent, under the blazing sky.

The visit to the Holy Spirit was a great success. Don Fabrizio, from love of quiet, had refrained from asking Concetta the meaning of her words; doubtless just one of the usual tiffs between cousins; anyway the coolness between the two young people kept off bother, confabulations, and decisions, so it had been welcome. On these premises the tomb of Blessed Corbèra was venerated with due respect by all, the nuns' watery coffee drunk with tolerance, the pink and greenish almond cakes crunched with satisfaction; the Princess inspected the wardrobe, Concetta talked to the nuns with her usual withdrawn kindliness, and he, the Prince, left on the refectory table the ten ounces of gold that he offered every time he came. It was true that on leaving Father Pirrone was found alone; but as he said that Tancredi had suddenly remembered an urgent letter and gone off on foot, no one took much notice.

On returning to the palace the Prince went up to the library, right in the middle of the façade under the clock and lightning conductor. From the great balcony, closed against the heat, could be seen the square of Donnafugata, vast, shaded by dusty plane trees. Opposite were some house fronts of exuberant design by a local architect, rustic monstrosities in soapstone, weathered by the years, upholding amid twists and curves balconies that were too small; other houses, among which was that of Don Calogero Sedàra, hid behind prim Empire fronts.

Don Fabrizio walked up and down the immense room; every now and again he paused and glanced out at the square: on one of the benches donated by himself to the commune three old men were roasting themselves in the sun; four mules stood tethered to a tree; a dozen or so urchins were chasing each other, shouting and brandishing wooden swords. Under the blazing midsummer sun the view could not have been more typical. On one of his crossings by the window, however, his eye was drawn to a figure that was obviously from the city—slim, well dressed. He screwed up his eyes: it was Tancredi; he recognized him, although already some way off, by the sloping shoulders and slim-fitting waist of his frock coat. He had changed his clothes; he was no longer in brown, as at the convent, but in Prussian blue—"my seduction color," as he himself called it. In one hand he held a cane with an enamel handle (doubtless the one bearing the Unicorn of the Falconeri and their motto, *Semper purus*), and he was walking with catlike tread, as if taking care not to get his shoes dusty.

Ten paces behind him followed a lackey carrying a tasselled box containing a dozen yellow peaches with pink cheeks. He sidestepped a sword-waving urchin, carefully avoided a urinating mule, and reached the Sedàras' door.

3

Leaving for a shoot · Troubles of Don Fabrizio · A letter from Tancredi · Game and the Plebiscite · Don Ciccio Tumeo lets himself go · On eating a toad · Small epilogue

THE rains had come, the rains had gone, and the sun was back on its throne like an absolute monarch kept off it for a week by his subjects' barricades, and now reigning once again, choleric but under constitutional restraint. The heat braced without burning, the light domineered but let colors live; from the soil cautiously sprouted clover and mint, and on faces appeared diffident hopes.

Don Fabrizio, with the dogs Teresina and Arguto and his retainer Don Ciccio Tumeo, would spend long hours out shooting, from dawn till afternoon. The effort was out of all proportion to the results, for the most expert shot finds difficulty in hitting a target which is scarcely ever there, and it was rarely that the Prince was able to take even a brace of pheasants home to the larder, or Don Ciccio to slap onto the kitchen table a wild rabbit, promoted—as is done in Sicily—*ipso facto* to the rank of hare.

A big bag would, anyway, have been a secondary pleasure for the Prince; the joy of those days out shooting lay elsewhere, subdivided in many tiny episodes. It began with shaving in a room still dark, by candlelight that projected every gesture emphatically over the painted architecture on the ceiling; it was whetted by crossing dormant drawing rooms, by glimpses in the flickering light of tables with playing cards lying in disorder amid chips and empty glasses, and catching sight among them of a Jack of Spades waving a manly greeting; by passing through the motionless garden under a gray light in which the earliest birds were twisting and turning to shake the dew off their feathers; by slipping through the ivy-hung wicket gate; by escaping, in fact. And then in the street, blamelessly innocent still in the early light, he would find Don Ciccio smiling into his yellowed mustache and swearing affectionately at the dogs; these, as they waited, were flexing their muscles under velvety fur. Venus still glimmered, a peeled grape, damp and transparent, but one could already hear the rumble of the solar chariot climbing the last slope below the horizon; soon they would meet the first flocks moving toward them, torpid as tides, guided by stones from shepherds in leather breeches; the wool looked soft and rosy in the early rays of the sun; then there would be obscure quarrels of precedence to be settled between sheep dogs and punctilious pointers, after which deafening interval they turned up a slope and found themselves in the immemorial silence of pastoral Sicily. All at once they were far from everything in space and still more so in time. Donnafugata with its palace and its newly rich was only a mile or two away, but it seemed a dim memory like those landscapes sometimes glimpsed at the distant end of a railway tunnel; its troubles and splendors appeared even more insignificant than if they belonged to the past, for compared to this remote unchangeable landscape they seemed part of the future, made not of stone and flesh but of the substance of some dream of things to come, extracts from a utopia thought up by a rustic Plato and apt to change at a whim into quite different forms or even found not to exist at all; deprived thus of that charge of energy which everything in the past continues to possess, they were a bother no longer.

Yes, Don Fabrizio had certainly had his worries those last two months; they had come from all directions, like ants making for a dead lizard. Some had crawled from crevices of the political situation; some had been flung on him by other people's passions; and some (these had the sharpest bite) had sprung up within himself, from his irrational reactions, that is, to politics and the whims of others ("whims" was his name when irritated for what in calm he called "passions"). He would review these worries every day, maneuver them, set them in column or extend them in open order on the parade ground of his own conscience, hoping to find in their evolutions a sense of finality that could reassure him; and not succeeding. In former years there had been far fewer bothers, and anyway his stay at Donnafugata had always been a period of rest; his worries used to drop their rifles, disperse into crags of the valleys and settle down there quietly, so intent on munching bread and cheese that their warlike uniforms were forgotten and they could be mistaken for inoffensive peasants. This year, though, they had all stayed on parade in a body, like mutinous troops shouting and brandishing weapons, arousing, in his home, the dismay of a Colonel who has given the order "Fall out" only to find his battalion standing there in closer and more threatening order than ever.

The arrival had been all right, with bands, fireworks, bells, gypsy songs, and *Te Deum;* but afterward! The bourgeois revolution climbing his stairs in Don Calogero's tail coat; Angelica's beauty, which had put the shy grace of his Concetta in the shade; Tancredi rushing at the inevitable changes, and even able to deck out his realistic motives with sensual infatuation; the scruples and deceptions of the Plebiscite; the endless little subterfuges he had to submit to, he, the Leopard, who for years had swept away difficulties with a wave of his paw.

Tancredi had been gone for more than a month and was now at Caserta bivouacking in the apartments of his King; from there every now and again he sent Don Fabrizio letters which the latter read with alternate frowns and smiles, and then put away in the remotest drawer of his desk. He had never written to Concetta, though he did not forget to send her a greeting with the usual sly affection; once he even wrote, "I kiss the hands of all the little Leopardesses and particularly Concetta's," phrases censored by paternal prudence when the letter was read out to the assembled family. Angelica was now visiting them almost daily, more seductive than ever, accompanied by her father or some old witch of a maid: officially these visits were made to her friends the girls, but in fact their climax obviously came at the moment when she asked with apparent indifference, "And what news of the Prince?" "Prince" in Angelica's mouth did not, alas, mean him, Don Fabrizio, but the little Garibaldino Captain; and this provoked a strange sensation in Salina, woven from the warp of the crude cotton of sensual jealousy and the woof of silken pleasure at his dear Tancredi's success; a sensation, when all was said and done, that was somewhat disagreeable. It was always he who answered this question; he would give a carefully considered account of what he knew, taking care, however, to present a well-arranged little bouquet of news, from which his cautious tweezers had extracted both thorns (descriptions of many a jaunt to Naples, obvious allusions to the legs of Aurora Schwarzwald, dancer at the San Carlo) and premature buds ("send news of the Signorina Angelica"—"In Ferdinand II's study I found a Madonna by Andrea del Sarto which reminded me of the Signorina Sedàra"). So he would put together an insipid picture of Tancredi which bore very little resemblance to the original, but did at least prevent anyone from saying that he himself was acting either as spoilsport or pimp. These verbal precautions corresponded to his own feelings about Tancredi's considered passion, but he found them tiresome too; anyway, they were only one sample of all the guile in language and behavior he had been forced to use for some time; he thought with regret of the year before, when he could say whatever went through his head, in the certainty that any silly remark would be treated as words from the Gospel, and any unconsidered comment as princely carelessness. And now that he had begun regretting the past, he would find himself, in moments of worst humor, slithering quite a way down that perilous slope; once, as he was putting sugar in a cup of tea which Angelica was holding out to him, he realized that he was envying the chances open to a Fabrizio Salina and Tancredi Falconeri of three centuries before, who would have rid themselves of urges to bed down with the Angelicas of their day without ever going before a priest, or giving a thought to the dowries of such local girls (which were anyway then nonexistent) and never needing to keep uncles on tenterhooks about saying or suppressing appropriate remarks. The impulse of atavistic lust (which was not really all lust, but partly a sensuality stemming from laziness) stung the civilized gentleman nearing fifty so sharply that it made him blush; somewhere, at infinite removes, he had been touched by scruples which he chose to call Rousseauesque, and felt deeply ashamed; which could also go to show how deep was his revulsion from the social circumstances in which he was so inextricably involved.

The sensation of finding himself a prisoner in a situation evolving more rapidly than foreseen was particularly acute that morning. The night before, in fact, the stagecoach bearing the irregular and scanty mail to Donnafugata in its canary-yellow box had brought a letter from Tancredi.

This proclaimed its importance even before reading, written as it was on sumptuous sheets of gleaming paper and in a harmonious script scrupulously tracing full strokes down and thin strokes up. It was obviously the "clean copy" of any number of disordered drafts. In it the Prince was not addressed by the name of "Uncle mine," which had become dear to him; the wily youth had thought of a formula, "dear Uncle Fabrizio," which had a number of merits: of putting off any suspicion of connivance, proclaiming from the very first line the importance of what was to follow, allowing the letter to be shown to anyone, and also of providing a link with the ancient pre-Christian beliefs which attributed a binding power to the exact invocation of a name.

"Dear Uncle Fabrizio," therefore, was informed that his "most affectionate and devoted nephew" had for the last three months been a prey to the most violent love, and that neither "the risks of war" (read: walks in the park of Caserta) nor "the many attractions of a great city" (read: the charms of the dancer Schwarzwald) had been able even for an instant to drive from his mind and heart the image of the Signorina Angelica Sedàra (here a long procession of adjectives to exalt the beauty, grace, virtue, and intellect of his beloved); then, in neat hieroglyphics of ink and sentiment, the letter went on to say that Tancredi had felt so conscious of his own unworthiness that he had tried to suffocate his ardor ("long but vain have been the hours dur-

ing which, amid the clamor of Naples or the austere company of my comrades-in-arms, I have tried to repress my
feelings"). But now love had overcome his reserve, and he
was begging his dearly beloved uncle to deign to request
Signorina Angelica's "most esteemed father" for her hand,
in his name and on his behalf. "You know, Uncle, that all
I can offer to the object of my affection is my love, my
name, and my sword." After this phrase, in connection with
which it should not be forgotten that romanticism was then
at high noon, Tancredi went on to long considerations of
the expediency, nay the necessity, of unions between families such as the Falconeris and the Sedàras (once he even
dared write "The House of Sedàra") being encouraged in
order to bring new blood into old families, and also to level
out classes, aims of the current political movement in Italy.
This was the only part of the letter that Don Fabrizio read
with any pleasure; and not just because it confirmed his
own previsions and crowned him with the laurels of a
prophet, but also (it would be harsh to say "above all")
because the style, with its hints of subdued irony, magically
evoked his nephew's image: the jesting nasal tone, the spar-
kling malice in his blue eyes, the mockingly polite smile.
And when he realized that this little Jacobin sally was
written out on exactly one single sheet of paper so that if
he wanted he could let others read the letter while subtracting this revolutionary chapter, his admiration for Tancredi's tact knew no bounds. After a brief résumé of recent
operations and an expression of the conviction that within a
year they would be in Rome, "predestined capital of the

new Italy," he thanked his uncle for the care and affection given him in the past, and ended by excusing himself for daring to confide him with this charge, "on which my future happiness depends." Then came greetings (for Don Fabrizio only).

A first reading of this extraordinary composition made Don Fabrizio's head spin: once again he noted how astoundingly fast all this had gone; put in modern terms, he could be said to be in the state of mind of someone today who thinks he has boarded one of the old planes which potter between Palermo and Naples, and suddenly finds himself shut inside a super Jet and realizes he will be at his destination almost before there will be time to make the sign of the Cross. Then the second affectionate layer of his nature came to the top, and he rejoiced at this decision of Tancredi's which would assure him an ephemeral carnal satisfaction and a perennial financial peace. He paused, then, for a moment to note the youth's extraordinary self-confidence in presuming his own wish already accepted by Angelica; but all these thoughts were swept away eventually by a sense of humiliation at being forced to deal with Don Calogero about subjects so intimate, and also of vexation at having to conduct delicate negotiations next day, with the use, what was more, of precaution and cunning alien to his presumably leonine nature.

Don Fabrizio revealed the contents of this letter to his wife only when they were lying in bed under the pale blue glow from the glass-hooded oil lamp. Maria Stella did not say a word at first, just made a series of signs of the Cross;

then she remarked that she should have crossed herself with her left hand and not with her right; after this supreme expression of amazement she loosed the thunderbolts of her eloquence. Sitting up in bed, her fingers rumpling the sheet while her words furrowed the lunar atmosphere of the enclosed room like angry scarlet torches: "I'd so hoped he would marry Concetta! He's a traitor, like all liberals of his kind; first he betrayed his King, now he betrays us! He, with that double face of his, those honeyed words and poisoned actions! That's what happens when one lets people into one's home who aren't of our own blood!" Here she let loose her cavalry charge in family scenes: "I always said so, but no one would listen to me. I never could endure that fop! You just lost your head about him!" In reality the Princess too had been subject to Tancredi's charm, and she loved him still; but the pleasure of shouting "I told you so" being the strongest any human being can enjoy, all truths and all feelings were swept along in its wake. "And now he has even had the impertinence to ask you, his uncle and Prince of Salina, father of the very girl he has deceived, to carry his squalid message to that slut's rascally father! You mustn't do it, Fabrizio, you mustn't do it, you shan't do it, you mustn't do it!" Her voice went up in tone, her body began to stiffen.

Don Fabrizio, still lying on his back, gave a sideways glance to assure himself that the valerian was on the night table. The bottle was there with a silver spoon across the stopper; in the glaucous half darkness of the room they shone like a reassuring beacon, built to withstand storms of hysteria. For a moment he thought of getting out of bed and fetching them; but he compromised by just sitting up too; thus he reacquired a position of prestige. "Now, Stella, my dear, don't be silly. You don't know what you are saying. Angelica is not a slut. She may become one, but for the moment she's a girl just like any other, prettier than others, and she simply wants to make a good marriage; she may even be a little in love with Tancredi, like everyone else. She'll have money; most of it was ours, but it's now well, almost too well, taken care of by Don Calogero; and Tancredi has great need of that; he's a gentleman, he's ambitious, he's a perfect sieve with money. As for Concetta, he never actually said a word to her, in fact it's she who's treated him badly ever since we got to Donnafugata. And he's not a traitor; he follows the times, that's all, in his politics and in his private life; and anyway he's a very lovable lad, you know that as well as I do, Stella my dear." Five huge fingers stroked the top of her tiny head. She was sobbing now; having been sensible enough to drink a sip of water, the fire of her rage had muted to self-pity. Don Fabrizio began to hope that he would not have to get out of the warm bed, face a barefoot crossing of the chilly room. Then to ensure his future peace he pretended to be angry: "And I'll have no shouting in my own house, in my own room, in my own bed! None of this 'You do this' and 'You won't do that.' I decide; I'd already decided long before it ever crossed your mind! That's enough now!"

The hater of shouting was himself bawling with all the

breath in his great chest. Thinking he had a table in front of him, he banged a great fist on his own knee, hurt himself, and calmed down too.

The Princess, alarmed, was whining in a low voice like a frightened puppy.

"Now let's sleep. Tomorrow I'm going out shooting and have to get up early. Enough! What's decided is decided. Good night, Stella, my dear." He kissed his wife first on her forehead and then on her lips. He lay down again and turned toward the wall. The shadow of his recumbent form was projected on the silken wall like the silhouette of a mountain range on a blue horizon.

Stella lay back too, and as her right leg grazed the left leg of the Prince she felt consoled and proud at having for a husband a man so vital and so proud. What did Tancredi matter . . . or even Concetta . . . ?

For the moment such tightrope balancing was suspended, along with all other thought, in the archaic and aromatic countryside, if it could be called that, where he went shooting every morning. The term "countryside" implies soil transformed by labor; but the scrub clinging to the slopes was still in the very same state of scented tangle in which it had been found by Phoenicians, Dorians, and Ionians when they disembarked in Sicily, that America of antiquity. Don Fabrizio and Tumeo climbed up and down, slipped and were scratched by thorns, just as any Archidamus or Philostratus must have been tired and scratched twenty-five centuries before. They saw the same objects, their clothes were soaked with just as sticky a sweat, the same indifferent breeze blew steadily from the sea, moving myrtles and broom, spreading a smell of thyme. The dogs' sudden pauses for thought, their tension waiting for prey, was the very same as when Artemis was invoked for the chase. Reduced to these basic elements, its face washed clear of worries, life took on a tolerable aspect. That morning, shortly before reaching the top of the hill, Arguto and Teresina began the hieratic dance of dogs who have scented prey; stretching, stiffening, prudently raising paws, repressing barks; a few minutes later a tiny beige-colored backside slid through the grass and two almost simultaneous shots ended the silent wait; at the Prince's feet Arguto placed an animal in its death throes.

It was a wild rabbit; its dun-colored coat had not been able to save it. Horrible wounds lacerated snout and chest. Don Fabrizio found himself stared at by big black eyes soon overlaid by a glaucous veil; they were looking at him with no reproof, but full of tortured amazement at the whole order of things; the velvety ears were already cold, the vigorous paws contracting in rhythm, still-living symbol of useless flight; the animal had died tortured by anxious hopes of salvation, imagining it could still escape when it was already caught, just like so many human beings. While sympathetic fingers were still stroking that poor snout, the animal gave a last quiver and died; Don Fabrizio and Don Ciccio had had their bit of fun, the former not only the pleasure of killing but also the solace of compassion.

When the hunters reached the top of the hill, there among the tamarisks and scattered cork trees appeared the real Sicily again, the one compared to which baroque towns and orange groves are mere trifles: aridly undulating to the horizon in hillock after hillock, comfortless and irrational, with no lines that the mind could grasp, conceived apparently in a delirious moment of creation; a sea suddenly petrified at the instant when a change of wind had flung waves into frenzy. Donnafugata lay huddled and hidden in an anonymous fold of the ground, and not a living soul was to be seen; the only signs of the passage of man were scraggy rows of vines. Beyond the hills on one side was the indigo smudge of the sea, more mineral and barren, even, than the land. The slight breeze moved over all, universalizing the smell of dung, carrion, and sage, cancelling, suppressing, reordering each thing in its careless passage; it dried up the little drops of blood which were the only residue of the rabbit, far away it ruffled the locks of Garibaldi, and farther still flung dust in the eyes of Neapolitan soldiers hurriedly reinforcing the battlements of Gaeta, deluded by a hope as vain as the rabbit's frenzied flight. The Prince and the organist rested under the circumscribed shadow of cork trees: they drank tepid wine from wooden bottles with a roast chicken from Don Fabrizio's haversack, ate little cakes called *muffoletti* dusted with raw flour which Don Ciccio had brought with him and the local grapes so ugly to look at and so good to eat; with great hunks of bread they satisfied the hungry dogs standing there in front of them, impassive as bailiffs bent on getting debts paid. Under that monarchic sun Don Fabrizio and Don Ciccio were near to dozing.

But though a shot had killed the rabbit, though the bored rifles of General Cialdini were now dismaying the Bourbon troops at Gaeta, though the midday heat was making men doze off, nothing could stop the ants. Attracted by a few chewed grape-skins spat out by Don Ciccio, along they rushed in close order, morale high at the chance of annexing that bit of garbage soaked with an organist's saliva. Up they came full of confidence, disordered but resolute; groups of three or four would stop now and again for a chat, exalting, perhaps, the ancient glories and future prosperity of ant hill Number Two under cork tree Number Four on the top of Mount Morco; then once again they would take up their march with the others toward a buoyant future; the gleaming backs of those imperialists seemed to quiver with enthusiasm, while from their ranks no doubt rose the notes of an anthem.

By some association of ideas which it would be inopportune to pursue, the activity of these insects prevented the Prince from sleeping and reminded him of the days of the Plebiscite for the Unification through which he had lived shortly before at Donnafugata itself. Apart from a sense of amazement, those days had left him many an enigma to solve; now, in sight of nature, which, except for ants, obviously did not have such bothers, he might perhaps find a solution for one of them. The dogs were sleeping stretched and crouched like figures in relief; the little rabbit, hanging from a branch with its head down, was swinging out diagonally under the constant surge of wind, but Tumeo, with the help of his pipe, still managed to keep his eyes open.

"And you, Don Ciccio, how did you vote on the twenty-first?"

The poor man started; taken by surprise at a moment when outside the stockade of precautions in which, like each of his fellow townsmen, he usually moved, he hesitated, not knowing what to reply.

The Prince mistook for alarm what was really only surprise, and felt irritated. "Well, what are you afraid of? There's no one here but us, the wind, and the dogs."

The list of reassuring witnesses was not really happily chosen; wind is a gossip by definition, the Prince was half Sicilian. Only the dogs were absolutely trustworthy and that only because they lacked articulate speech. But Don Ciccio had now recovered; his peasant astuteness had suggested the right reply—nothing at all. "Excuse me, Excellency, but there's no point in your question. You know that everyone in Donnafugata voted 'yes.'"

Don Fabrizio did know this; and that was why this reply merely changed a small enigma into an enigma of history. Before the voting many had come to him for advice; all of them had been exhorted, sincerely, to vote "yes." Don Fabrizio, in fact, could not see what else there was to do: whether treating it as a *fait accompli* or as an act merely theatrical and banal, whether taking it as historical necessity or considering the trouble these humble folk might get into if their negative attitude were known. He had noticed, though, that not all had been convinced by his words; into play had come the abstract Machiavellianism of Sicilians, which so often induced these people, with all their generosity, to erect complex barricades on the most fragile of foundations. Like clinicians adept at treatment based on fundamentally false analyses of blood and urine which they are too lazy to rectify, the Sicilians of that time ended by killing off the patient, that is themselves, by a niggling and hair-splitting rarely grounded on any real understanding of the problems involved and even less of their interlocutors. Some who had spent their lives under the aegis of the Leopard felt it impossible for a Prince of Salina to vote in favor of the Revolution (as the recent changes were still called in those remote parts), and they interpreted his advice as ironical, intended to effect a result in practice opposite to his words. These pilgrims (and they were the best) had come out of his study winking at each other—as far as their respect for him would allow—proud at having penetrated the meaning of the princely words, and rubbing their hands in self-congratulation at their own perspicacity just when this was most completely in eclipse. Others, on the other hand, after having listened to him, went off looking sad, convinced that he was a turncoat or opportunist, and more than ever determined to take no notice of what he said but to follow instead the age-old proverb about preferring a known evil to an untried good. These were reluctant to ratify the new national reality for personal reasons too: either from religious faith, or from having received favors from the former regime and not been sharp enough to insert themselves into the new one, or finally because during the upsets of the liberation period they had lost some capons and sacks of beans, and been cuckolded either by Garibaldi volunteers or Bourbon levies. He had, in fact, the disagreeable but distinct impression that about fifteen of them would vote "no," a tiny minority certainly, but noticeable in the small electorate of Donnafugata. Taking into consideration that the people who came to him represented the flower of the inhabitants, and that there must also be some unconvinced among the hundreds of electors who had not dreamed of setting foot inside the palace, the Prince had calculated that Donnafugata's compact affirmative would be varied by about forty negative votes.

The day of the Plebiscite was windy and gray, and tired groups of youths had been seen going through the streets of the town with placards carrying "Yes" and the same on pieces of paper stuck in the ribbons of their hats. Among the papers and refuse swirled about by the wind were a few verses of *La Bella Gigugin* transformed into a kind of Arab wail, a fate to which any gay tune sung in Sicily is bound to succumb. They had also seen two or three "foreign faces" (that is, from Girgenti) installed in *Zzu* Menico's tavern, where they were declaiming about the "magnificent and progressive future" of the new Sicily united to resurgent Italy. A few peasants were standing listening, mutely, stunned by overwork or starved by unemployment. These cleared their throats and spat continuously, but kept silent; so silent that it must have been then (as Don Fabrizio said afterward) that the "foreign faces" decided to put, among the four major arts, Mathematics above Rhetoric.

The Prince went to vote about four in the afternoon, flanked on the right by Father Pirrone, on the left by Don Onofrio Rotolo; frowning and fair-skinned, he proceeded slowly toward the Town Hall, frequently putting up a hand to protect his eyes lest the breeze, loaded with all the filth collected on its way, should bring on the conjunctivitis to which he was subject; and he remarked to Father Pirrone that though the air would have been like a putrid pool without the wind, yet health-giving gusts did seem to drag up a lot of dirt with them. He was wearing the same black frock coat in which two years before he had gone to pay his respects at Caserta to poor King Ferdinand, who had been lucky enough to die in time to avoid this day of dirty wind, when the seal would be set on his incapacity. But had it really been incapacity? One might as well say that a person succumbing to typhus dies from incapacity. He remembered the King busy putting up dikes against the floods of useless documents; and suddenly he realized how much unconscious appeal to pity there was in those unattractive features. Such thoughts were disagreeable, as are all those that make us understand things too late, and the Prince's face went solemn and dark as if he were following an invisible funeral carriage. Only the violent impact of his feet on loose stones in the street showed his internal conflict; it is superfluous to mention that the ribbon on his top hat was innocent of any piece of paper, but for the eyes of those who knew him a "yes" and a "no" alternated under the glistening of the felt.

On reaching a little room in the Town Hall used as the

voting booth he was surprised to see all the members of
the committee get up as his great height filled the doorway; a few peasants who had arrived before were motioned
aside, and so without having to wait Don Fabrizio handed
his "yes" into the patriotic hands of Don Calogero Sedàra.
Father Pirrone, though, did not vote at all, as he had been
careful not to get himself listed as resident in the town.
Don Nofrio, obeying the express desires of the Prince, gave
his own monosyllabic opinion about the complicated Italian
question: a masterpiece of concision carried through with
the good grace of a child drinking castor oil. After which
all were invited for "a sip" upstairs in the Mayor's study;
but Father Pirrone and Don Nofrio put forward good reasons, one of abstinence, the other of stomach-ache, and remained below. Don Fabrizio had to face the refreshments
alone.

Behind the Mayor's writing desk gleamed a brand-new
portrait of Garibaldi and (already) one of the new King
from Piedmont, Victor Emmanuel, luckily hung to the
right; the first handsome, the second ugly; both, however, made brethren by prodigious growths of hair which
nearly hid their faces altogether. On a small table was a
plate with some ancient biscuits covered with fly droppings
and a dozen little squat glasses brimming with rosolio:
four red, four green, four white, the last in the center: an
ingenuous symbol of the new national flag which tempered
the Prince's remorse with a smile. He chose the white
liquor for himself, presumably because the least indigest-
ible and not, as some thought, a tardy homage to the Bour-

bon standard. Anyway, all three varieties of rosolio were equally sugary, sticky, and revolting. They had the good taste not to give toasts. But, as Don Calogero said, great joys are silent. Don Fabrizio was shown a letter from the authorities of Girgenti announcing to the industrious citizens of Donnafugata the concession of a contribution of two thousand lire for sewerage, a work which would be completed before the end of 1961, so the Mayor assured them, stumbling into one of those *lapsus* whose mechanism Freud was to explain many decades later; and the meeting broke up.

Before dusk the three or four whores of Donnafugata (there were some there, too, not organized but each hard at work on her own) appeared in the square with tricolor ribbons in their manes in protest against the exclusion of women from the vote; the poor creatures were jeered at even by the most advanced liberals and forced back to their lairs. This did not prevent the newspaper *Giornale di Trinacria* from telling the people of Palermo four days later that at Donnafugata "some gentle representatives of the fair sex wished to show their faith in the new and brilliant destinies of their beloved Country, and demonstrated in the main square amid general acclamation from the patriotic population."

After this the electoral booths were closed and the scrutators got to work; late that night the central balcony of the Town Hall was flung open and Don Calogero appeared with a tricolor sash over his middle, flanked by two ushers with lighted candelabra which the wind blew out at once.

To the invisible crowd in the shadows below he announced that the Plebiscite at Donnafugata had had the following results:

Voters listed, 515; Voted, 512; Yes, 512; No, zero.

Applause and hurrahs rose from the dark background of the square; on her little balcony Angelica, with her funereal maid, clapped lovely rapacious hands; speeches were made; adjectives loaded with superlatives and double consonants reverberated and echoed in the dark from one wall to another; amid the thunder of fireworks messages were sent off to the King (the new one) and to the General; a tricolor rocket or two climbed up from the village into the blackness toward the starless sky. By eight o'clock all was over, and nothing remained except the darkness as on any other night, as always.

On the top of Monte Morco all was clear now, in bright light; but deep in Don Fabrizio's heart the gloom of that night still lay stagnant. His discomfort had become more irksome, vaguer; it had no connection at all with the great matters of which the Plebiscite marked the start of a solution: the major interests of the Kingdom (of the Two Sicilies), and of his own class, his personal advantages came through all these events battered but still lively. In the circumstance he could not well expect more. No, his discomfort was not of a political nature and must have had deeper roots, down in one of those reasons which we call irrational because they are buried under layers of self-ignorance. Italy was born in that sullen night at Donnafugata, born right there in that forgotten little town, just as much as in the sloth of Palermo or the clamor of Naples; but an evil fairy, of unknown name, must have been present; anyway Italy was born and one had to hope that she would live on in that form; any other would be worse. Agreed. And yet this persistent disquiet of his must mean something; during that too brief announcement of figures, just as during those too emphatic speeches, he had a feeling that something, someone, had died, God only knew in what corner of the country, in what corner of the popular conscience.

The cool air had dispersed Don Ciccio's somnolence; the massive grandeur of the Prince dispelled his fears; now all that remained afloat on the surface of Don Ciccio's conscience was resentment, useless of course but not ignoble. He stood there, spoke in dialect, and gesticulated, a pathetic puppet who in some absurd way was right.

"I, Excellency, voted 'no.' 'No,' a hundred times 'no.' I know what you told me: necessity, unity, expediency. You may be right; I know nothing of politics. Such things I leave to others. But Ciccio Tumeo is honest, poor though he may be, with his trousers in holes" (and he slapped the carefully mended patches in his shooting breeches), "and I don't forget favors done me! Those swine in the Town Hall just swallowed up my opinion, chewed it, and then spat it out transformed as they wanted. I said black and they made me say white! The one time when I could say what I thought, that bloodsucker Sedàra went and annulled it, behaved as if I never existed, as if I never meant a thing,

I, Francesco Tumeo La Manna, son of Leonardo, organist of the Mother Church at Donnafugata, a better man than he is! To think I'd even dedicated to him a mazurka I composed at the birth of that . . ." (he bit his thumb to rein himself in), "that mincing daughter of his!"

At this point calm descended on Don Fabrizio, who had finally solved the enigma; now he knew who had been killed at Donnafugata, at a hundred other places, in the course of that night of dirty wind: a new-born babe: good faith; just the very child who should have been cared for most, whose strengthening would have justified all the silly vandalisms. Don Ciccio's negative vote, fifty similar votes at Donnafugata, a hundred thousand "noes" in the whole Kingdom, would have had no effect on the result, would in fact have made it, if anything, more significant; and this maiming of souls would have been avoided. Six months before they used to hear a rough despotic voice saying, "Do what I say or you'll catch it!" Now there was an impression already of such a threat being replaced by the soapy tones of a moneylender: "But you signed it yourself, didn't you? Can't you see? It's quite clear. You must do as we say, for here are the I.O.U.s; your will is identical with mine."

Don Ciccio was still thundering on: "For you nobles it's different. *You* can be ungrateful about an extra estate, but *we* must be grateful for a bit of bread. It's different again for profiteers like Sedàra, with whom cheating is a law of nature. Small folk like us have to take things as they come. You know, Excellency, that my father, God rest his soul, was gamekeeper at the Royal shoot of Sant'Onofrio back in Ferdinand IV's time, when the English were here? It was a hard life, but the green Royal livery and the silver plaque conferred authority. Queen Isabella, the Spaniard, was Duchess of Calabria then, and it was she who had me study, let me be what I am now, organist of the Mother Church, honored by Your Excellency's kindness; when my mother sent off a petition to Court, in our years of greatest need, back came five gold ounces, sure as death, for they were fond of us there in Naples, they knew we were decent folk and faithful subjects; when the King came he used to clap my father on the shoulder. 'Don Lionà,' he said, 'I wish we'd more like you, devoted to the Throne and to my Person.' Then the officer in attendance used to hand out the gold. Alms, they call it now, that really Royal generosity; and they call it that so as not to give any themselves; but it was a just reward for loyalty. And if those holy Kings and lovely Queens are looking down at us from heaven today, what would they say? 'The son of Don Leonardo Tumeo betrayed us!' It's lucky the truth is known in Paradise! Yes, Excellency, I know, people like you have told me, such things from royalty mean nothing, they're just part of the job. That may be true, in fact it is true. But we'd get those five gold ounces, that's a fact, and they helped us through the winter. And now that I could repay the debt my 'no' becomes a 'yes'! I used to be a 'faithful subject'; I've become a 'filthy pro-Bourbon.'"

Don Fabrizio had always liked Don Ciccio, partly because of the compassion inspired in him by all who from youth had thought of themselves as dedicated to the arts, and in old age, realizing they had no talent, still carried on the same activity at lower levels, pocketing withered dreams; and he was also touched by the dignity of his poverty. But now he also felt a kind of admiration for him, and deep down at the very bottom of his proud conscience a voice was asking if Don Ciccio had not perhaps behaved more nobly than the Prince of Salina. And the Sedàras, all the various Sedàras, from the petty one who violated figures at Donnafugata to the major ones at Palermo and Turin, had they not committed a crime by choking such consciences? Don Fabrizio could not know it then, but a great deal of the slackness and acquiescence for which the people of the South were to be criticized during the next decades was due to the stupid annulment of the first expression of liberty ever offered them.

Don Ciccio had said his say. And now his genuine but rarely shown side of "austere man of principle" was taken over by one much more frequent and no less genuine, that of snob. For Tumeo belonged to the zoological species of "passive snob," one unjustly reviled, particularly today. Of course the word "snob" was unknown in the Sicily of 1860; but just as tuberculosis existed before Koch, so in that remote era there were people for whom to obey, imitate, and above all avoid distressing those whom they considered of higher social rank than themselves, was the supreme law of life. Snobbery, in fact, is the opposite of envy. At that time a man of this type went under various names: he was called "devoted," "attached," "faithful"; and life was happy

for him since a nobleman's most fugitive smile was enough
to flood an entire day with sun; and as he appeared under
such affectionate names, the restorative graces were more
frequent than they are today. Now Don Ciccio's frankly
snobbish nature made him fear causing Don Fabrizio distress, and he searched diligently for ways to disperse any
frowns he might be causing on the Prince's Olympian
brow; the best means to hand was suggesting they should
start shooting again; and so they did. Surprised in their
afternoon naps, a few wretched woodcock and another rabbit fell under the marksmen's fire, particularly accurate
and careful that day, as both Salina and Tumeo were identi-
fying those innocent creatures with Don Calogero Sedàra.
But the shots, the flying feathers, the bits of skin glittering
for an instant in the sun, were not enough to soothe the
Prince that day; as the hours passed and return to Donnafugata drew near he felt more and more oppressed, worried, humiliated at the thought of the imminent conversation with the plebeian Mayor, and his having called in his
heart those two woodcock and the rabbit "Don Calogero"
had been no use after all; though he had already decided
to swallow the horrid toad, he still felt a need for more
ample information about his adversary, or rather, for a
sounding out of public opinion about the step he was about
to take. So for the second time that day Don Ciccio was
surprised by a sudden point-blank question.

"Listen, Don Ciccio; you see so many people, what do
they really think of Don Calogero at Donnafugata?"

Tumeo, in truth, felt he had already shown his opinion

of the Mayor quite clearly; and he was just about to say so when into his mind came rumors he had heard about Tancredi's making up to Angelica; and he was suddenly overwhelmed with regret at letting himself be drawn into expressing downright judgments which must certainly be anathema to the Prince if what he assumed was true; in another compartment of his mind meanwhile he was congratulating himself at not having said anything positive against Angelica; and the faint ache which he still felt in his right forefinger had the effect of a soothing balsam.

"After all, Excellency, Don Calogero Sedàra is no worse than lots of others who have come up in the last few months." The homage was moderate but enough to allow Don Fabrizio to insist, "You see, Don Ciccio, I'm most interested to know the truth about Don Calogero and his family."

"The truth, Excellency, is that Don Calogero is very rich, and very influential too; that he's a miser (when his daughter was at school he and his wife used to eat a fried egg between them) but knows how to spend when he has to; and as every coin spent in the world must end in someone's pocket he now finds many people dependent on him; when he's a friend he really is a friend, one must say that for him: he lets his land on very harsh terms and the peasants kill themselves to pay, but a month ago he lent fifty gold ounces to Pasquale Tripi, who had helped him at the time of the landings: without interest, too, which is the greatest miracle ever known since Santa Rosalia stopped the plague at Palermo. He's clever as the Devil, too; Your

Excellency should have seen him last April or May: up and down the whole district he went like a bat; by trap, horse, mule; foot, in rain or sun; and whenever he passed secret groups were formed, to prepare the way for those that were to come. He's a scourge of God, Excellency, a scourge of God. And we haven't seen the beginning of Don Calogero's career. In a few months he'll be Deputy in the Turin Parliament; in a few years, when Church property is put up for sale, he'll pay next to nothing for the estates of Marca and Fondachello and become the biggest landowner in the province; that's Don Calogero, Excellency: the new man; a pity he has to be like that, though."

Don Fabrizio remembered a conversation with Father Pirrone some months before in the sunlit observatory. What the Jesuit had predicted had come to pass. But wasn't it perhaps good tactics to insert himself into the new movement, make at least part use of it for a few members of his own class? The bother of his imminent interview with Don Calogero lessened.

"But the rest of his family, Don Ciccio, what are they really like?"

"Excellency, no one has laid eyes on Don Calogero's wife for years, except me. She only leaves the house to go to early Mass, the five o'clock one, when it's empty. There's no organ-playing at that hour; but once I got up early just to see her. Donna Bastiana came in with her maid, and as I was hiding behind a confessional I could not see very much; but at the end of Mass the heat was too much for the poor woman and she took off her black veil.

Word of honor, Excellency, she was lovely as the sun; one can't blame Don Calogero, who's a beetle of a man, for wanting to keep her away from others. But even in the best-kept houses secrets come out; servants talk; and it seems Donna Bastiana is a kind of animal: she can't read or write, or tell the time by a clock; she can scarcely talk; just a beautiful mare, voluptuous and uncouth; she's incapable even of affection for her own daughter! Good for bed, and that's all."

Don Ciccio, who, as pupil of queens and follower of princes, considered his own simple manners perfect, smiled with pleasure. He had found a way of getting some of his own back on this suppressor of his personality. "Anyway," he went on, "one couldn't expect much else. You know whose daughter Donna Bastiana is, Excellency?" He turned, rose on tiptoe, pointed to a distant group of huts which looked as if they were slithering off the edge of the hill, nailed there just by a wretched-looking bell tower: a crucified hamlet. "She's the daughter of one of your peasants from Runci, Peppe Giunta, he was called, so filthy and so savage that everyone called him Peppe 'Mmerda; excuse the word, Excellency." Satisfied, he twisted one of Teresina's ears around a finger. "Two years after Don Calogero had eloped with Bastiana they found him dead on the path to Rampinzeri, with twelve bullets in his back. Always lucky, is Don Calogero, for the old man was getting uppish, they say."

Much of this was known to Don Fabrizio and had already been totted up in his mind; but the nickname of

Angelica's grandfather was new to him; it opened up profound historical perspectives and made him glimpse other abysses, compared to which Don Calogero himself seemed a flower bed in a garden. The Prince began to feel the ground giving way under his feet; how ever could Tancredi swallow this? And what about himself? He found himself trying to work out the relationship between the Prince of Salina, uncle of the bridegroom, and the grandfather of the bride; he found none, there wasn't any. Angelica was just Angelica, a flower of a girl, a rose merely fertilized by her grandfather's nickname. *Non olet*, he repeated, *non olet*; in fact, *optime foeminam ac contubernium olet*.

"You've mentioned everything, Don Ciccio, savage mothers and fecal grandfathers, but not what interests me: the Signorina Angelica."

The secret of Tancredi's matrimonial intentions, although still embryonic until a few hours before, would certainly have been told then had it not been luckily camouflaged. No doubt the young man's frequent visits to Don Calogero's home had been noticed, as also his ecstatic smiles and little attentions, normal and insignificant in a city but symptoms of violent passion in the eyes of the virtuous folk of Donnafugata. The main scandal had been the first; the old man roasting in the sun and the children duelling in the dust had seen all, understood all, and repeated all; and on the aphrodisiac and seductive properties of those dozen peaches had been consulted the most expert witches and abstruse treatises on potions, chiefly that by Rutilio Benincasa, the Aristotle of the rustic proletariat. Luckily, there had come about a phenomenon relatively frequent among Sicilians: malice had masked truth; everyone had built up a puppet of a libertine Tancredi fixing his lascivious desires on Angelica; he was maneuvering to seduce her, that was all. The thought of any possible marriage between a Prince of Falconeri and a granddaughter of Peppe 'Mmerda did not even cross the minds of these country folk, who thus rendered to feudal families a homage equivalent to that rendered by the blasphemer to God. Tancredi's departure had cut short these fantasies and they were not mentioned again. In this respect Tumeo had been like the others, so he greeted the Prince's question with the amused air assumed by old men discoursing on the follies of the young.

"As to the Signorina, Excellency, there's nothing to say about her; she speaks for herself: her eyes, her skin, her figure are all there to be seen and appreciated by anyone. Don Tancredi has understood the language they speak, I think; or shouldn't I suggest such a thing? She has all the beauty of the mother with none of the grandfather's stink of manure; and she's intelligent, too. You've seen how those few years in Florence have transformed her completely? A real lady she's become," went on Don Ciccio, insensible to subtleties in such matters, "a complete lady. When she returned from school and invited me home she played my old mazurka; badly, but it was a delight to watch her, those black locks, those eyes, those legs, that breast. . . . Uh! No stink of manure there! Her sheets must smell like Paradise!"

The Prince gave a start of annoyance; so touchy is the pride of class, even in a moment of decline, that these orgiastic praises of the beauties of his future niece offended him; how dared Don Ciccio express himself with this lascivious lyricism about a future Princess of Falconeri? It is true, of course, that the poor man knew nothing yet; he would have to be told all; but anyway the news would be public in three hours. He decided at once and turned to Tumeo a smile feline but friendly. "Calm yourself, my dear Don Ciccio, calm yourself; at home I have a letter from my nephew charging me to ask on his behalf for Signorina Angelica's hand in matrimony; so from now on you will talk of her with your usual respect. You are the first to know the news, but for that privilege you must pay: when we get back to the palace you'll be locked up with Teresina in the gun room; you'll have time to clean and oil all the guns, and you will be set at liberty only after Don Calogero's visit; I want nothing to leak out before."

Taken by surprise like this, all Don Ciccio's snobberies and precautions collapsed together like a group of ninepins hit in the middle. All that survived was an age-old feeling.

"How foul, Excellency! A nephew of yours ought not to marry the daughter of those who're your enemies who have stabbed you in the back! To try to seduce her, as I thought, was an act of conquest; this is unconditional surrender. It's the end of the Falconeris, and of the Salinas too."

Having said this, he bent his head and longed in anguish for the earth to open under his feet. The Prince had gone purple; even his ears, even the whites of his eyes seemed flushed with blood. He clenched his fists and took a step toward Don Ciccio. But he was a man of science, used, after all, to seeing pros and cons; and anyway under that leonine aspect he was a skeptic. He had put up with so much that day already: the result of the Plebiscite, the nickname of Angelica's grandfather, those bullets in the back. And Tumeo was right; in him spoke clear tradition. But the man was a fool: this marriage was not the end of everything, but the beginning of everything. It was in the very best of traditions.

His fists unclenched; the marks of his nails were impressed on his palms. "Let's go home, Don Ciccio, there are some things you can't understand. Now you'll remember what we agreed, won't you?"

And as they climbed down toward the road, it would have been difficult to tell which of the two was Don Quixote and which was Sancho Panza.

When Don Calogero's arrival was announced at exactly half past four the Prince had not yet finished his toilet; he sent a message asking the Mayor to wait a minute in his study and went on placidly beautifying himself. He plastered his hair with *lemo-liscio*, Atkinson's lime and glycerine, a dense whitish lotion which arrived in cases from London and whose name suffered the same ethnic changes as songs; he rejected the black frock coat and chose instead a very pale lilac one which seemed more suited to the presumably festive occasion; he dallied a little longer to

tweak out with pincers an impudent fair hair which had
succeeded in getting through free that morning in his hurried shave; he had Father Pirrone called; before leaving
the room he took from a table an extract from the *Blätter
für Himmelsforschung* and with the rolled paper made the
sign of the Cross, a gesture of devotion which in Sicily has
a nonreligious meaning more frequently than is realized.

As he crossed the two rooms preceding the study he tried
to imagine himself as an imposing Leopard with smooth,
scented skin preparing to tear a timid jackal to pieces; but
by one of those involuntary associations of ideas which are
the scourge of natures like his, he found flicking into his
memory one of those French historical pictures in which
Austrian marshals and generals, covered with plumes and
decorations, are filing in surrender past an ironical Napoleon; they are more elegant, undoubtedly, but it is the
squat little man in the gray topcoat who is the victor; and
so, put out by these inopportune memories of Mantua and
Ulm, it was an irritated Leopard that entered the study.

Don Calogero was standing there, very small, very badly
shaved; he would have looked like a jackal had it not been
for eyes glinting intelligence; but as this intelligence of his
had a material aim opposed to the abstract one to which the
Prince's was supposed to tend, this was taken as a sign of
slyness. Devoid of the instinct for choosing the right clothes
for the occasion which was innate in the Prince, the Mayor
had thought it proper to dress up almost in mourning; he
was nearly as black as Father Pirrone, but while the latter
was sitting in a corner with the marmoreally abstract air of

priests who wish to avoid influencing the decisions of others, the Mayor's face expressed a sense of avid expectancy almost painful to behold. They plunged at once into the skirmish of insignificant words which precede great verbal battles. But it was Don Calogero who launched the main attack.

"Excellency," he asked, "have you had good news from Don Tancredi?" In little towns in those days the Mayor was always able to examine the post unofficially, and perhaps he had been warned by the unusually elegant writing paper. The Prince, when this occurred to him, began to feel annoyed.

"No, Don Calogero, no. My nephew's gone mad . . ."

But there exists a deity who is protector of princes. He is called Courtesy. And he often intervenes to prevent leopards from unfortunate slips. But he has to be paid heavy tribute. As Pallas intervened to curb the intemperances of Odysseus, so Courtesy appeared to Don Fabrizio to stop him on the brink of the abyss; but the Prince had to pay for his salvation by becoming explicit for once in his life. With perfect naturalness, without a second's hesitation, he ended the phrase, ". . . mad with love for your daughter, Don Calogero. So he wrote to me yesterday."

The Mayor preserved a surprising equanimity. He gave a slight smile and began examining the ribbon on his hat; Father Pirrone's eyes were turned to the ceiling, as if he were a master mason charged with judging its solidity. The Prince was put out: that silence on both their parts even deprived him of the petty satisfaction of arousing surprise. So it was with relief that he realized Don Calogero was about to speak.

"I knew it, Excellency, I knew it. They were seen to kiss on Tuesday, the twenty-fifth of September, the day before Don Tancredi's departure. In your garden, near the fountain. Laurel hedges aren't always as thick as people think. For a month I have been waiting for your nephew to make some move, and I was thinking just now of coming to ask Your Excellency what his intentions were."

Don Fabrizio felt as if he were assailed by numbers of stinging hornets. First, as is proper to every man not yet decrepit, that of carnal jealousy. So Tancredi had tasted that flavor of strawberries and cream which to him would always be unknown! Then came a sense of social humiliation at finding himself an accused instead of a bearer of good news. Third, personal vexation, that of one who thought he had everything in his control and then finds that a good deal has been happening without his knowledge. "Don Calogero, let's not change the cards we have on the table. Remember, it was *I* who called *you*. I wished to tell you of a letter from my nephew which arrived yesterday. In it he declares his passion for your daughter, a passion of whose intensity I . . ." (here the Prince hesitated a moment because lies are sometimes difficult to tell before gimlet eyes like the Mayor's) ". . . I was completely ignorant till now; and at the end of it he charges me to ask you for Signorina Angelica's hand."

Don Calogero went on smiling impassively; Father Pirrone had transformed himself from architectural expert into Moslem sage and, with four fingers of his right hand crossed in four fingers of his left, was rotating his thumbs around each other, turning and changing their direction with a great display of choreographic fantasy. The silence lasted a long time, the Prince lost patience. "Now, Don Calogero, it is I who am waiting for you to declare your intentions."

The Mayor's eyes had been fixed on the orange fringe of the Prince's armchair; he covered them for an instant with his right hand, then raised them; now they looked candid, brimming with amazed surprise as if that action had really changed them.

"Excuse me, Prince" (by the sudden omission of "Excellency" Don Fabrizio knew that all was happily consummated), "but joy and surprise had taken my words away. I'm a modern parent, though, and can give no definite answer until I have questioned the angel who is the consolation of our home. But I also know how to exercise a father's sacred rights. All that happens in Angelica's heart and mind is known to me, and I think I can say that Don Tancredi's affection, which honors us all, is sincerely returned."

Don Fabrizio was overcome with sincere emotion; the toad had been swallowed; the chewed head and gizzards were going down his throat; he still had to crunch up the claws, but that was nothing compared to the rest; the worst was over. With this sense of liberation, he began to feel his affection for Tancredi coming to the fore again, and imagined those narrow blue eyes of his glittering as they read the happy reply; he imagined, or recalled rather, the first months of a love-match with the frenzies and acrobatics of the senses approved and encouraged by all the hierarchies of angels, benevolent though surely surprised. And he foresaw Tancredi's security of life later on, his chances for developing talents whose wings would have been clipped by lack of money.

The nobleman rose to his feet, took a step toward the surprised Don Calogero, raised him from his armchair, clasped him to his breast; the Mayor's short legs were suspended in the air. For a moment that room in a remote Sicilian province looked like a Japanese print of a huge violet iris with a hairy fly hanging from a petal. When Don Calogero touched the floor again, Don Fabrizio thought, "I really must give him a pair of English razors; this won't do."

Father Pirrone switched off the turbine of his thumbs; he got up and squeezed the Prince's hand. "Excellency, I invoke the protection of God on this marriage; your joy has become mine." To Don Calogero he extended the tips of his fingers without a word. Then with a knuckle he tapped a barometer hanging on the wall: it was falling; bad weather ahead. He sat down and opened his breviary.

"Don Calogero," said the Prince, "the love of these two young people is the basis, the only foundation, of their future happiness. We all know that. But we men of a certain age, men of experience, we have to think of other things too. There is no point in my telling you how illustrious is the family of Falconeri; it came to Sicily with

Charles of Anjou, flourished under Aragonese, Spanish, Bourbon kings (if I may name them in your presence), and I am sure that they will also prosper under the new dynasty from the mainland (may God preserve it)." (It was impossible to tell how much the Prince was being ironic or how much he was being mistaken.) "They were Peers of the Realm, Grandees of Spain, Knights of Santiago, and, when they have a fancy to be Knights of Malta, they need only raise a finger and the Via Condotti pours diplomas out on them without a moment's hesitation, so far at least." (This perfidious insinuation was entirely lost on Don Calogero, who was quite ignorant of the statutes of the Sovereign Order of the Knights of Malta.) "I am sure that your daughter will decorate the ancient trunk of the Falconeri by her rare beauty, and emulate in her virtues those of the saintly Princesses of the line, the last of whom, my sister, God rest her soul, will certainly bless the bride and bridegroom from heaven." Don Fabrizio felt moved again, remembering his dear Giulia whose wasted life had been a perpetual sacrifice to the frenzied extravagance of Tancredi's father. "As for the boy, you know him; and if you did not, I am here to guarantee him in every possible way. There is endless good in him, and it is not only I who say so. Isn't that true, Father Pirrone?"

The excellent Jesuit, dragged from his reading, found himself suddenly facing an unpleasant dilemma. He had been Tancredi's confessor, and he knew quite a number of his little failings: none of them very serious, of course, but such as to detract quite a good deal from the endless goodness of which the Prince had spoken; and all of them such (he almost felt like saying) as to guarantee the firmest marital infidelity. This, of course, could not actually be said both for sacramental reasons and from worldly convention. On the other hand he liked Tancredi, and though he disapproved of the wedding with all his heart, he would never say a word which could either impede it or in any way cloud its course. He took refuge in Prudence, most tractable of the cardinal virtues. "The fund of goodness in our dear Tancredi is great indeed, Don Calogero, and sustained by Divine Grace and by the earthly virtues of Signorina Angelica he may become, one day, an excellent Christian husband." The prophecy, risky but prudently conditional, passed muster.

"But, Don Calogero," went on the Prince, chewing on the last gristly bits of toad, "if it is pointless to tell you of the antiquity of the Falconeris, it is unfortunately also pointless, since you already know it, to tell you that my nephew's economic circumstances are not equal to the greatness of his name. Don Tancredi's father, my brother-in-law Ferdinando, was not what is called a provident parent; his magnificent scale of life, and the irresponsibility of his administrators, have gravely shaken the patrimony of my dear nephew and former ward; the great estates around Mazzara, the pistachio woods of Ravanusa, the mulberry plantations of Oliveri, the palace in Palermo, all, all have gone; you know that, Don Calogero."

Don Calogero did indeed know that: it had been the greatest migration of swallows in living memory—a memory which still brought terror, though not prudence, to the whole of the Sicilian nobility, while it was a font of delight for all the Sedàras. "During the period of my guardianship all I succeeded in saving was the villa, the one near my own, by juridical quibbles and also thanks to a sacrifice or two on my own part which I made joyfully, both in memory of my sainted sister Giulia and because of my own affection for the dear lad. It's a fine villa: the staircase was designed by Marvuglia, the drawing rooms frescoed by Serenario; but at the moment the room in best repair can scarcely be used as a stall for goats."

The last shreds of toad had been nastier than he had expected: but they had gone down too, in the end. Now he had only to wash out his mouth with some phrase which was pleasant as well as sincere. "But, Don Calogero, the result of all these disasters, of all this heartbreak, has been Tancredi. There are certain things known to people like us; and maybe it is impossible to obtain the distinction, the delicacy, the fascination of a boy like him without his ancestors' having romped through a half-dozen fortunes. At least so it is in Sicily; it's a kind of law of nature, like those which regulate earthquakes and drought."

He paused a moment as a lackey came in bearing two lighted lamps on a tray. As they were being set in place the Prince made a silence vibrant with heartfelt pleasure reign in the study. "Tancredi is no ordinary boy, Don Calogero," he went on. "He is far more than merely gentlemanly and elegant; though he has not studied much, he knows about the important things: men, women, the feel and sense of the times. He is ambitious, and rightly so; he will go far; and your Angelica, Don Calogero, will be lucky to mount the ladder with him. Also, in Tancredi's company one may have moments of irritation, but never of boredom; and that means a great deal."

It would be an exaggeration to say that the Mayor appreciated the worldly subtleties of this part of the Prince's speech; on the whole it just confirmed him in his conviction of Tancredi's astuteness and opportunism; and what he needed at home was a man astute and able, no more. He thought himself, he felt himself, to be the equal of anyone; and he was even sorry to notice in his daughter a genuine affection for the handsome youth.

"Prince, all these things I knew, and others too. And they don't matter to me at all." He wrapped himself round once more in a cloak of sentimentality. "Love, Excellency, love is all, as I know myself." And he may have been sincere, poor man, if his definition of love were admitted. "But I'm a man of the world and I want to put my cards on the table too. There's no point in talking about my daughter's qualities: she's the blood in my heart, the liver in my guts; I've no one else to leave what I have, and what's mine is hers. But it's only right that the young people should know what they can count on at once. In the marriage contract I will assign to my daughter the estate of Settesoli, of six hundred and forty-four *salmi*, that is ten hundred and ten hectares, as they want us to call them nowadays, all wheat, first-class land, airy and cool; and a hundred and eighty *salmi* of olive groves and vineyards at Gibildolce; and on the wedding day I will hand over to the bridegroom twenty linen sacks each containing ten thousand ounces of gold. I'll only have a pittance left myself," he added, knowing well he would not, and not wanting to be believed, "but a daughter's a daughter. And with that they can do up all the staircases by Marruggia and all the ceilings by Sorcionario that exist. Angelica must be properly housed."

Ignorant vulgarity exuded from his every pore; even so, the two listeners were astounded; Don Fabrizio needed all his self-control not to show surprise; Tancredi's coup was far bigger than he had ever imagined. A sensation of revulsion came over him again, but Angelica's beauty, the bridegroom's grace, still managed to veil in poetry the crudeness of the contract. Father Pirrone did let his tongue cluck on his palate; then, annoyed at having shown his own amazement, he tried to rhyme the improvident sound by making his chair and shoes squeak and by crackling the leaves of his breviary, but he failed completely; the impression remained.

Luckily, an impromptu remark from Don Calogero, the only one in the conversation, got both of them out of their embarrassment. "Prince," he said, "I know that what I am about to say will have no effect on you who descend from the loves of the Emperor Titus and Queen Berenice; but the Sedàras are noble too; till I came along we'd been an unlucky lot, buried in the provinces and undistinguished, but I have the documents in order, and one day it will be known that your nephew has married the Baronessina Sedàra del Biscotto; a title granted by his Majesty

Ferdinand IV for work on the port of Mazzara. I have to put the papers through; there's only one link missing."

A hundred years ago this business of a missing entry, of getting such papers "through," was an important element in the lives of many Sicilians, causing alternating exaltation and depression to thousands of decent or not so decent people; this subject is too important to be treated fleetingly, but we will content ourselves with saying that Don Calogero's heraldic impromptu gave the Prince the incomparable artistic satisfaction of seeing a type realized in all its details, and that the depressed laugh he gave ended in a sweetish taste of nausea.

After this the conversation drifted off into a number of aimless ruts: Don Fabrizio remembered Tumeo shut up in the darkness of the gun room; for the nth time in his life he deplored the length of country calls and ended by wrapping himself in hostile silence. Don Calogero understood, promised to return next morning with Angelica's undoubted consent, and said goodbye. He was accompanied through two of the drawing rooms, embraced again, and began descending the stairs as the Prince, towering above him, watched this little conglomeration of astuteness, ill-cut clothes, money, and ignorance who was now to become almost a part of the family getting smaller and smaller.

Holding a candle in his hand, he then went to free Tumeo, who was sitting resignedly in the dark smoking his pipe. "I'm sorry, Don Ciccio, but you'll understand, I had to do it."

"I do understand, Excellency, I do understand. Did everything go off all right?"

"Perfectly, couldn't be better." Tumeo mouthed some congratulations, put the leash back on the collar of Teresina, sleeping exhausted from the hunt, and picked up the day's bag.

"Take those woodcock of mine too, won't you? They're not enough for us all, anyway. Goodbye, Don Ciccio, come and see us soon. And excuse everything." A powerful clap on the shoulder served as sign of reconciliation and a reminder of power; the last faithful retainer of the House of Salina went off to his own poor rooms.

When the Prince returned to his study he found that Father Pirrone had slipped away to avoid discussions. And he went toward his wife's room to tell her all that had happened. The sound of his vigorous rapid steps announced his arrival ten yards ahead. He crossed the girls' sitting room; Carolina and Caterina were winding a skein of wool, and as he passed got to their feet and smiled; Mademoiselle Dombreuil hurriedly took off her spectacles and replied demurely to his greeting; Concetta had her back to him; she was bent over her embroidery frame and, not hearing her father's steps, did not even turn.

4

A S meetings due to the marriage contract became more frequent, Don Fabrizio found an odd admiration growing in him for Sedàra's qualities. He became used to the ill-shaven cheeks, the plebeian accent, the odd clothes, and the persistent odor of stale sweat, and he began to realize the man's rare intelligence. Many problems that had seemed insoluble to the Prince were resolved in a trice by Don Calogero; free as he was from the shackles imposed on many other men by honesty, decency, and plain good manners, he moved through the jungle of life with the confidence of an elephant which advances in a straight line, rooting up trees and trampling down lairs, without even noticing scratches of thorns and moans from the crushed. Reared and tended in tranquil vales across which blew the courtesies of "please," "I'd be so grateful," "How very kind," the Prince, when talking to Don Calogero, now found himself on an open heath swept by searing winds, and although continuing in his heart to prefer defiles in the hills he could not help admiring this surge and sweep which drew from the plane trees and cedars of Donnafugata notes never heard before.

Bit by bit, almost without realizing it, Don Fabrizio told Don Calogero about his own affairs, which were numerous, complex, and little known to himself; this was not due to any defect of intelligence, but to a kind of contemptuous indifference about matters he considered low, though deep down this attitude was really due to laziness and the ease with which he had always got out of difficulties by selling off a few more hundred of his thousands of acres.

Don Calogero's advice, after listening to the Prince's accounts and reorganizing them for himself, was both opportune and immediately effective; but the eventual result of such advice, cruelly efficient in conception and feeble in application by the easygoing Don Fabrizio, was that in years to come the Salina family were to acquire a reputation for treating dependents harshly, a reputation quite unjustified in reality but which helped to destroy its prestige at Donnafugata and Querceta, without in any way halting the collapse of the family fortunes.

It is only fair to mention that more frequent contact with the Prince had a certain effect on Sedàra too. Until that moment he had met aristocrats only on business (of buying and selling) or through their very rare and long-brooded invitations to parties, circumstances in which this most singular of social classes does not show at its best. During such meetings he had formed the opinion that the aristocracy consisted entirely of sheeplike creatures, existing merely in order to give their wool to his clipping shears and their names and incomprehensible prestige to his daughter. But since getting to know Tancredi during the period after Garibaldi's landing, he had found himself dealing, unexpectedly, with a young noble as cynical as himself, capable of striking a sharp bargain between his own smiles and titles and the attractions and fortunes of others, while knowing how to dress up such "Sedàra-ish" actions with a grace and fascination which he, Don Calogero, felt he did not himself possess, but which influenced him without his realizing it and without his being able in any way to discern its origins. When he got to know Don Fabrizio better, he found there again the pliability and incapacity for self-defense that were characteristic of his imaginary sheep-noble, but also a strength of attraction different in tinge, but similar in intensity, to young Falconeri's; he also found a certain energy with a tendency toward abstraction, a disposition to seek a shape for life from within himself and not in what he could wrest from others. This abstract energy made a deep impression on Don Calogero, although with a direct impact not filtered through words as has been attempted here; much of this fascination he noticed simply came from good manners, and he realized how agreeable can be a well-bred man, who at heart is only someone who eliminates the unpleasant aspects of so much of the human condition and exercises a kind of profitable altruism (a formula in which the usefulness of the adjective made him tolerate the uselessness of the noun). Gradually Don Calogero came to understand that a meal in common need not necessarily be all munching and grease stains; that a conversation may well bear no resemblance to a dog fight; that to give precedence to a woman is a sign of strength and not, as he had believed, of weakness; that sometimes more can be obtained by saying "I haven't explained myself well" than "I can't understand a word"; and that the adoption of such tactics can result in a greatly increased yield from meals, arguments, women, and questions.

It would be rash to affirm that Don Calogero drew an immediate profit from what he had learned; he did try to shave a little better and complain a little less about the waste of laundry soap; but from that moment there began, for him and his family, that process of continual refining which in the course of three generations transforms innocent peasants into defenseless gentry.

Angelica's first visit to the Salina family as a bride-to-be was impeccably stage-managed. Her bearing was so perfect that it might have been suggested word by word by Tancredi, but this was ruled out by the slow communications of the period; one possible explanation was that he had given her some suggestions even before their official engagement: a risky hypothesis for anyone able to measure the young Prince's foresight, but not entirely absurd. Angelica arrived at six in the evening, dressed in pink and white; her soft black tresses were shadowed by a big autumnal straw hat on which bunches of artificial grapes and golden ears of wheat discreetly evoked the vineyards of Gibildolce and the granaries of Settesoli. She sloughed off her father in the entrance hall, then with a swirl of wide skirts floated lightly up the many steps of the inner staircase and flung herself into the arms of Don Fabrizio; on his whiskers she implanted two big kisses which were returned with genuine affection; the Prince paused perhaps just a second longer than necessary to breathe in the scent of gardenia on adolescent cheeks. After this Angelica blushed, took half a step back: "I'm so, so happy . . . ," then came close again, stood on tiptoe, and murmured into his ear, "Uncle mine!"; a highly successful line, comparable in its perfect timing almost to Eisenstein's baby carriage, and which, explicit and secret as it was, set the Prince's simple heart aflutter and yoked him to the lovely girl for ever. Meanwhile Don Calogero was coming up the stairs, and said how very sorry his wife was she could not be present, but the night before she had slipped at home and twisted her left foot, which was most painful. "Her ankle's like an eggplant, Prince." Don Fabrizio, exhilarated by the verbal caress, and forewarned by Tumeo's revelations that his offer would never be put to the proof, said that he would give himself the pleasure of calling upon the Signora Sedàra at once, a suggestion which dismayed Don Calogero and made him, in order to reject it, think up a second indisposition of his spouse's, this time a violent headache which forced the poor woman to remain in the dark.

Meanwhile the Prince gave his arm to Angelica. They crossed a number of dark salons, just lit enough by the dim glimmer of oil lamps for them to see their way; but at the end of the splendid perspective of rooms glittered the "Leopold Drawing Room," where the rest of the family was gathered, and their procession through empty darkness toward a light center of intimacy had the rhythm of a Masonic initiation.

The family was crowding around the door; the Princess had withdrawn her own reservations before the wrath of her husband, who had not so much rejected them as blasted them to nothingness; she kissed her lovely future niece again and again and squeezed her to her bosom with such energy that the girl found stamped on her skin the setting of the famous Salina ruby necklace which Maria Stella had insisted on wearing, though it was daylight, in sign of a major celebration. The sixteen-year-old Francesco Paolo was pleased at having this exceptional chance of kissing Angelica too, under the impotently jealous eyes of his father. Concetta was particularly affectionate; her joy was so intense that the tears even came to her eyes. The other sisters drew close around her with noisy gaiety just because they were not moved. Even Father Pirrone, who in his saintly way was not insensible to female fascination, in which he saw an undeniable proof of Divine Goodness, felt all his own opposition melt away before the warmth of her grace (with a small *g*), and he murmured to her, "*Veni, sponsa de Libano.*" (He had to check himself then to avoid other warmer verses rising to his memory.) Mademoiselle

Dombreuil, as befits a governess, wept with emotion, kneading the girl's plump shoulders in her disappointed fingers and crying, "*Angelicà, Angelicà, pensons à la joie de Tancrède.*" Only Bendicò, in contrast to his usual sociability, crouched behind a console table and growled away in the back of his throat until energetically called to task by an indignant Francesco Paolo with still-quivering lips.

Lighted candles had been set in twenty-four of the forty-eight branches of the chandelier, and each of these candles, candid and at the same time ardent, seemed like a virgin in the throes of love; the two-colored Murano flowers on their stems of curved glass looked down, admired the girl who entered, and gave her a fragile and iridescent smile. The great fireplace was lit more in sign of joy than to warm the tepid room, and the light of the flames quivered on the floor, loosing intermittent gleams from the dull gold of the furniture; it really did represent the domestic hearth, symbol of home, and its brands were sparks of desire, its embers were ardors contained.

The Princess, who possessed to eminent degree the faculty of reducing emotions to the least common denominator, began narrating sublime episodes from Tancredi's childhood; so insistent was she about these that it really began to seem as if Angelica should consider herself lucky to be marrying a man who had been so reasonable at the age of six as to submit to necessary enemas without a fuss, and so bold at twelve as to have stolen a handful of cherries. As this episode of banditry was being recalled, Concetta burst out laughing. "That's a habit Tancredi hasn't yet been able to rid himself of," she said. "D'you remember, Papa, how a couple of months ago he took those peaches we'd been so looking forward to?" Then she suddenly looked dour, as if she were chairwoman of an association for owners of damaged orchards.

Don Fabrizio's voice quickly put such trifling in its place; he talked of Tancredi as he was now, of the quick attentive youth, always ready with a remark which enraptured those who loved him and exasperated everyone else; he told of Tancredi's introduction to the Duchess of San-something-or-other during a visit to Naples, and how she had been so taken with him that she wanted him to visit her morning, noon, and night, whether she happened to be in her drawing room or her bed; all because, said she, no one knew how to tell *les petits riens* like Tancredi; and although Don Fabrizio hurriedly added that Tancredi could have been no more than sixteen at the time and the Duchess over fifty, Angelica's eyes flashed, for she had definite information about the habits of Palermitan youths and strong intuitions about those of Neapolitan Duchesses.

Anyone deducing from this attitude of Angelica that she loved Tancredi would have been mistaken; she had too much pride and too much ambition to be capable of that annihilation, however temporary, of one's own personality without which there is no love; apart from that she was too young and inexperienced to be able to appreciate yet his genuine qualities, all subtle nuances; but although she did not love him, she was, then, in love with him, a very different thing; his blue eyes, his affectionate teasing, certain suddenly serious tones of his voice gave her, even in memory, quite a definite turn, and in those days her one longing was to be gripped by those hands of his; presently she would forget them and find a substitute as she did, in fact, later, but for the moment she yearned for him to seize her. So the revelation of this possible love-affair (which was, in fact, nonexistent) gave her a twinge of that most absurd of tortures, retrospective jealousy; a twinge soon dissipated, however, by a cool appraisal of the advantages, erotic and otherwise, of marriage to Tancredi.

Don Fabrizio went on praising Tancredi. In his affection he got to the point of talking about him as a kind of Mirabeau. "He's begun early and well," said he, "and will go far." Angelica's smooth forehead bowed in assent. Actually she did not care at all about Tancredi's political future; she was one of the many girls who consider public events as part of a separate universe, and she could not even imagine that a speech by Cavour might in time, through a thousand minute links, influence her own life and change it. She was thinking, "We've got the stuff, and that's enough for us; as to going far . . ." Such youthful simplicities she was to discard completely when, years later, she became one of the most venomous string pullers for Parliament and Senate.

"And then, Angelica, you have no idea yet how amusing Tancredi is! He knows everything, sees an unexpected side everywhere. When one's with him and he's in form, the world seems even funnier than it usually does, sometimes more serious, too." That Tancredi was amusing, Angelica already knew; that he was capable of revealing new worlds, she not only hoped but had some reason to suspect ever since the twenty-fifth of last September, day of that famous kiss, the only one officially noticed, in the shelter of that treacherous laurel hedge, for it had been something much subtler and tastier, entirely different from the only other sample in her experience, one given her over a year before by a gardener's boy at Poggio a Cajano. But Angelica cared very little about the wit or even the intelligence of her fiancé, far less in any case than did sweet old Don Fabrizio —really *so* sweet, though so "intellectual" too. In Tancredi she saw her chance of gaining a fine position in the noble world of Sicily, a world which to her was full of marvels very different from those which it contained in reality; and she also wanted him as a lively partner in bed. If he was superior in spirit too, all the better; but she for her part didn't bother much about that. There was always amusement to be had. In any case those were ideas for the future; for the moment, whether witty or stupid, she would have liked to have him there, stroking at least her neck under the tresses, as he had once done.

"Oh God, oh God, how I wish he were with us now!"

The exclamation moved them all, both by its evident sincerity and the ignorance that caused her to make it, and brought that very successful first visit to an end. For shortly afterward Angelica and her father made their farewells: preceded by a stable lad with a lighted lantern, the uncertain gold of whose gleams set alight the red of fallen plane leaves, father and daughter returned to their home whose entrance had been forbidden to Peppe 'Mmerda, Angelica's grandfather, by bullets in the kidneys.

Now that Don Fabrizio felt serene again, he had gone back to his habit of evening reading. In autumn, after the Rosary, as it was now too dark to go out, the family would gather around the fire waiting for dinner, and the Prince, standing up, would read out to his family extracts from modern novels, exuding dignified benevolence from every pore.

Those were years when novels were helping to form those literary myths which still dominate European minds today; but in Sicily, partly because of its traditional impermeability to anything new, partly because of the general ignorance of any language whatsoever, partly also, it must be said, because of a nagging and strict Bourbon censorship which worked through the Customs, no one had heard of Dickens, Eliot, Sand, Flaubert, or even Dumas. A couple of Balzac's volumes had, through various subterfuges, it is true, reached the hands of Don Fabrizio, who had appointed himself family censor; he had read them and then lent them, in disgust, to a friend he didn't like, saying that they were by a writer with a talent undoubtedly vigorous but also extravagant and "obsessed" (today he would have said "monomaniacal"): a hasty judgment, obviously, but not without a certain acuteness. The level of these readings was therefore somewhat low, conditioned as it was by respect for the virginal shyness of the girls, the religious scruples of the Princess, and the Prince's own sense of dignity, which would have energetically refused to let his united family hear any "filth."

It was about the tenth of November and getting toward the end of their stay at Donnafugata. The rain was pouring down and a gale slapping gusts of rain angrily on the windowpanes; in the distance was a roll of thunder; every now and again a few drops found their way down the primitive Sicilian chimney, sizzled a moment on the fire, and dotted with black the glowing brands of olive wood. He was reading *Angiola Maria* and that evening had just reached the last few pages; the description of the heroine's journey through the icy Lombard winter froze the Sicilian hearts of the young ladies, even in their warm armchairs. All of a sudden there was a great scuttle in the room next door, and in came Mimí the valet breathing hard. "Excellency," he cried, forgetting all his style, "Excellency, Signorino Tancredi's arrived! He's in the courtyard seeing his luggage unloaded. Think of it! Madonna, in this weather!" And off he rushed.

Surprise swept Concetta into a time which no longer corresponded with reality, and "Darling!" she exclaimed. But the very sound of her own voice led her back to the comfortless present and, of course, such a brusque change from a secret warm climate to an open frozen one was most painful; fortunately, the exclamation was submerged in the general excitement and not heard.

Preceded by Don Fabrizio's long steps, they all rushed toward the stairs; the dark drawing rooms were hurriedly crossed; down they went; the great gate was flung wide

on to the outer stairs and the courtyard below; the wind
rushed in, making the canvases of the portraits quiver and
sweeping with it dampness and a smell of earth; against a
sky lit by flashes of lightning the trees in the garden swayed
and rustled like torn silk. Don Fabrizio was just about to
pass through the front door when on the top step outside
appeared a heavy shapeless mass; it was Tancredi wrapped
up in the huge blue cloak of the Piedmontese Cavalry, so
soaked that he must have weighed a ton and looked quite
black. "Careful, Uncle; don't touch me, I'm a sponge!"
The light of the lantern on the stairs showed a glimpse of
his face. He came in, undid the chain which held the cloak
at the collar, and let fall the garment, which flopped on the
floor with a squelch. He smelled like a wet dog; he hadn't
taken off his boots for the last three days; but to Don
Fabrizio, embracing him, he was the lad more beloved than
his own sons, for Maria Stella a dear nephew most basely
calumniated, for Father Pirrone the sheep always lost and
always found, for Concetta a dear ghost resembling her lost
love. Even Mademoiselle Dombreuil kissed him with her
mouth so unused to caresses and cried, poor girl, *"Tancrède, Tancrède, pensons à la joie d'Angelicà,"* so few
strings had her own bow, forced as she always was to echo
the joys of others. Bendicò also found again his dear comrade in play, one who knew better than anyone else how to
blow into a snout through a closed fist; but he showed his
ecstasy in his own doggy way by leaping frenziedly around
the room and taking no notice of his beloved.

It was a moving moment, this grouping of the family

around the returned youth, all the dearer as he was not really a member of it, all the happier as he was coming to gather both love and a sense of perennial security. A moving moment—but a long one, too. When the first transports were spent, Don Fabrizio noticed that on the threshold were standing two other figures, also dripping and also smiling. Tancredi noticed them too and began to laugh. "Excuse me, all of you, but the excitement quite made me forget. Aunt," he said, turning to the Princess, "I've allowed myself to bring a dear friend, Count Carlo Cavriaghi; anyway you know him, he used often to come up to the villa when he was with the General. And this other is Lancer Moroni, my servant." The soldier smiled all over his dull, honest face, and stood there at attention while from the thick cloth of his overcoat the water dripped down onto the floor. But the young Count did not stand at attention; taking off his soaking shapeless cap, he kissed the Princess's hand, smiled, and dazzled the girls with his little blond mustache and his unsuppressible rolling *r*. "And to think they told me that it never rained down here! Heavens, the last two days we might have been in the sea itself." Then he became serious: "But, Falconeri, where is the Signorina Angelica? You've dragged me all the way here from Naples to show me her. I see many a beauty, but not her." He turned to Don Fabrizio: "You know, Prince, according to him she's the Queen of Sheba! Let's go at once to worship this creature *formosissima et nigerrima*. Come on, you stubborn oaf!"

By such talk he brought the language of the officers'

mess into the proud hall with its armored and beribboned ancestors; and everyone was amused. But Don Fabrizio and Tancredi knew how things stood: they knew Don Calogero, they knew his Beautiful Beast of a wife, the incredible state of that rich man's home; things unknown in candid Lombardy.

Don Fabrizio intervened. "Listen, Count: you thought it never rained in Sicily and now you can see it's pouring. We wouldn't like you to think there isn't pneumonia in Sicily too, and then find yourself in bed with a high temperature. Mimí," he said to the valet, "light the fire in the Signorino Tancredi's room and in the green room of the guest wing. Prepare the little room next door for the soldier. And you, Count, go and get thoroughly dry and change your clothes. I'll send you up some punch and biscuits. And dinner is at eight, in two hours." Cavriaghi was too used to military service not to bow at once to the voice of authority; he saluted and followed meekly behind the valet. Behind him Moroni dragged along the military boxes and curved sabers in their green flannel wrappings.

Meanwhile Tancredi was writing, "Dearest Angelica, I've come, and for you. I'm head over heels in love, but also wet as a frog, filthy as a lost dog, and hungry as a wolf. The very minute I've cleaned myself up and consider myself worthy of appearing before the loveliest creature in the world, I will hurry over to you; in two hours. My respects to your dear parents. To you . . . nothing for the moment." The text was submitted for the approval of the Prince; the latter had always been an admirer of

Tancredi's epistolary style; he laughed, and approved in full. Donna Bastiana would have plenty of time to catch some other imaginary disease; and the note was at once sent across the square.

Such was the general zest and jollity that a quarter of an hour was enough for the two young men to dry, clean up, change uniforms, and meet once again in the "Leopold Room" around the fire; there they drank tea and brandy and let themselves be admired. At that period nothing could have been less military than the families of the Sicilian aristocracy; no Bourbon officers had ever been seen in the drawing rooms of Palermo, and the few Garibaldini who had penetrated them gave more the impression of picturesque scarecrows than real military men. So those two young officers were in fact the first the Salina girls had ever seen, close to; in their double-breasted uniforms, Tancredi's with the silver buttons of the Lancers, Carlo's with the gilt ones of the Bersaglieri, the first with a high black velvet collar bordered with orange, the other with crimson, they sat stretching toward the embers legs encased in blue cloth and black cloth. On their sleeves were the silver and gold stars amid twirls and dashes and endless loops: a delight for girls used only to severe frock coats and funereal tail coats. The edifying novel lay upside down behind an armchair.

Don Fabrizio did not quite understand: he remembered both the young men in lobster red and very carelessly turned out. "Shouldn't you Garibaldini be wearing a red shirt, though?"

The two turned on him as if a snake had bitten them. "Garibaldini, Garibaldini indeed, Uncle! We were once, and now that's over! Cavriaghi and I, thanks be to God, are officers in the regular army of His Majesty, King of Sardinia for another few months, and shortly to be of Italy. When Garibaldi's army broke up we had the choice: to go home or stay in the King's army. He and I and a lot of others went into the *real* army. We couldn't stand that rabble long, could we, Cavriaghi?"

"Heavens, what dreadful people! Good for ambushes and looting, that's all! Now we're with decent fellows, and we're real officers!" And he plucked at his little mustache with a grimace of adolescent disgust.

"We had to drop rank, you know, Uncle. They didn't seem to think much of our military experience. From Captain I've become Lieutenant again, as you see!" And he showed the two stars on his shoulder straps. "He from being Lieutenant is now Second Lieutenant. But we're as happy as if we'd got a promotion. With our uniforms, we're now respected in quite another way."

"I should think so," interrupted Cavriaghi. "People aren't afraid we'll steal their chickens."

"You should have seen what it was like from Palermo to here, when we stopped at post stations to change horses! All we had to say was 'Urgent orders on His Majesty's service,' and horses appeared like magic; and we'd show them our orders, which were actually the bills of the Naples hotel wrapped up and sealed!"

Having had their say on military changes, they passed

on to vaguer subjects of conversation. Concetta and Cavriaghi had sat down together a little apart, and the young Count showed her the present which he had brought her from Naples: the *Poems* of Aleardo Aleardi magnificently bound for the purpose. A princely crown was deeply incised into the dark blue leather with her initials, *C. C. S.*, beneath. Below that again, in large vaguely Gothic lettering, were the words *Sempre sorda*—Forever deaf.

Concetta was amused, and laughed. "Why deaf, Count? I can hear C. C. S. all right!"

The face of the young Count flamed with boyish passion. "Blind and deaf, yes, deaf, Signorina, deaf to my sighs and deaf to my groans! And blind, too, blind to the begging in my eyes. If you only knew what I suffered when you left Palermo to come here; not a wave, not a sign as the carriage vanished down the drive. And you expect me not to call you deaf? 'Cruel' is what I really should have written."

His somewhat literary excitement was chilled by the girl's reserve. "Count, you must be very tired after your long journey, your nerves are not quite in order; calm yourself. Why not read me a nice poem?"

While the Bersagliere was reading out the gentle verse in a voice charged with emotion and amid pauses full of distress, Tancredi in front of the fireplace was taking from his pocket a small blue satin box. "Here's the ring, Uncle, the ring I'm giving to Angelica; or rather the one you must hand to her in my name." He pressed the clasp and there was a dark sapphire cut in a clear octagon, and clustering close around it a multitude of tiny flawless diamonds. A slightly gloomy jewel, but in close harmony with the funereal taste of the times, and one obviously worth the two hundred gold ounces sent by Don Fabrizio. In reality it had cost a good deal less; in those months of fleeing and sacking, there were superb jewels to be picked up cheap in Naples; from the difference in price had come a brooch, a memento for Schwarzwald. Concetta and Cavriaghi were also called to admire it, but they did not move, as the young Count had already seen it and Concetta was putting off that pleasure till later. The ring went from hand to hand, was admired, praised, and Tancredi was congratulated on his good taste. Don Fabrizio asked, "But what about the measurements? We'll have to send the ring to Girgenti to have it adjusted to the right size." Tancredi's eyes sparkled with fun. "There's no need for that, Uncle; the measurement is exact; I'd taken it before." And Don Fabrizio was silenced; here, he recognized, was a master.

The little box had made the whole round of the fireplace and come back to the hands of Tancredi when from behind the door was heard a subdued "May I?" It was Angelica. In the rush and excitement she had snatched up, to protect her from the pouring rain, one of those huge peasants' capes of rough cloth called a *scappolare*. Wrapped in the stiff dark blue folds, her body looked very slim; under the wet hood her green eyes looked anxious and bewildered, eagerly sensual.

The sight of her, and the contrast between the beauty of her face and the rusticity of her clothes, was like a whiplash to Tancredi; he got up, ran to her without a word, and kissed her on the mouth. The box which he held in his right hand tickled her bent neck. Then he pressed the spring, took the ring, put it on her engagement finger; the box dropped to the floor. "There, darling, that's for you, from your Tancredi." Then irony broke in: "And thank Uncle for it, too." Then he embraced her again; sensual anticipation made them both tremble; the room, the by-standers, seemed very far away; and he really felt as if by those kisses he were taking possession of Sicily once more, of the lovely faithless land which the Falconeris had lorded over for centuries and which now, after a vain re-volt, had surrendered to him again, as always to his peo-ple, its carnal delights and its golden crops.

As a result of this welcome arrival the family's return to Palermo was put off, and there followed two weeks of en-chantment. The gale which had accompanied the journey of the two officers had been the last of a series; after it came the resplendent St. Martin's summer, which is the real season of pleasure in Sicily: weather luminous and blue, oasis of mildness in the harsh progression of the sea-sons, inveigling and leading on the senses with its sweet-ness, luring to secret nudities by its warmth. Not that there was any erotic nudity at the palace of Donnafugata, just an air of excited sensuality all the sharper for being carefully restrained. Eighty years before, the Salina palace had been a meeting place for those obscure pleasures which appealed to the dying eighteenth century; but the severe regency of the Princess Carolina, the neoreligious fervor of the Restoration, the straightforward sensuality of Don Fabrizio, had eventually caused its bizarre extravagances to be forgotten; the little powdered demons had been put to flight; they still eixsted, of course, but only as sleeping embryos, hibernating under piles of dust in some attic of the vast building. The lovely Angelica's entry into the palace had made them stir a little, as may be remembered; but it was the arrival of two young men in love which really awoke the instincts lying dormant in the house; and these now showed themselves everywhere, like ants wakened by the sun, no longer poisonous, but livelier than ever. Even the architecture, the rococo decoration itself, evoked thoughts of fleshly curves and taut erect breasts; and every opening door seemed like a curtain rustling in a bed-alcove.

Cavriaghi was in love with Concetta; but boy that he was, not only in appearance like Tancredi but deep within, his love found expression in the easy rhymes of poets such as Prati and Aleardi, and in dreaming of moonlight elopements whose logical sequence he did not dare contemplate and which Concetta's "deafness" obviated from the start anyway. One cannot know if in the seclusion of that green room of his he did not abandon himself to more definite hopes; certain it is that to the love-scenery of that autumn in Donnafugata his only contribution was the sketching in of clouds and evanescent horizons and not the creation of architectural masses. The two girls Carolina and Caterina, however, played their parts excellently in the symphony of desires traversing the whole palace that November and

mingling with the murmur of the fountains, the pawing of
the horses in heat in the stables, and the tenacious burrow-
ing of nuptial nests by woodworms in the old furniture.
The two girls were young and attractive and, though with
no particular loves of their own, found themselves immersed in the currents emanating from the others; often the
kiss which Concetta denied to Cavriaghi, the embrace from
Angelica which left Tancredi unsatisfied, would reverberate
around the girls and graze their untouched bodies; and they
too would find themselves dreaming about locks of hair
damp with sweat, about whimpers of pleasure. Even poor
Mademoiselle Dombreuil, by dint of functioning as lightning conductor, was drawn into the turbid and laughing vor-
tex, just as psychiatrists become infected and succumb to the
frenzies of their patients. When after a day of hide-and-
seek and moralizing ambushes she lay down on her lonely
bed, her own withered breasts would quiver as she muttered indiscriminate invocations to Tancredi, to Carlo, to
Fabrizio. . . .

Center and motor of this sensual agitation were, of
course, one couple, Tancredi and Angelica. Their certain
marriage, though not very close, extended its reassuring
shadow in anticipation on the parched soil of their mutual
desires. Difference of class made Don Calogero consider
their long periods alone together as quite normal with the
nobility, and made Princess Maria Stella think habitual
to those of the Sedàras' rank the frequency of Angelica's
visits and a freedom of bearing which she would certainly
not have found proper in her own daughters. And so An-

gelica's visits to the palace became more and more frequent
until they were almost constant, and she ended by being
only accompanied there formally by her father, who would
return at once to his office and to the finding or weaving of
hidden plots, or by a maid who would vanish into the servants' quarters to drink coffee and bore the unfortunate palace domestics.

Tancredi wanted Angelica to know the whole palace
with its inextricable complex of guest rooms, state rooms,
kitchens, chapels, theaters, picture galleries, odorous tack
rooms, stables, stuffy conservatories, passages, stairs, terraces
and porticoes, and particularly a series of abandoned and
uninhabited apartments which had not been used for many
years and formed a mysterious and intricate labyrinth of
their own. Tancredi did not realize (or he realized perfectly
well) that he was drawing the girl into the hidden center of
the sensual cyclone; and Angelica at that time wanted whatever Tancredi did. Their wanderings through the almost
limitless building were interminable; they would set off as
if for some unknown land, and unknown indeed it was because in many of those apartments and corners not even Don
Fabrizio had ever set foot (a cause of great satisfaction to
him, for he used to say that a palace of which one knew
every room wasn't worth living in).

The two lovers embarked for Cythera on a ship made
of dark and sunny rooms, of apartments sumptuous or
squalid, empty or crammed with remains of heterogeneous
furniture. They would set off accompanied by Cavriaghi or
by Mademoiselle Dombreuil (Father Pirrone, with the wis-

dom of his Order, had always refused his company), sometimes by both; outer decency was saved. But in the palace of
Donnafugata it was not difficult to mislead anyone wanting
to follow; this just meant slipping into a passage (these
were very long, narrow, and tortuous, with grilled windows
which could not be passed without a sense of anguish),
turning through a gallery, going up some handy stairs,
and the two young people were far away, invisible, alone
as if on a desert island. All that remained to survey them
was some faded pastoral portrait made unseeing by the
painter's inexperience, or a shepherdess glancing down con-
senting from some obliterated fresco.

Cavriaghi anyway would soon tire, and when he found
his route leading through a room he knew or some staircase down into the garden he would slip off, both to please
his friend and to go and sigh over Concetta's ice-cold
hands. The governess would hang on longer, but not in-
definitely; for some time her unanswered calls could be
heard fading farther and farther away: *"Tancrède, Angelicà, où êtes-vous?"* Then silence would fall again, except
for the scuffle of rats in the ceilings above, or the rustle of
some centuries-old and forgotten letter sent wandering by
the wind over the floor: excuses for pleasant frights, for
the reassuring contact of flesh with flesh. And with them
always was Eros, malicious and tenacious, drawing the
young couple into a game full of risk and fun. Both of
them were still very near childhood, and they enjoyed the
game in itself, enjoyed being followed, being lost, being
found again; but when they touched each other their sharp-

ened senses would overwhelm them, and his five fingers entwined in hers with that gesture dear to uncertain sensualists, the gentle rub of fingertips on the pale veins of the back of the hand, confusing their whole being, preluding more insinuating caresses.

Once she had hidden behind an enormous picture propped on the floor, and for a short time *Arturo Corbèra at the Siege of Antioch* formed a protection for the girl's hopeful anxiety; but when she was found, with her smile veined in cobwebs and her hands veiled in dust, she was clasped tight, and though she kept on saying again and again, "No, Tancredi, no," her denial was in fact an invitation, for all he was doing was staring with his blue eyes into her green ones. One luminous cold morning she was trembling in a dress that was still summery; he squeezed her to him, to warm her, on a sofa covered in tattered silk; her odorous breath moved the hair on his forehead; they were moments ecstatic and painful, during which desire became torment, restraints upon it a delight.

The rooms in the abandoned apartments had neither a definite layout nor a name, and like the explorers of the New World, they would baptize the rooms they crossed with the names of their joint discoveries. A vast bedroom in whose alcove stood the ghost of a bed adorned with a canopy hung with skeleton ostrich feathers was remembered afterward as "the feather room"; a staircase with steps of smooth crumbling slate was called by Tancredi "the staircase of the lucky slip." A number of times they really did not know where they were; all this twisting and turning, backing and following, and pauses full of murmuring contact, made them lose their way so that they had to lean out of some paneless window to gather from an angle of the courtyard or a view of the garden which wing of the palace they were in. But sometimes they could not find their way even so, as the window did not give on to one of the great courts but on to some inner yard, anonymous itself and never entered, marked only by the corpse of some cat or the usual little heap of spaghetti and tomato sauce either vomited or flung there; and from another window they would find themselves looking into the eyes of some pensioned-off old maidservant. One afternoon inside a cupboard they found four chimes, that music which delighted the affected simplicity of the eighteenth century. Three of these, buried in dust and cobwebs, remained mute; but the last, which was more recent and shut tighter into its dark wooden box, started up its cylinder of bristling copper and the little tongues of raised steel suddenly produced a delicate tune, all in clear, silvery tones: the famous *Carnival of Venice*; they rhymed their kisses with those notes of disillusioned gaiety; and when their embrace loosened they were surprised to notice that the notes had ceased for some time and that their action had left no other trace than a memory of ghostly music.

Once the surprise was of a different kind. In one of the rooms in the old guest wing they noticed a door hidden by a cupboard; the centuries-old lock soon gave way to fingers pleasantly entwined in forcing it: behind it a long narrow staircase wound up in gentle curves of pink marble steps.

At the top was another door, open, and covered with thick but tattered padding; then came a charming but odd little apartment, of six small rooms gathered around a medium-sized drawing room, all, including the drawing room, with floors of whitest marble, sloping away slightly toward a small lateral gutter. On the low ceilings were some very unusual reliefs in colored stucco, fortunately made almost indecipherable by damp; on the walls were big surprised-looking mirrors, hung too low, one shattered by a blow almost in the middle, and each fitted with contorted rococo candle brackets. The windows gave on to a segregated court, a kind of blind and deaf well, which let in a gray light and had no other openings. In every room and even in the drawing room were wide, too wide sofas, showing nails with traces of silk that had been torn away; spotty arm-rests; on the fireplaces were delicate intricate little marble intaglios, naked figures in paroxysms but mutilated by some furious hammer. The damp had marked the walls high up and also low down at a man's height, where it had assumed strange shapes, an odd thickness, dark tints. Tancredi, disturbed, would not let Angelica touch a cupboard on the wall of the drawing room, which he shut up himself. It was deep but empty, except for a roll of dirty stuff standing upright in a corner; inside was a bundle of small whips, switches of bull's muscle, some with silver handles, others wrapped halfway up in a charming old silk, white with little blue stripes, on which could be seen three rows of blackish marks; and metal instruments for inexplicable purposes. Tancredi was afraid of himself too. "Let's go, my dear, there's nothing interesting here." They shut the door carefully, went down the stairs again in silence, and put the cupboard back where it was before; and all the rest of that day Tancredi's kisses were very light, as if given in a dream and in expiation.

After the Leopard, in fact, the whip seemed the most frequent object at Donnafugata. The day after their discovery of the enigmatic little apartment the two lovers found another kind of whip. This was not, it is true, in the secret apartment but in the venerated one called the Apartment of the Saint-Duke, where in the middle of the seventeenth century a Salina had withdrawn as if into a private monastery, there to do penance and prepare his own journey toward Heaven. They were small low rooms, with floors of humble brick, whitewashed walls, like those of the poorest peasants. The last of these opened on to a balcony which overlooked the yellow expanse of estate after estate, all immersed in sad light. On one wall was a huge crucifix, more than life-sized; the head of the martyred God touched the ceiling, the bleeding feet grazed the floor; the wound in the ribs seemed like a mouth prevented by brutality from pronouncing the words of ultimate salvation. Next to the Divine Body there hung from a nail a lash with a short handle, from which dangled six strips of now hardened leather ending in six lumps of lead as big as walnuts. This was the "discipline" of the Saint-Duke. In that room Giuseppe Corbèra, Duke of Salina, had scourged himself alone, in sight of his God and his estates, and it must have seemed to him that the drops of his own blood were about to rain down on the land and redeem it; in his holy exaltation it must have seemed that only through this expiatory baptism could these estates really become his, blood of his blood, flesh of his flesh, as the saying is. But now many of them had left for ever and a large number of those which could be seen from up there belonged to others —to Don Calogero, even; to Don Calogero, thus to Angelica, thus to his future son-in-law. This proof of blackmail through beauty, parallel to that other blackmail through blood, made Tancredi's head whirl. Angelica was kneeling and kissing the pierced feet of Christ. "There," said Tancredi, "you're like that whip there, you're used for the same ends." And he showed her the whip; and because Angelica did not understand and raised her smiling head, lovely but vacuous, he bent down and as she genuflected gave her a rough kiss which made her moan, for it bruised her lip and rasped her palate.

So the pair of them spent those days in dreamy wanderings, in the discovery of hells redeemed by love, of forgotten paradises profaned by love itself. The urge to put a stop to the game and draw the prize became more and more pressing for them both; in the end they stopped searching, but went off absorbed into the remotest rooms, those from which no cry could reach anyone from the outside world. But there never would be a cry; only invocations and low moans. There they would both lie, close but innocent, pitying each other. The most dangerous places for them were the rooms of the old guest wing: private, in good order, each with its neat rolled-up mattress which would spread out again at a mere touch of the hand. One day not Tancredi's mind, which had no say in the matter, but all his blood had decided to put an end to it; that morning Angelica, like the beautiful bitch that she was, had said, "I'm your novice," recalling to him, with the clarity of an invitation, their first mutual onrush of desire; and already the woman had surrendered and offered, already the male was about to overwhelm the man, when the clang of the church bell almost straight above their heads added its own throb to the others; their interlaced mouths disentangled for a smile. They came to themselves; and next day Tancredi had to leave.

Those were the best days in the life of Tancredi and Angelica, lives later to be so variegated, so erring, against the inevitable background of sorrow. But that they did not know then; and they were pursuing a future which they deemed more concrete than it turned out to be, made of nothing but smoke and wind. When they were old and uselessly wise their thoughts would go back to those days with insistent regret; they had been days when desire was always present because it was always overcome, when many beds had been offered and refused, when the sensual urge, because restrained, had for one second been sublimated in renunciation, that is into real love. Those days were the preparation for a marriage which, even erotically, was no success; a preparation which, however, was in a way sufficient to itself, exquisite and brief, like those melodies which outlive the forgotten works they belong to and hint in their delicate and veiled gaiety at themes which later in the finished work were to be developed without skill, and fail.

When Angelica and Tancredi returned to the world of the living from their exile in the universe of extinct vices, forgotten virtues, and, above all, perennial desire, they were greeted with amiable irony. "How silly of you, children, to get so dusty. What a state you're in, Tancredi!" Don Fabrizio would smile; and his nephew would go off to get himself dusted. Cavriaghi sat astride a chair, conscientiously smoking a "Virginia," and looked at his friend washing his face and collar and snorting at seeing the water turn black as coal. "I don't deny it, Falconeri; the Signorina Angelica is the loveliest thing I've ever seen; but that's not a justification. Heavens, do restrain yourself a bit; today you've been alone together three whole hours; if you're so much in love then get married at once and don't let people laugh at you. You should have seen the face the Father made today when he came out of his office and found you were still sailing about in that ocean of rooms! Brakes, my dear fellow, brakes, that's what you need! You Sicilians have so few of them!"

He pontificated away, enjoying inflicting his wisdom on his older comrade, on "deaf" Concetta's cousin. But Tancredi, as he dried his hair, was furious; to be accused of having no brakes, he who had enough to stop a train! On the other hand the good Bersagliere was not entirely in the wrong: appearances had to be thought of too; though he had gone moralist like this from envy now it was obvious that his courtship of Concetta was getting nowhere. And then Angelica! That delicious taste of blood today, when he'd bitten the inside of her lip! That soft bending of hers under his embrace! But it was true, there was no sense in it all really. "Tomorrow we'll go and visit the church with a full escort, Father Pirrone and Mademoiselle Dombreuil!"

Angelica meanwhile was changing her dress in the girls' room. "*Mais Angelicà, est-il Dieu possible de se mettre dans un tel état?*" Mademoiselle Dombreuil was wailing indignantly, as the lovely creature, in undershirt and petti-coats, was washing her arms and neck. The cold water sub-dued her excitement and she had to admit to herself that the governess was right: was it worth getting so tired and so dusty and making people smile? For what? Just to be gazed in the eyes, to be stroked by those slender fingers, little more . . . and her lip was still smarting. "That's enough now. Tomorrow we'll stay in the drawing room with the others." But next day those same eyes, those same fingers would cast their spell again, and the two would go back once more to their mad game of hide-and-seek.

The paradoxical result of all these separate but con-vergent resolutions was that at dinner in the evening the pair most in love were the calmest, reposing on their illu-sory good intentions for next day; and they would muse ironically on the love-relationships of the others, however minor. Concetta had disappointed Tancredi; when at Na-ples he had felt a certain remorse about her, and that was why he had brought Cavriaghi along with him in the hope

of the Milanese replacing him with his cousin; pity also
played a part in his foresight. In a subtle but easygoing
way, astute as he was, he had seemed when he arrived almost to be commiserating with her at his own abandon-
ment, and pushed forward his friend. Nothing doing: Concetta unravelled her little spool of schoolgirl gossip and
looked at the sentimental little Count with icy eyes behind
which there almost seemed a certain contempt. A silly girl,
that; no good making any more efforts. What more did she
want, anyway? Cavriaghi was a handsome lad, well set up,
with a good name and flourishing dairy farms in Brianza;
in fact he was one of whom that rather chilling term, "a
good match," could be used. Ah: so Concetta wanted him,
Tancredi, did she? He had wanted her too once; she was
less beautiful, much less rich than Angelica, but she had
something in her which the girl from Donnafugata would
never possess. Life is a serious matter, though. Concetta
must have realized that. Why had she begun treating him
so badly, then? Turning on him at the Holy Spirit Convent, so many times after? The Leopard, yes, the Leopard,
of course; but there must be limits even for that proud
beast. "Brakes is what you want, my dear cousin, brakes!
You Sicilian girls have so few of them!"

But in her heart Angelica agreed with Concetta: Cavriaghi lacked dash; after loving Tancredi, to marry Cavriaghi would be like a drink of water after a taste of this
Marsala in front of her. Concetta, of course, understood
that from her own experience. But those other two sillies,
Carolina and Caterina, were making fishes' eyes at Cav-

riaghi and swooning away every time he went near them. Well, then! With her own lack of family scruples, she just could not understand why one of the two didn't try to nab the little Count from Concetta for herself. "Boys at that age are like little dogs; one only has to whistle and they come straight away. Silly girls! With all those scruples, and taboos and pride, they won't get anyone in the end."

In the smoking room, conversations between Tancredi and Cavriaghi, the only two smokers in the house and so the only exiles, also assumed a certain tone. The little Count ended by confessing to his friend the failure of his own amorous hopes. "She's too beautiful, too pure for me; she doesn't love me; it was rash for me to hope; but I'll leave here with regret like a dagger in my heart. I've not even dared make a definite proposal. I feel that to her I'm just a worm, and she's right. I must find a she-worm to put up with me." And his nineteen years made him laugh at his own discomfiture.

From the height of his own assured happiness Tancredi tried to console him: "You see, I've known Concetta all her life; she's the sweetest creature in the world: a mirror of all the virtues; but she's a little too reserved, too withdrawn. I'm afraid she has too high an opinion of herself; and then she's Sicilian to the very marrow: she's never left here; she might never feel at home in a place where one has to arrange a week ahead for a plate of macaroni!"

Tancredi's little joke, one of the earliest expressions of national unity, managed to make Cavriaghi smile again; pains and sorrows did not stay with him long. "But I'd have laid in *cases* of macaroni for her, of course! Anyway what's done is done; I only hope your uncle and aunt, who've been so sweet to me, won't hold it against me that I've come and thrust myself among you pointlessly." He was reassured quite sincerely, for Cavriaghi had made himself liked by everyone except Concetta (and perhaps by Concetta too, in a way) for the boisterous good humor which he combined with the most plaintive sentimentality; then they talked of something else—that is, they talked of Angelica.

"You know, Falconeri, you *are* a lucky dog! To go and find a jewel like Signorina Angelica in this pigsty (excuse my calling it that, my dear fellow). What a beauty, good God, what a beauty! Lucky rascal, leading her round for hours in the remotest corners of this house as huge as our own cathedral! And not only lovely, but clever and cultured too; and good as well; one can see that in her eyes, in that sweet innocence of hers."

Cavriaghi went on ecstatically about Angelica's goodness, under Tancredi's amused glance. "The really good person in all this is you yourself, Cavriaghi." The phrase slipped unnoticed over that Milanese optimism. Then, "Listen," said the young Count, "you'll be leaving in a few days; don't you think it's time I was introduced to the mother of the young Baroness?"

This was the first time—and from a Lombard voice— that Tancredi heard his future wife called by a title. For a second he did not realize whom the other was talking of. Then the prince in him rebelled. "Baroness? What d'you

193

mean, Cavriaghi? She's a dear, sweet creature whom I love, and that's quite enough."

That it really was "quite enough" was not actually true, but Tancredi was perfectly sincere; atavistically used to great possessions, it seemed to him that the estates of Gibildolce and Settesoli, all those bags of gold, had been his since the time of Charles of Anjou, always.

"I'm sorry, but I don't think you'll be able to meet Angelica's mother; she's leaving tomorrow for a mud cure at Sciacca; she's very ill, poor thing."

He stubbed the end of his "Virginia" in the ash tray. "Let's go into the drawing room, shall we? We've been bears here for long enough."

One day about that time Don Fabrizio received a letter from the Prefect of Girgenti, written in a style of extreme courtesy, announcing the arrival at Donnafugata of the Cavaliere Aimone Chevalley di Monterzuolo, Secretary to the Prefecture, who wanted to talk to him, the Prince, about a subject very close to the Government's heart. Surprised, Don Fabrizio sent off his son, Francesco Paolo, to the post station next day to receive the *missus dominicus* and invite him to stay at the palace, an act both of hospitality and of true compassion, consisting in not abandoning the body of the Piedmontese to the thousands of little creatures which would have tortured him in the cavelike hostelry of *Zzu* Menico.

The post coach arrived at dusk with an armed guard on

the box and a few glum faces inside. From it also alighted Chevalley di Monterzuolo, recognizable at once by his exhausted appearance and suspicious smile. He had been in Sicily for a month, in the most strictly native part of the island what was more, bounced there straight from his little property near Montferrat. Timid and congenitally bureaucratic, he found himself much out of his element. His head had been stuffed with the tales of brigands by which Sicilians love to test the nervous resistance of new arrivals, and for a month he saw every usher in his office as a murderer, and every wooden paper cutter on his desk as a dagger; also the oil in the cooking had upset his insides.

There he stood now, in the twilight, with his valise of beige cloth, peering at the very unpromising aspect of the street in the midst of which he had been dumped. The inscription "Corso Vittorio Emanuele," whose blue letters on a white ground adorned the half-ruined house opposite him, was not enough to convince him that he was in a place which was, after all, part of his own nation; and he did not dare to ask the way from any of the peasants propped against the near-by walls like caryatids, in his certainty of not being understood and his fear of an easy knife thrust in the guts, still dear to him however upset.

When Francesco Paolo came up and introduced himself he screwed up his eyes at first, as he thought he was done for; but the fair-haired youth's calm honest air reassured him a little, and when he realized that he was being invited to stay at the Salina palace he was both surprised and relieved. The journey in the dark to the palace was marked by a constant exchange of Piedmontese and Sicilian courtesies (the two most punctilious in Italy) in connection with the valise, which in the end was carried by both gentlemanly contenders, although it was very light.

When he reached the palace, the bearded faces of the armed keepers standing about in the first courtyard once more disturbed the soul of Chevalley di Monterzuolo; while the distant cordiality of the Prince's greeting, together with the evident luxury of the rooms he glimpsed, flung him into contrary worries. Member of one of those families of the petty Piedmontese squirearchy which live in dignified restraint on their own land, this was the first time he found himself a guest at a great house, and this redoubled his shyness; meanwhile the bloodthirsty anecdotes he had been told at Girgenti, the staggeringly primitive aspect of the town, the "bravos" (as he called them to himself) encamped in the courtyard, filled him with terror; so that he went down to dinner in the grip of contrasting fears, at finding himself in an ambiance above his normal habits and at feeling an innocent traveller in a bandits' lair.

At dinner he ate well for the first time since setting foot on the shores of Sicily, and the charm of the girls, the austerity of Father Pirrone, and the grand manner of Don Fabrizio convinced him that the palace of Donnafugata was not the antechamber of Capraro the bandit, and that he would probably leave there alive. His greatest consolation was the presence of Cavriaghi, who, he was told, had been staying there for ten days and looked in excellent health and also on excellent terms with that young Falconeri, a friendship between a Sicilian and a Lombard which seemed almost miraculous to him. At the end of dinner he went up to Don Fabrizio and requested a private interview, as he wished to leave again next morning; but the Prince clapped him on the shoulder and with a most Leopardlike smile exclaimed, "Not at all, my dear Cavaliere, you're in my home now and I'll hold you as hostage for as long as I like; you won't leave tomorrow morning, and to be quite sure of it I shall deprive myself of the pleasure of a private talk with you until the afternoon." This phrase, which would have terrified the excellent Secretary three hours before, now rather cheered him. That evening Angelica was not there, and so they played a hand of whist; at a table with Don Fabrizio, Tancredi, and Father Pirrone, he won two rubbers and gained three lire and thirty-five centimes; after which he withdrew to his own room, enjoyed the cleanliness of the linen, and fell into the trustful sleep of the just.

Next morning Tancredi and Cavriaghi led him around the garden, and showed him the picture gallery and tapestry collection. They also trotted him a little around the town; under the honey-colored sun of that November day it seemed less sinister than it had the night before; he even saw a smile here and there, and Chevalley di Monterzuolo began to reassure himself even about rustic Sicily. Tancredi noticed this and was at once assailed by the singular island itch to tell foreigners tales that were revolting but unfortunately quite true. They were passing in front of a pleasant little palace whose façade was decorated with crude stucco-work.

"That, my dear Chevalley, is the home of Baron Mútolo; now it's closed and empty, as the family live in Girgenti since the Baron's son was captured ten years ago by brigands."

The Piedmontese began to tremble. "Poor things, I wonder how much they paid to free him."

"No, no, they didn't pay a thing; they were in financial straits already and had no ready money, like everybody else here. But they got the boy back all the same; by installments, though."

"What d'you mean, Prince?"

"By installments, I said, by installments: bit by bit. First arrived the index finger of his right hand. A week later his left foot; and finally in a great big basket, under a layer of figs (it was August), the head; its eyes were staring and there was congealed blood on the corner of the lips. I didn't see it, I was a child then; but I'm told it wasn't a pretty sight. The basket was left on that very step there, the second one up to the door, by an old woman with a black shawl on her head; no one recognized her."

Chevalley's eyes went rigid with horror; he had already heard the story before this, but seeing now in the sunshine the very step on which the bizarre gift had been put was a different matter. His bureaucratic mind came to his help. "What an inept police those Bourbons had. Very soon, when our Carabinieri come, they'll put an end to all this."

"No doubt, Chevalley, no doubt."

Then they passed in front of the Civilians' Club, which had its daily show of iron chairs and men in mourning out in the shade of the plane trees in the square. Bows, smiles. "Take a good look, Chevalley, impress the scene on your memory: twice a year or so one of these gentlemen here is left stone dead on his own little armchair; a rifle shot in the uncertain light of dusk, and nobody ever knows who it was that shot him." Chevalley felt the need to lean on Cavriaghi's arm so as to sense a little Northern blood near him.

Shortly afterward, at the top of a steep alley, through multicolored festoons of drawers out to dry, they saw the simple baroque front of a little church. "That is Santa Ninfa. The parish priest was killed in there five years ago as he was saying Mass."

"Horrors! Shooting in church!"

"Oh, no shooting, Chevalley. We are too good Catholics for misbehavior of that kind. They just put poison in the Communion wine; more discreet, more liturgical, I might say. No one ever knew who did it; the priest was a most excellent person; he had no enemies."

Like a man who wakes up in the night to see a skeleton sitting at the foot of the bed on his own trousers, and saves himself from panic by forcing himself to believe it's just a joke by drunken friends, so Chevalley took refuge in the idea that he was having his leg pulled. "Very amusing,

Prince, really entertaining! You should write novels, you know; you tell these stories very well." But his voice was trembling; Tancredi took pity on him, and although on their way home they passed three or four places which were almost more evocative, he abstained from telling their tales, and talked about Bellini and Verdi, perennial curative unctions for national wounds.

At four in the afternoon the Prince sent to tell Chevalley that he was waiting for him in his study. This was a little room with walls lined by glass cases containing gray pheasants with pink claws, thought rare, and found in past shoots. One wall was ennobled by a high, narrow bookcase, crammed full of back numbers of mathematical reviews. Above the great armchair meant for visitors hung a constellation of family miniatures: Don Fabrizio's father, Prince Paolo, heavy in face and sensual in lip as a Moor, with the ribbon of St. Januarius diagonally across his black Court uniform; Princess Carolina as a widow, her fair hair heaped into a towering coiffure, and with severe blue eyes; the Prince's sister, Giulia, Princess of Falconeri, sitting on a bench in a garden, with the crimson splotch of a small parasol laid on the ground to her right and to her left the yellow splotch of Tancredi at three years old offering her wild flowers (Don Fabrizio had thrust this miniature into his pocket secretly while the bailiffs were making their inventory for the sale at Villa Falconeri). Beneath that was his eldest son, Paolo, in tight white leather breeches, just about to mount an arrogant horse with a curving neck and flashing eyes; various unidentifiable uncles and aunts, covered with jewels or pointing sorrowfully at the bust of some extinct dear one. But in the center of the constellation, acting as a kind of polestar, shone a bigger miniature; this was of Don Fabrizio himself at the age of about twenty, with his very young wife leaning her head on his shoulder in an act of complete loving abandon. She was dark-haired, he rosy in the blue and silver uniform of the Royal Guards, smiling with pleasure, his face framed in his first and very fair long whiskers.

Chevalley, as soon as he sat down, began explaining the mission with which he had been charged. "After the happy annexation, I mean after the glorious union of Sicily and the Kingdom of Sardinia, the Turin Government intends to nominate a number of illustrious Sicilians as Senators of the Kingdom. The provincial authorities have been charged with drawing up a list of personalities to be proposed for the Central Government's examination, and eventually for Royal nomination, and, of course, at Girgenti your name was mentioned at once, Prince: a name illustrious for its antiquity, for the personal prestige of its bearer, for scientific merit; and also for the dignified and liberal attitude assumed during recent events." The little speech had been prepared for some time; it had even been the object of a number of pencil notes in the little book which was now in the hip pocket of Chevalley's trousers. But Don Fabrizio gave no sign of life; his eyes only just showed through his heavy lids. Motionless, the great paw with its blondish hairs completely covered a dome of St. Peter's in alabaster on the table.

Accustomed by now to the deafness of the loquacious Sicilians whenever a proposal was made to them, Chevalley did not let himself be discouraged. "Before sending the list to Turin my superiors thought it proper to inform you in person and see if this proposal met with your approval. To ask for your assent, for which the Government hopes greatly, has been the object of my mission here: a mission which has also given me the honor and the pleasure of getting to know you and your family, this magnificent palace, and picturesque Donnafugata."

Flattery always slipped off the Prince like water off the leaves of water lilies: it is one of the advantages enjoyed by men who are at once proud and used to being so. "This fellow here seems to be under the impression he's come to do me a great honor," he was thinking. "To me, who am what I am, among other things a Peer of the Kingdom of Sicily, which must be more or less the same as a Senator. It's true that one must value gifts in relation to those who offer them; when a peasant gives me his bit of cheese he's making me a bigger present than the Prince of Làscari when he invites me to dinner. That's obvious. The difficulty is that the cheese is nauseating. So all that remains is the heart's gratitude, which can't be seen, and the nose wrinkled in disgust, which can be seen only too well."

Don Fabrizio's ideas about the Senate were very vague; in spite of every effort his thoughts kept leading him back to the Roman Senate: to Senator Papirius breaking a staff on the head of Gallus, who had been rude; to the horse Incitatus, made a Senator by Caligula, an honor which even his son Paolo might have thought excessive. He was irritated at finding recurring to him insistently a phrase which was sometimes used by Father Pirrone: *"Senatores boni viri, senatus autem mala bestia."* Nowadays there was also an Imperial Senate in Paris, though that was only an assembly of profiteers with big salaries. There was or had been a Senate in Palermo too, though it had only been a committee of civil administrators—what administrators! Low work for a Salina. He decided to be frank. "But, Cavaliere, do explain what being a Senator means; the newspapers under our last monarchy never allowed information about the constitutional system of other Italian States to be printed, and a week's visit of mine to Turin a couple of years ago was not enough to enlighten me. What is it? A simple title of honor? A kind of decoration, or are there legislative, deliberative functions?"

The Piedmontese, representative of the only liberal State in Italy, rose to the bait. "But, Prince, the Senate is the High Chamber of the Kingdom! In it the flower of Italy's politicians, chosen by the wisdom of the Sovereign, will examine, discuss, approve, or disapprove the laws proposed by the Government for the progress of the country; it functions at the same time as spur and as brake: it incites good actions and prevents bad ones. When you have accepted a seat in it, you will represent Sicily on an equality with the other elected Deputies, you will make us hear the voice of this lovely country which is only now coming into sight of the modern world, with so many wounds to heal, so many just desires to be granted."

Chevalley would perhaps have continued for some time in this vein if Bendicò, from behind the door, had not asked "the wisdom of his Sovereign" to admit him. Don Fabrizio made as if to get to his feet and open the door, but slowly enough to allow the Piedmontese time to open it himself; Bendicò meticulously sniffed around Chevalley's trousers, after which, having decided this was a good man, the dog lay down under the window and slept.

"Just listen to me, Chevalley, will you? If it were merely a question of some honor, a simple title to put on a visiting card, no more, I should be pleased to accept; I feel that at this decisive moment for the future of the Italian State it is the duty of us all to support it, and to avoid any impression of disunity in the eyes of those foreign States which are watching us with alarm or with hope, both of which will be shown unjustified but which do at the moment exist."

"Well, then, Prince, why not accept?"

"Be patient now, Chevalley, I'll explain in a moment; we Sicilians have become accustomed, by a long, a very long hegemony of rulers who were not of our religion and who did not speak our language, to split hairs. If we had not done so we'd never have coped with Byzantine tax gatherers, with Berber Emirs, with Spanish Viceroys. Now the bent is endemic, we're made like that. I said 'support,' I did not say 'participate.' In these last six months, since your Garibaldi set foot at Marsala, too many things have been done without our being consulted for you to be able now to ask a member of the old governing class to help develop things and carry them through. I do not wish to discuss now whether what was done was done well or badly; for my part I believe it to have been done very badly; but I'd like to tell you at once what you'll understand only after spending a year among us.

"In Sicily it doesn't matter whether things are done well or done badly; the sin which we Sicilians never forgive is simply that of 'doing' at all. We are old, Chevalley, very old. For more than twenty-five centuries we've been bearing the weight of a superb and heterogeneous civilization, all from outside, none made by ourselves, none that we could call our own. We're as white as you are, Chevalley, and as the Queen of England; and yet for two thousand and five hundred years we've been a colony. I don't say that in complaint; it's our fault. But even so we're worn out and exhausted."

Chevalley was disturbed now. "But that is all over now, isn't it? Now Sicily is no longer a conquered land, but a free part of a free State."

"The intention is good, Chevalley, but it comes too late; and anyway I've already said that it is mainly our fault. You talked to me a short while ago about a young Sicily facing the marvels of the modern world; for my part I see instead a centenarian being dragged in a Bath chair around the Great Exhibition in London, understanding nothing and caring about nothing, whether it's the steel factories of

Sheffield or the cotton spinners of Manchester, and thinking of nothing but drowsing off again amid beslobbered pillows and with a pot under the bed."

He was still talking slowly, but the hand around St. Peter's had tightened; later the tiny cross surmounting the dome was found snapped. "Sleep, my dear Chevalley, sleep, that is what Sicilians want, and they will always hate anyone who tries to wake them, even in order to bring them the most wonderful of gifts; and I must say, between ourselves, I have strong doubts whether the new Kingdom will have many gifts for us in its luggage. All Sicilian expression, even the most violent, is really wish-fulfillment: our sensuality is a hankering for oblivion, our shooting and knifing a hankering for death; our laziness, our spiced and drugged sherbets, a hankering for voluptuous immobility, that is, for death again; our meditative air is that of a void wanting to scrutinize the enigmas of nirvana. That is what gives power to certain people among us, to those who are half awake: that is the cause of the well-known time lag of a century in our artistic and intellectual life; novelties attract us only when they are dead, incapable of arousing vital currents; that is what gives rise to the extraordinary phenomenon of the constant formation of myths which would be venerable if they were really ancient, but which are really nothing but sinister attempts to plunge us back into a past that attracts us only because it is dead."

Not all of this was understood by the good Chevalley, and the last phrase he found particularly obscure; he had seen the variously painted carts being drawn along by horses decorated with feathers, he had heard tell of the heroic puppet shows, but he had thought, too, they were genuine old traditions. He said, "Aren't you exaggerating a little, Prince? I myself have met emigrant Sicilians in Turin—Crispi, for example—who seemed anything but asleep."

The Prince said irritably, "When there are so many of us there are bound to be exceptions; anyway, I've already mentioned some of us who are half awake. As for this young man Crispi, not I, certainly, but you perhaps may be able to see if as an old man he doesn't fall back into our voluptuous torpor; they all do. I've explained myself badly; I said Sicilians, I should have added Sicily, the atmosphere, the climate, the landscape of Sicily. Those are the forces which have formed our minds together with and perhaps more than foreign dominations and ill-assorted rapes; this landscape which knows no mean between sensuous slackness and hellish drought; which is never petty, never ordinary, never relaxed, as a country made for rational beings to live in should be; this country of ours in which the inferno around Randazzo is a few miles from the loveliness of Taormina Bay; this climate which inflicts us with six feverish months at a temperature of a hundred and four; count them, Chevalley, count them: May, June, July, August, September, October; six times thirty days of sun sheer down on our heads; this summer of ours which is as long and glum as a Russian winter and against which we struggle with less success; you don't know it yet, but fire could be said to snow down on us as on the accursed cities of the Bible; if a Sicilian worked hard in any of those months he would expend energy enough for three; then water is either lacking altogether or has to be carried from so far that every drop is paid for by a drop of sweat; and then the rains, which are always tempestuous and set dry river beds to frenzy, drown beasts and men on the very spot where two weeks before both had been dying of thirst.

"This violence of landscape, this cruelty of climate, this continual tension in everything, and these monuments, even, of the past, magnificent yet incomprehensible because not built by us and yet standing around like lovely mute ghosts; all those rulers who landed by main force from every direction, who were at once obeyed, soon detested, and always misunderstood, their only expressions works of art we couldn't understand and taxes which we understood only too well and which they spent elsewhere: all these things have formed our character, which is thus conditioned by events outside our control as well as by a terrifying insularity of mind."

The ideological inferno evoked in this little lecture disturbed Chevalley even more than the bloodthirsty tales of that morning. He tried to say something, but Don Fabrizio was now too worked up to listen.

"I don't deny that a few Sicilians may succeed in breaking the spell, once off the island; but they would have to leave it very young; by twenty it's too late: the crust is formed; they will remain convinced that their country is basely calumniated, like all other countries, that the civilized norm is here, the oddities are elsewhere. But do please excuse me, Chevalley, I've let myself be carried away and I've probably bored you. You haven't come all this way to hear Ezekiel deplore the misfortunes of Israel. Let us return to the subject of our conversation: I am most grateful to the Government for having thought of me for the Senate, and I ask you to express my most sincere gratitude to them. But I cannot accept. I am a member of the old ruling class, inevitably compromised with the Bourbon regime, and tied to it by chains of decency if not of affection. I belong to an unfortunate generation, swung between the old world and the new, and I find myself ill at ease in both. And what is more, as you must have realized by now, I am without illusions; what would the Senate do with me, an inexperienced legislator who lacks the faculty of self-deception, essential requisite for wanting to guide others? We of our generation must draw aside and watch the capers and somersaults of the young around this ornate catafalque. Now you need young men, bright young men, with minds asking 'how' rather than 'why,' and who are good at masking, at blending, I should say, their personal interests with vague public ideals." He was silent, left St. Peter's alone. Then he went on, "May I give you some advice to hand on to your superiors?"

"That goes without saying, Prince; it will certainly be heard with every consideration; but I still venture to hope that instead of advice you may give your consent."

"There is a name I should like to suggest for the Senate: that of Calogero Sedàra. He has more the qualities to sit there than I have: his family, I am told, is an old one or soon will be; he has more than what you call prestige, he has power; he has outstanding practical merits instead of scientific ones; his attitude during the May crisis was not so much irreproachable as actively useful; as to illusions, I don't think he has any more than I have, but he's clever enough to know how to create them when needed. He's the man for you. But you must be quick, as I've heard that he intends to put up as candidate for the Chamber of Deputies."

There had been much talk about Sedàra at the Prefecture; his activities both as Mayor and as private citizen were well known. Chevalley gave a start; he was an honest man, and his esteem for the legislative chambers was paralleled by the purity of his intentions; so he thought it best not to say a word in reply, and he did well not to compromise himself, as ten years later Don Calogero did in fact gain the Senate. But though honest, Chevalley was no fool: he certainly lacked those quick wits which in Sicily usurp the name of intelligence, but he could assess slowly and firmly and also he had not the Southern insensibility to the distress of others. He understood Don Fabrizio's bitterness and discomfort, he reviewed for an instant the misery, the abjection, the black indifference of which he had been witness for the last month; during the past few hours he had envied the Salina opulence and grandeur, but now his mind went back tenderly to his own little vineyard, his Monterzuolo near Casale, ugly, mediocre, but serene and alive. And he found himself pitying this Prince without hopes as much as the children without shoes, the malaria-ridden women, the guilty victims whose names reached his office every morning; all were equal, at bottom, all were comrades in misfortune segregated in the same well.

He decided to make a last effort. As he got up his voice was charged with emotion. "Prince, do you seriously refuse to do all in your power to alleviate, to attempt to remedy the state of physical squalor, of blind moral misery in which this people of yours lies? Climate can be overcome, the memory of evil days cancelled, for the Sicilians must want to improve; if honest men withdraw the way will be open for those with no scruples and no vision, for Sedàra and his like; and then everything will be as before for more centuries. Listen to your conscience, Prince, and not to the proud truths that you have spoken. Collaborate."

Don Fabrizio smiled at him, took him by the hand, made him sit beside him on the sofa. "You're a gentleman, Chevalley, and I consider it a privilege to have met you; you are right in all you say; your only mistake was saying that 'the Sicilians must want to improve.' I'll tell you a personal anecdote. Two or three days before Garibaldi entered Palermo I was introduced to some British naval officers from one of the warships then in the harbor to keep an eye on things. They had heard, I don't know how, that I own a house down on the shore facing the sea, with a terrace on its roof from which can be seen the whole circle of hills around the city; they asked to visit this house of mine and look at the landscape where the Garibaldini were said to be operating, as they could get no clear idea of it from their ships. In fact Garibaldi was already at Gibilrossa.

They came to my house, I accompanied them up on to the roof; they were simple youths, in spite of their reddish whiskers. They were ecstatic about the view, the light; they confessed, though, that they had been horrified at the squalor and filth of the streets around. I didn't explain to them that one thing was derived from the other, as I have tried to with you. Then one of them asked me what those Italian volunteers were really coming to do in Sicily. *'They are coming to teach us good manners,'* I replied in English. *'But they won't succeed, because we think we are gods.'*

"I don't think they understood, but they laughed and went off. That is my answer to you too, my dear Chevalley: the Sicilians never want to improve for the simple reason that they think themselves perfect; their vanity is stronger than their misery; every invasion by outsiders, whether so by origin or, if Sicilian, by independence of spirit, upsets their illusion of achieved perfection, risks disturbing their satisfied waiting for nothing; having been trampled on by a dozen different peoples, they consider they have an imperial past which gives them a right to a grand funeral. Do you really think, Chevalley, that you are the first who has hoped to canalize Sicily into the flow of universal history? I wonder how many Moslem imams, how many of King Roger's knights, how many Swabian scribes, how many Angevin barons, how many jurists of the Most Catholic King have conceived the same fine folly; and how many Spanish viceroys too, how many of Charles III's reforming functionaries! And who knows now what happened to them all! Sicily wanted to sleep in spite of their invocations; for why should she listen to them if she herself is rich, if she's wise, if she's civilized, if she's honest, if she's admired and envied by all, if, in a word, she is perfect?

"Now even people here are repeating what was written by Proudhon and some German Jew whose name I can't remember, that the bad state of things, here and elsewhere, is all due to feudalism; that is, my fault, as it were. Maybe. But there's been feudalism everywhere, and foreign invasions too. I don't believe that your ancestors, Chevalley, or the English squires or the French seigneurs governed Sicily any better than did the Salinas. The results were different. The reason for the difference must lie in this sense of superiority that dazzles every Sicilian eye, and which we ourselves call pride while in reality it is blindness. For the moment, for a long time yet, there's nothing to be done. I am sorry; but I cannot lift a finger in politics. It would only get bitten. These are things one can't say to a Sicilian; and if you'd said them yourself, I too would have objected.

"It's late, Chevalley; we must go and dress for dinner. For a few hours I have to act the part of a civilized man."

Chevalley left early next morning, and Don Fabrizio, who had arranged to go out shooting, was able to accompany him to the post station. With them was Don Ciccio Tumeo, carrying on his shoulders the double weight of two shotguns, his and Don Fabrizio's, and within himself the bile of his own trampled virtue.

In the livid light of five-thirty in the morning Donna-

fugata was deserted and apparently despairing. In front of
every house the refuse of squalid meals accumulated along
leprous walls; trembling dogs were routing about with a
greed that was always disappointed. An occasional door was
already open and the smell of sleep spread out into the
street; by glimmering wicks mothers scrutinized the eye-
lids of their children for trachoma; almost all were in
mourning, and many had been the wives of those carcasses
one stumbles over on the turns of mountain tracks. The
men were coming out gripping their hoes to look for someone who might give them work, God willing; subdued
silence alternated with exasperated screams of hysterical
voices; away over toward the Convent of the Holy Spirit
a tin-colored dawn was beginning to tinge leaden clouds.

Chevalley thought, "This state of things won't last;
our lively new modern administration will change it all."
The Prince was depressed: "All this shouldn't last; but it
will, always; the human 'always,' of course, a century, two
centuries . . . and after that it will be different, but worse.
We were the Leopards, the Lions; those who'll take our
place will be little jackals, hyenas; and the whole lot of us,
Leopards, jackals, and sheep, we'll all go on thinking ourselves the salt of the earth." They thanked each other and
said goodbye. Chevalley hoisted himself up onto the post
carriage, propped on four wheels the color of vomit. The
horse, all hunger and sores, began its long journey.

Day had just dawned; the little light that managed to
pass through the quilt of clouds was held up once more by
the immemorial filth on the windows. Chevalley was alone;

amid bumps and shakes he moistened the tip of his index finger with saliva and cleaned a pane for the width of an eye. He looked out: in front of him, under the ashen light, the landscape lurched to and fro, irredeemable.

5

Father Pirrone's arrival at San Cono · Conversation
with his friends and the herbalist · Family troubles of a
Jesuit · The troubles solved · Interview with the "man
of honor" · Return to Palermo

FATHER Pirrone's origins were rustic; he had been born at San Cono, a tiny hamlet which is now, thanks to the bus, almost a satellite star in the solar system of Palermo, but a century ago belonged as it were to a planetary system of its own, being four or five cart-hours from the Palermo sun.

The father of our Jesuit had been overseer of two properties belonging to the Abbey of Sant'Eleuterio in the region of San Cono. An overseer's job was then most perilous for the health both of soul and of body, as it necessitated odd acquaintanceships and the accumulated knowledge of many a tale which might bring on ills that could suddenly stretch the patient dead at the foot of some rustic wall, with all those stories locked inside him, lost irrevocably to idle curiosity. But Don Gaetano, Father Pirrone's father, had man-

aged to avoid this occupational disease by rigorous hygiene
based on discretion and a careful use of preventive reme-
dies; and he had died peacefully of pneumonia, one sunny
Sunday in February when a soughing wind was felling the
almond blossom. He left his widow and three children
(two girls and the priest) relatively well off; wise man that
he was, he had managed to save up some of the incredibly
meager salary paid by the abbey, and at the moment of his
demise owned a little almond grove at the back of the valley, a row or two of vines on the slopes, and some stony
pasturage farther up: all poor man's stuff, of course, but
enough to confer a certain weight amid the depressed econ-
omy of San Cono. He was also owner of a small, rigidly
square house, blue outside and white in, four rooms down
and four up, at the very entrance to the village on the Palermo road.

Father Pirrone had left that house at the age of sixteen,
when his successes at the parish school and the benevolence
of the Mitered Abbot of Sant'Eleuterio had set him on the
road toward the Archiepiscopal seminary; but every few
years he had returned there, to bless the marriage of one
of his sisters or to give a (in the worldly sense) superfluous
absolution to the dying Don Gaetano, and he had come
back now, at the end of February, 1861, for the fifteenth
anniversary of his father's death; a day gusty and clear,
just like that other one.

Getting there had meant a five-hour shaking in a cart
with his feet dangling behind a horse's tail; but once he
had overcome his nausea at the patriotic pictures newly

painted on the cart panels, culminating in a rhetorical presentation of a flame-colored Garibaldi arm in arm with an aquamarine Santa Rosalia, they had been a pleasant five hours. The valley rising from Palermo to San Cono mingles the lushness of the coast with the harshness of the interior, and is swept by sudden gusts of cleansing wind, famous for being able to deviate the best-aimed bullets, so that marksmen faced with ballistic problems preferred to exercise elsewhere. Then the carter, who had known the dead man well, launched out into lengthy reminiscences of his merits, reminiscences which, although not always adapted to a son's and a priest's ear, had flattered his practiced listener.

His arrival was greeted with happy tears. He embraced and blessed his mother, whose deep widow's weeds set off nicely her white hair and rosy hue, and greeted his sisters and nephews, looking askance among the latter at Carmelo, who had had the bad taste to put a tricolor cockade in his cap in token of rejoicing. As soon as he got into the house he was assailed as always by sweet youthful memories; nothing was changed, from the red-brick floor to the sparse furniture; the same light entered the small narrow windows; Romeo, the dog, barking briefly in a corner, was exactly like another hound, its great-great-grandfather, his companion in violent play; and from the kitchen arose the centuries-old aroma of simmering meat sauce made of extract of tomatoes, onions, and goat's meat, for macaroni on festive occasions. Everything expressed the serenity achieved by the dead man's labors.

Soon they moved off to church for the commemorative Mass. That day San Cono looked its best, basking almost proudly in its exhibition of different manures. Sly goats with dangling black udders, and numbers of little Sicilian piglets, dark and slim as minute colts, were running among the people and up the steep tracks; and as Father Pirrone had become a kind of local glory, many women, children, and even youths crowded around him to ask for his benediction or remind him of old days.

After local gossip in the sacristy with the parish priest, and attendance at Mass, he moved to the tombstone in a side chapel; the women kissed the marble amid sobs, the son prayed out loud in his archaic Latin; and when they got home the macaroni was ready and much enjoyed by Father Pirrone, whose palate had not been spoiled by the culinary delicacies of Villa Salina.

Then toward evening his friends came to greet him and met in his room. A three-branched copper lantern hung from the ceiling and spread a dim light from its oil burners; in a corner was the bed with its varicolored mattress and stifling pink-and-yellow quilt; another corner of the room was bounded by high stiff matting, hiding honey-colored wheat taken weekly to the mill for the family's needs; on the walls hung pockmarked engravings, St. Anthony showing the Divine Infant, St. Lucia her gouged-out eyes, and St. Francis Xavier haranguing crowds of plumed and naked Indians; outside in the starry dusk, the wind blew and in its way was the only one to commemorate the dead. In the center of the room, under the lamp, was a big squat brazier surrounded by a strip of polished wood on which people put their feet; all around, on hemp chairs, sat the guests. There were the parish priest, the two Schirò brothers, local landowners, and Don Pietrino, the old herbalist; they came looking glum and remained looking glum, because, while the women were busy below, they sat talking of politics, hoping to hear consoling news from Father Pirrone, who came from Palermo and must know a lot as he lived with the "nobles." The desire for news had been appeased and that for consolation disappointed, for their Jesuit friend, partly from sincerity and partly also from tactics, painted them a very black future. The Bourbon tricolor still hung over Gaeta but the blockade was tight and the powder magazines in the fortress were being blown up one by one, and nothing could be saved there now except honor: not much, that is; Russia was friendly but distant, Napoleon III shifty and close, and of the risings in Basilicata and Terre di Lavoro the Jesuit spoke little because deep down he was rather ashamed of them. They must, he told them, face up to the reality of this atheist and rapacious Italian State now in formation, to these laws of expropriation, to conscription which would spread from Piedmont all the way down here, like cholera. "You'll see," was his not very original conclusion, "you'll see they won't even leave us eyes to weep with."

These words were followed by the traditional chorus of rustic complaints. The Schirò brothers and the herbalist already felt the new fiscal grip; the former had had extra contributions and additions here and there, the latter an overwhelming shock: he had been called to the Town Hall and told that if he didn't pay twenty lire every year he wouldn't be allowed to sell his potions. "But I go and gather the grasses, these holy herbs God made, with my own hands in the mountains, rain or shine, on certain days and nights of the year. I dry them in the sun, which belongs to everybody, and I grind them up myself, with my own grandfather's mortar. What have you people at the Town Hall to do with it? Why should I pay you twenty lire? Just for nothing like that?"

The words came muffled from a toothless mouth, but his eyes were dark with genuine rage. "Am I right or not, Father? You tell me!"

The Jesuit was fond of him; he remembered him as a man already grown, in fact already bent from continual wandering and stooping, when he himself had been a boy throwing stones at the birds; and he was also grateful because he knew that when the old man sold one of his potions to women he always said they would be useless without many a Hail Mary and a Gloria. But he prudently preferred to ignore what was in the potions, or the hopes with which the clients asked for them.

"You're right, Don Pietrino, a hundred times right. Why, of course! But if those people didn't take money off you and other poor souls like you, how could they afford to make war on the Pope and steal what's his?"

The conversation meandered on in the mild lamplight, quivering as the wind penetrated the heavy shutters. Father Pirrone expatiated on the future and the inevitable confiscation of ecclesiastical property: goodbye then to the mild rule of the abbey in these parts; goodbye to the plates of soup distributed in bad winters; and when the younger Schirò had the impudence to say that a few poor peasants might perhaps get some land of their own, his voice froze into sharp contempt. "You'll see, Don Antonino, you'll see. The Mayor will buy everything up, pay the first installments, and then do just what he likes. It's already happened in Piedmont!"

They ended by going off scowling even more than when they'd come, and with enough complaints to last two months. The only one to stay was the herbalist, who would not be going to bed that night as there was a new moon and he had to gather rosemary on the Pietrazzi rocks; he had brought a lantern with him and would be setting off straight from there.

"But tell me, Father, you who live with the nobles, what do they say about all these great doings? What does the Prince of Salina say, so tall and quick-tempered and proud?"

Father Pirrone had more than once asked himself this question, and it was not an easy one to answer, particularly as he had taken little notice or interpreted as exaggeration what Don Fabrizio had told him one morning in the observatory nearly a year ago. He knew now, but he could find no way of translating it into comprehensible terms for Don Pietrino, who, though far from a fool, had more understanding of the anticatarrhal, laxative, and even aphrodisiac properties of his herbs than of such abstractions.

"You see, Don Pietrino, the 'nobles,' as you call them, aren't so easy to understand. They live in a world of their own, of joys and troubles of their own; they have a very strong collective memory, and so they're put out by things which wouldn't matter at all to you and me, but which to them seem vitally connected with their fortunes, memories, and hopes. Divine Providence has willed that I should become a humble member of the most glorious Order in an Eternal Church whose eventual victory has been assured; you are at the other end of the scale, by which I don't mean the lowest but the most different. When you find a thick bush of marjoram or a well-filled nest of Spanish flies (you look for those too, Don Pietrino, I know) you are in direct communication with the natural world which the Lord created with undifferentiated possibilities of good and evil until man could exercise his own free will on it; and when you're consulted by old women and by pretty young girls, you are plunging back into the dark abyss of centuries that preceded the light from Golgotha."

The old man looked at him in amazement; he had wanted to know if the Prince of Salina was satisfied or not with the latest changes, and the other was talking to him about aphrodisiacs and light from Golgotha. "All that reading's driven him off his head, poor man."

"But the 'nobles' aren't like that; all they live by has been handled by others. They find us ecclesiastics useful to reassure them about eternal life, just as you herbalists are here to procure them soothing or stimulating drinks. And by that I don't mean they're bad people; quite the contrary. They're just different; perhaps they appear so strange to us because they have reached a stage toward which all those who are not saints are moving, that of indifference to earthly goods through surfeit. Perhaps it's because of that they take so little notice of things that are of great importance to us; people on the mountains don't worry about mosquitoes in the plains, nor do the inhabitants of Egypt about umbrellas. Yet the former fear landslides, the latter crocodiles, which are no worry to us. For them new fears have appeared of which we're ignorant; I've seen Don Fabrizio get quite testy, wise and serious though he is, because of a badly ironed collar to his shirt; and I know for certain that the Prince of Làscari didn't sleep for a whole night from rage because he was wrongly placed at one of the Viceroy's dinners. Now don't you think that a human being who is put out only by bad washing or protocol must be happy, and thus superior?"

Don Pietrino could understand nothing at all now: all this was getting more and more nonsensical, what with shirt collars and crocodiles. He was still upheld, though, by a basis of good rustic common sense. "But if that's what they're like, Father, they'll all go to hell."

"Why? Some will be lost, others saved, according to how they've lived in that conditioned world of theirs. Salina himself, for instance, might just scrape through; he plays his own game properly, follows the rules, doesn't cheat. God punishes those who voluntarily contravene the Divine Laws which they know and voluntarily turn down a bad road; one who goes his own way, so long as he doesn't

misbehave along it, is always all right. If you, Don Pietrino, sold hemlock instead of mint, knowingly, you'd be
in for it; but if you thought you'd picked the right one,
Gnà Zana would die the noble death of Socrates and you'd
go straight to heaven with a cassock and wings of purest
white."

The death of Socrates was too much for the herbalist; he
had given up and was fast asleep. Father Pirrone noticed
this and was pleased, for now he would be able to talk
freely without fear of being misunderstood; and he felt a
need of talking, so as to fix into a pattern of phrases some
ideas obscurely milling in his head.

"And they do a lot of good, too. If you knew, for instance, the families otherwise homeless that find shelter in
those palaces! And the owners ask for no return, not even
immunity from petty theft! They do it not from ostenta-
tion but from a sort of obscure atavistic instinct which prevents them from doing anything else. Although it may not
seem so, they are in fact less selfish than many others; the
splendor of their homes, the pomp of their receptions, have
something impersonal about them, something not unlike
the grandeur of churches and of liturgy, something which
is in fact *ad maiorem gentis gloriam*; and that redeems a
great deal: for every glass of champagne drunk by themselves they offer fifty to others; when they treat someone
badly, as they do sometimes, it is not so much their personality sinning as their class affirming itself. *Fata crescunt.*
For instance, Don Fabrizio has protected and educated his
nephew Tancredi and so saved a poor orphan who would

have otherwise been lost. You say that he did it because the young man is a noble too, and that he wouldn't have lifted a finger for anyone else. That's true, but why should he lift a finger if sincerely, in the deep roots of his heart, all 'others' seem to him botched attempts, china figurines come misshapen from the potter's hands and not worth putting to the test of fire?

"You, Don Pietrino, if you weren't asleep at this moment, would be jumping up to tell me that the 'nobles' are wrong to have this contempt for others, and that all of us, equally subject to the double slavery of love and death, are equal before the Creator; and I would have to agree with you. But I'd add that not only the 'nobles' are to be blamed for despising others, since that is quite a general vice. A university professor despises a parish schoolmaster even if he doesn't show it, and since you're asleep I can tell you without reticence that we clergy consider ourselves superior to the laity, we Jesuits superior to the other clergy, just as you herbalists despise tooth-pullers who in their turn deride you. Doctors, on the other hand, jeer at both tooth-pullers and herbalists, and are themselves treated as fools by their patients who expect to be kept alive with hearts or livers in a hopeless state; lawyers, to magistrates, are just bores who try to deflect the course of the law, and on the other hand literature is full of satires against the pomposity, ignorance, and often worse of those very judges. The only people who also despise themselves are laborers; when they've learned to jeer at others the circle will be closed and we'll have to start all over again.

"Have you ever thought, Don Pietrino, how many names of jobs have become insults? From carter and fishwife to *reître* or *pompier* in French? People don't think of the merits of carters and fishwives; they just look at their marginal defects and call them all rough and vulgar; and as you can't hear me, I may tell you that I'm perfectly aware of the exact current meaning of the word 'Jesuit.'

"Then these nobles put a good face on their own disasters: I've seen one who'd decided to kill himself next day, poor man, looking beaming and happy as a boy on the eve of his first Communion; while if you, Don Pietrino, had to drink one of your own herb drinks you'd make the village ring with your laments. Rage is gentlemanly; complaints are not. I could give you a recipe, in fact: if you meet a 'gentleman' who's querulous, look up his family tree; you'll soon find a dead branch.

"It's a class difficult to suppress because it's in continual renewal and because if needs be it can die well, that is it can throw out a seed at the moment of death. Look at France; they let themselves be massacred with elegance there and now they're back as before. I say as before, because it's differences of attitude, not estates and feudal rights, which make a noble.

"They tell me that in Paris nowadays there are Polish counts who've been forced into exile and poverty by revolts and despotism; they drive cabs, but frown so at their middle-class customers that the poor things get into the cab, without knowing why, as humbly as dogs in church.

"And I can tell you too, Don Pietrino, that if, as has often happened before, this class were to vanish, an equivalent one would be formed straight away with the same qualities and the same defects; it might not be based on blood any more, but possibly on . . . on, say, the length of time lived in a place, or on greater knowledge of some text considered sacred."

At this point his mother's steps were heard on the wooden stairs; she laughed as she came in. "Whom d'you think you're talking to, son? Can't you see your friend's fast asleep?"

Father Pirrone looked a little abashed; he did not reply but just said, "I'll go outside with him now. Poor man, he's got to spend all night out in the cold." He took the wick from the lantern and lit it from one of the ceiling lamps, getting up on tiptoe and splashing his cassock with oil; then he put it back and shut its little door. Don Pietrino was sailing in dreams; saliva was dribbling from a lip and spreading over his collar. It took some time to wake him up. "Excuse me, Father, but you were saying such confusing things." They smiled, went downstairs, and out. Night submerged the little house, the village, the valley; the near-by mountains could just be seen, surly as always; the wind had calmed but it was very cold; the stars were glittering away, producing thousands of degrees of heat which were not enough to warm one poor old man. "Poor Don Pietrino! Would you like me to go and get you another cloak?"

"Thank you, I'm used to it. We'll meet tomorrow, then you'll tell me what the Prince of Salina feels about the Revolution."

"I can tell you that at once and in a few words: he says there's been no revolution and that all will go on as it did before."

"More fool he! Doesn't it seem a revolution to you when the Mayor wants me to pay for the grass God created and which I gather myself? Or have you gone off your head too?"

The light of the lantern went jerking off and eventually vanished into shadows thick as felt.

Father Pirrone thought what a mess the world must seem to one who knew neither mathematics nor theology. "O Lord, only Thy Omniscience could have devised so many complications."

Another sample of these complications faced him next morning. When he went down, ready to say Mass in the parish church, he found his sister Sarina chopping onions in the kitchen. The tears in her eyes seemed bigger than her activity warranted.

"What is it, Sarina? Any trouble? Don't let it depress you; the Lord afflicts and consoles."

His affectionate tone dissipated the remains of the poor woman's reserve; she began sobbing loudly, with her face on the greasy tabletop. Among the sobs could always be heard the same words, "Angelina, Angelina. . . . If Vicenzino knew he'd kill them both. . . . Angelina. . . . He'd kill them both!"

His hands thrust into his wide black sash, with only his thumbs showing, Father Pirrone stood looking at her. It wasn't difficult to understand: Angelina was Sarina's adolescent daughter; Vicenzino, whose fury was so feared, was her father and his brother-in-law; the only unknown part of the equation was the name of the other person involved, Angelina's presumed lover.

The Jesuit had seen her for the first time the day before as a full-grown girl, after having left her a snivelling child seven years before. She seemed about eighteen and was very plain indeed, with the jutting mouth of so many peasant girls around these parts, and frightened dog's eyes. He had noticed her on his arrival and in his heart in fact made rather uncharitable comparisons between her, plebeian as the diminutive of her own name, and Angelica, sumptuous as that name of hers from Ariosto, who had recently disturbed the peace of the Salina household.

The trouble must be serious, and here he was right in the middle of it; he remembered what Don Fabrizio had once said: every time one sees a relative one finds a thorn; then he was sorry for having remembered that. He extracted his right thumb from his sash, took off his hat, and clapped his sister's quivering shoulder. "Come on now, Sarina, don't do that! Luckily, I'm here. Crying's no use. Where is Vicenzino?" Vicenzino had gone off to Rimato to see the Schirós' keeper. All the better; they could talk things over without fear of surprise. Between sobs, sucked tears, and nose snuffling, out the whole squalid story came: Angelina (or rather 'Ncilina) had let herself be seduced; the disaster had happened during St. Martin's summer; she used to go to meet her lover in Donna Nunziata's hayloft; now she'd been with child three months; in a panic she had confessed all to her mother; soon her belly would begin showing and Vicenzino would raise hell. "He'll kill me too, he will, because I didn't tell him; he's what they call 'a man of honor'!"

In fact with his low forehead, ornamental tufts of hair on the temples, lurching walk, and perpetual swelling of the right trouser pocket where he kept a knife, it was obvious at once that Vicenzino was "a man of honor," one of those violent cretins capable of any havoc.

Now Sarina was overcome by a new fit of sobbing, stronger than the first because she'd been seized by renewed remorse for having been unworthy of her husband, that mirror of chivalry.

"Sarina, Sarina, stop it now! Don't do that! The young man must marry her, he will marry her. I'll go to his home, talk to him and his family, everything will be all right. Then Vicenzino will know only about the engagement and his precious honor will remain intact. But I must know who the man is. If you know, tell me."

His sister raised her head; her eyes now showed another fear, no longer the animal one of the knife thrusts, but a more restricted, a keener one which the brother could not for the moment place.

"It was Santino Pirrone! Turi's son! And he did it out of spite, spite against me, against our mother, against our father's memory! I've never spoken to him; they all said he was a good boy—but he's a swine, a true son of that father of his. I remembered afterward: I always used to see him passing here in November with two friends and a red geranium behind his ear. Red of hell, that was, red of hell!"

The Jesuit took a chair and sat down next to the poor woman. Obviously he would have to be late for Mass. This was serious. Turi, the father of the seducer Santino, was an uncle of his; the brother, in fact the elder brother, of his dead father. Twenty years ago he had worked together with the dead man in his job as overseer, just at the moment of the latter's greatest and most meritorious activity. Later the brothers had quarrelled, one of those family quarrels we all know with deeply entangled roots, impossible to cure because neither side speaks out clearly, each having much to hide. The fact was that when the dead man acquired the little almond grove, his brother Turi had said that half of it really belonged to him because half the money for it, or half the work, he had put in himself; but the deeds bore only the name of the dead Gaetano. Turi stormed up and down the roads of San Cono foaming at the mouth; the dead man's prestige was in danger, friends intervened, and the worst was avoided; the almond grove remained Gaetano's property, but the gulf between the two branches of the Pirrone family became unbridgeable; Turi did not even go to his brother's funeral and was just called the "swine," that was all, in his sister's house. The Jesuit had been told of all this by letters dictated to the parish priest, and had formed some ideas of his own about it which he did not express from filial reverence. The little almond grove now belonged to Sarina.

It was all quite obvious; no love or passion played any part: just a dirty trick to revenge another dirty trick. But it could be set right; the Jesuit thanked Providence for having brought him to San Cono at that very time. "Listen, Sarina, I'll settle all this in a couple of hours, but you've got to help me; half of Chibbaro" (that was the almond grove) "must go as 'Ncilina's dowry. There's no other way out of it; the silly girl has been the ruin of you." And he thought of how the Lord, to bring about His justice, can even use bitches in heat.

Sarina lost her temper. "Half of Chibbaro! To that swine, never! Better dead!"

"All right. Then after Mass I'll go and talk to Vicenzino. Don't be afraid, I'll try to calm him down." He put his hat back on his head and his hands into his sash, and waited patiently, sure of himself.

Any edition of Vicenzino's furies, even though revised and expurgated by a Jesuit priest, were always illegible to the unhappy Sarina, who began weeping for the third time; gradually her sobs lessened and then stopped. She got up: "May God's Will be done; you fix it, it's beyond me. But our lovely Chibbaro! All that sweat of our father's!"

Her tears were just about to start again, but the priest had already gone.

After celebrating the Divine Sacrifice and accepting coffee from the parish priest, the Jesuit went straight to his Uncle Turi's home. He had never been there before but knew it was a shack at the very top of the village near

Mastro Ciccu the blacksmith's. He soon found it, and as
there were no windows and the door was open to let in a
little sun, he stopped on the threshold; in the darkness inside he could see heaps of mules' harness, saddlebags, sacks;
Don Turi earned his living as a mule driver, now helped
by his son.

"*Doràzio!*" called Father Pirrone. This was an abbrevia-
tion of the form of *Deo gratias* (*agamus*) used by clerics
asking permission to enter. An old man's voice shouted,
"Who is it?" and someone got up at the back of the room
and came toward the door. "It's your nephew, Father
Saverio Pirrone. I wanted to talk to you if I may."

It was not much of a surprise to Turi; a visit by Father
Pirrone or some representative must have been expected
for at least two months. Uncle Turi was a vigorous straight-
backed old man baked through and through by sun and
hail, with the sinister furrows on his face which trouble
traces on people who are not good.

"Come in," he said without a smile. He stood aside and
even went grudgingly through the action of kissing the
priest's hand. Father Pirrone sat down on one of the big
wooden saddles. The place looked very wretched indeed:
two chickens were grubbing away in a corner, and everything smelled of manure, wet washing, and evil poverty.

"Uncle, we've not met for years, but that's not all my
fault; I'm seldom at home, as you know, but you never
come near my mother, your sister-in-law; I'm sorry to hear
that."

"I'll never set foot in that house again. Just passing it

turns my stomach! Turi Pirrone never forgets an injury, even after twenty years!"

"Oh yes, of course, yes indeed. But here I am today like the dove from Noah's Ark, to assure you that the flood is over. I'm very glad to be here and I was very happy yesterday when they told me at home that your son Santino is engaged to my niece Angelina; they are two fine young people, I'm told, and their union will put an end to the quarrel between our families which, if I may say so, has always grieved me."

Turi's face expressed a surprise too obvious not to be false. "If it weren't for your habit, Father, I'd say you were lying. You must have been listening to tales from those females of yours. Santino has never even mentioned Angelina to me; he's far too good a son to go against his father's wish."

The Jesuit admired the old man's astuteness and the smoothness of his lying.

"Apparently, Uncle, I've been misinformed; why, they told me that you'd agreed on the dowry and would both be coming to our place today to make it official. But the nonsense these idle females talk! Even if it's not true, though, it does show what's in those good hearts of theirs. Well, Uncle, there's no point in my staying here; I'm going straight home to reprove my sister. And excuse me, won't you; I'm very pleased to find you so well."

The old man's face was beginning to show a certain greedy interest. "Wait, Father. Give us another laugh with this gossip of yours; what dowry were the females talking of?"

"Oh, I don't know! I think I heard something about half of Chibbaro! 'Ncilina, they said, was very dear to them and no sacrifice was too much to ensure peace in the family!"

Don Turi stopped laughing. He got up. "Santino!" he began bawling as loudly as if calling a recalcitrant mule. And as no one came he shouted louder still, "Santino, Blood of the Madonna, where are you?" Then when he saw Father Pirrone quiver he put a hand over his mouth with a gesture unexpectedly servile.

Santino was seeing to the animals in the little yard. He entered shyly with a whip in his hands. He was a fine-looking lad of twenty-two, tall and slim like his father, with eyes not yet embittered. He had seen the Jesuit pass through the village the day before, as had everyone else, and he recognized him at once. "This is Santino. And this is your cousin Father Saverio Pirrone. You can thank God the Reverend Father is here, or I'd have cut your ears off. What's all this love-making without your own father knowing? Children are born for their parents and not to run after skirts."

The young man looked ashamed, perhaps not because of disobedience but because of his father's past consent, and did not know what to say; he got out of the difficulty by putting his whip on the floor and going to kiss the priest's hand. The latter showed his teeth in a smile and sketched a benediction. "God bless you, my son, though I don't think you deserve it."

The old man continued, "As your cousin here has gone on begging me, I've given my consent in the end. Why didn't you tell me before, though? Now clean yourself up and we'll go down to Angelina's now."

"A moment, Uncle, just a moment." It occurred to Father Pirrone that he ought to say a word to the "man of honor," who knew nothing as yet. "Back home they'll be sure to want to get things ready; anyway, they told me they'd be expecting you at seven this evening. Come then, and it'll be a pleasure to see you." And off he went, after embracing father and son.

When Father Pirrone got back to the little square house he found his brother-in-law Vicenzino already home, so all he could do to reassure his sister was wink at her from behind her proud husband's back; but as they were both Sicilians that was quite enough. Then he told his brother-in-law that he wanted to talk to him, and the two went off to the scraggy little arbor at the back of the house. The swaying edge of the Jesuit's cassock traced a kind of uncrossable mobile frontier around him; the fat buttocks of the "man of honor" waggled, perennial symbol of threatening pride. Their conversation was actually quite different from what the priest had foreseen. Once assured of the imminence of 'Ncilina's marriage, the "man of honor" showed complete indifference about what her behavior had been. But at the first mention of a dowry his eyes rolled, the veins in his temples swelled, and the rolling of his gait became more marked; from his mouth came a gurgle of low obscene oaths and announcements of murderous intentions; his hand, which had not made a single gesture in defense of his daughter's honor, began clutching the right pocket of his trousers to show that in defense of his almond trees he was ready to spill the very last drop of other people's blood.

Father Pirrone let the stream of abuse run out, merely making quick signs of the Cross at the frequent curses; of the gesture announcing a massacre he took no notice at all. During a pause he put in, "Of course I want to contribute to a general settlement too. You know the private agreement ensuring me the ownership of whatever was due to me from our father's estate? I'll send that back to you from Palermo, torn up."

This balm had an immediate effect. Vicenzino, intent on computing the value of the anticipated inheritance, was silent; and through the cold sunny air came the cracked notes of a song which had suddenly burst from 'Ncilina as she swept out her uncle's room.

In the late afternoon Uncle Turi and Santino came to pay their visit, quite spruced up and wearing very white shirts. The engaged couple sat on chairs side by side and broke out now and again into loud wordless giggles in each other's faces. They were really pleased, she at "settling" herself and having this big handsome male at her disposal, he at following his father's advice and now owning not only half an almond grove but a slave too. And no one now found the red geranium he had put in his buttonhole to be any reflection of hell.

Two days later Father Pirrone left to return to Palermo. As he was jolted along he went over impressions that were not entirely pleasant: that brutish love-affair come to fruition in St. Martin's summer, that wretched half almond grove reacquired by means of calculated courtship, seemed to him the rustic poverty-stricken equivalent of other events recently witnessed. Nobles were reserved and incomprehensible, peasants explicit and clear; but the Devil twisted them both around his little finger all the same.

At Villa Salina he found the Prince in excellent spirits. Don Fabrizio asked if he had enjoyed his four days away and if he had remembered to give his mother his, the Prince's, greetings. He knew her, in fact; she had stayed at the villa six years before and pleased both Prince and Princess by her serene widowhood. The Jesuit had entirely forgotten about the greetings and was silent; then he said that his mother and sister had charged him with bearing His Excellency their respects, which as an invention was less grievous a sin than a lie. "Excellency," he added then, "I wanted to ask you if you could give orders for me to have a carriage tomorrow; I must go to the Archbishopric to ask for a dispensation; a niece of mine has got engaged to her cousin."

"Of course, Father Pirrone, of course, if you wish; but I have to go down to Palermo myself the day after tomorrow; you could come with me; or are you really in such a rush?"

6

Going to a ball · The ball; entrance of Pallavicino and of the Sedàras · Don Fabrizio's discontent · The ballroom · In the library · Don Fabrizio dances with Angelica · Supper; conversation with Pallavicino · The ball fades; the return home

T

HE Princess Maria Stella climbed into the carriage, sat down on the blue satin cushions, and gathered around her as many rustling folds of her dress as she could. Meanwhile Concetta and Carolina were also climbing in; they settled down facing her, their identical pink dresses exhaling a faint scent of violets. Then a heavy foot on the running board made the barouche heel over on its high springs; Don Fabrizio was getting in too. The carriage was crammed: waves of silk, ribs of three crinolines, billowed, clashed, entwined almost to the height of their heads; beneath was a tight press of stockings, girls' silken slippers, the Princess's bronze-colored shoes, the Prince's patent-leather pumps; each suffered from the others' feet and could find nowhere to put his own.

The mounting steps were folded, the footman received

his orders. "To Palazzo Ponteleone." He got back onto the box, the groom holding the horses' bridles moved aside, the coachman gave an imperceptible click of his tongue, and the barouche slid into motion.

They were going to a ball.

Palermo at the moment was passing through one of its intermittent periods of worldliness; there were balls everywhere. After the coming of the Piedmontese, after that incident at Aspromonte, now that the specters of violence and sequestration had fled, the few hundred people who made up "the world" never tired of meeting each other, always the same ones, to exchange mutual congratulations on still existing.

So frequent were the various and yet identical parties that the Prince and Princess of Salina had moved to their town palace for three weeks so as not to have to make the long drive from San Lorenzo almost every night. The ladies' dresses would arrive from Naples in long black cases like coffins, and there would be a hysterical coming and going of milliners, hairdressers, and shoemakers, of exasperated servants carrying excited notes to dressmakers. The Ponteleone ball was to be one of the most important of the short season: important for all concerned because of the grandeur of the family, the splendor of the palace, and the number of guests; particularly important for the Salinas, who would be presenting Angelica, their nephew's lovely bride-to-be, to "society." It was still only half past ten, rather early to appear at a ball if one is Prince of Salina, whose arrival should be timed for when a fete is at its height. But this time they had to be early if they wanted to be there for the entry of the Sedàras, who were the sort of people ("they don't *know* yet, poor things") to take literally the hours on the gleaming invitation card. It had taken a good deal of trouble to get one of those cards sent to them; no one knew them, and the Princess Maria Stella had had to make a visit to Margherita Ponteleone ten days before; all had gone smoothly, of course, but even so it had been one of those little thorns that Tancredi's engagement had inserted into the Leopard's delicate paws.

The short drive to Palazzo Ponteleone was through a tangle of dark alleys, and they went at a walk: Via Salina, Via Valverde, down the slope of the Bambinai, so gay in daytime with its little shops of waxen figures, so dreary by night. The horseshoes sounded muffled amid the dark houses, asleep or pretending to sleep.

The girls, incomprehensible beings for whom a ball was fun and not a tedious worldly duty, were chatting away gaily in low voices; the Princess Maria Stella felt her bag to assure herself she'd brought her little bottle of smelling salts; Don Fabrizio was enjoying in anticipation the effect of Angelica's beauty on all those who did not know her and of Tancredi's luck on all those who knew him too well. But a shadow lay across his content: what would Don Calogero's tail coat be like? Certainly not like the one worn at Donnafugata; he had been put into the hands of Tancredi, who had dragged him off to the best tailor and even been present at fittings. Officially the result had seemed to satisfy him the other day; but in confidence he'd said, "The coat is the best we can do; Angelica's father lacks *chic*." That was undeniable; but Tancredi had guaranteed a perfect shave and decently polished shoes. That was something.

Where the Bambinai slope comes out by the apse of San Domenico the carriage stopped; there was a faint tinkle, and around the corner appeared a priest bearing a ciborium with the Blessed Sacrament; behind, a young acolyte held over him a white canopy embroidered in gold; in front, another bore a big lighted candle in his left hand and in his right a little silver bell which he was shaking with obvious enjoyment. These were the Last Sacraments; in one of those barred houses someone was in a death agony. Don Fabrizio got out and knelt on the pavement, the ladies made the sign of the Cross, the tinkling faded into the alleys tumbling down toward San Giacomo, and the barouche, with its occupants given a salutary warning, set off again toward its destination, now close by.

They arrived, they alighted in the portico; the coach vanished into the immensity of the courtyard, whence came the sound of pawing horses and the gleams of equipages arrived before.

The great stairs were of rough material but superb proportions; rustic flowers spread simple scents at the sides of every step; on the landing between flights the amaranthine liveries of two footmen, motionless under their powder, set a note of bright color in the pearly gray surroundings. From two high little grated windows came a gurgle of laughter and childish murmurs; the small Ponteleone grandchildren, excluded from the party, were looking on, making fun of the guests. The ladies smoothed down silken folds; Don Fabrizio, *gibus* under an arm, was head and shoulders above them all, although a step behind. At the door of the first drawing room they met their host and hostess: he, Don Diego, white-haired and paunchy, saved from looking plebeian only by his caustic eyes; she, Donna Margherita, with the hooked features of an old priest between coruscating tiara and a triple strand of emeralds.

"You've come early! All the better! But don't worry, *your* guests haven't appeared yet." A new thorn pierced the sensitive fingertips of the Leopard. "Tancredi's here already too." There in the opposite corner of the drawing room was standing their nephew, black and slim as an adder, surrounded by three or four young men whom he was making roar with laughter at little tales that were quite certainly indecent; but his eyes, restless as ever, were fixed on the entrance door. Dancing had already begun, and through three, four, five antechambers came the notes of the orchestra from the ballroom.

"We're also expecting Colonel Pallavicino, who did so well at Aspromonte."

This phrase from the Prince of Ponteleone was not so simple as it sounded. On the surface it was a remark without political meaning, mere praise for the tact, the delicacy, the respect, the tenderness almost with which the Colonel had had a bullet fired into General Garibaldi's foot; and for the accompaniment too, the bowing, kneeling, and hand-kissing of the wounded Hero lying under a chestnut tree

on a Calabrian hillside, smiling from emotion and not from
irony as he might well have done (for Garibaldi, alas,
lacked a sense of humor).

In an intermediate stage of the princely psyche the
phrase had a technical meaning and was intended to praise
the Colonel for having made the proper dispositions and
carrying out successfully against the same adversary what
Landi had so unaccountably failed to do at Calatafimi. At
heart, though, Ponteleone thought that the Colonel had
"done well" in managing to stop, defeat, wound, and cap-
ture Garibaldi and, in so doing, saving the compromise so
laboriously achieved between the old and the new.

Evoked, created almost by the approving words and
still more approving thoughts, the Colonel now appeared
at the top of the stairs. He was moving amid a tinkle of
epaulettes, chains, and spurs in his well-padded double-
breasted uniform, a plumed hat under his arm and a curved
saber propped on his left wrist. He was a man of the world
and of graceful manners, well versed, as all Europe knew
by now, in hand-kissings dense with meaning; every lady
whose fingers were brushed that night by his perfumed mustache was able to re-evoke from first-hand knowledge the
historical incident already so highly praised in the popular
press.

After sustaining the shower of praise poured over him
by the Ponteleones, after squeezing the two fingers held
out to him by Don Fabrizio, Pallavicino merged into the
scented froth of a group of ladies. His consciously virile
features showed above their snowy white shoulders, and

an occasional phrase came over: "I was sobbing, Countess, sobbing like a child"; or, "He was handsome and calm as an archangel." His male sentimentality enchanted ladies reassured already by the musketry of his Bersaglieri.

Angelica and Don Calogero were late, and the Salina family were thinking of plunging into the other rooms when Tancredi was seen to detach himself from his little group and move like a dart toward the entrance: the expected pair had arrived. Above the measured swirl of her pink crinoline Angelica's white shoulders merged into her strong soft arms; her head looked small and proud on its smooth youthful neck adorned with intentionally modest pearls. And when from the opening of her long kid glove she drew a hand which though not small was perfectly shaped, on it was seen glittering the Neapolitan sapphire.

In her wake came Don Calogero, a rat escorting a flaming rose; though his clothes had no elegance, this time they were at least decent. His only mistake was wearing in his buttonhole the cross of the Order of the Crown of Italy recently conferred on him; but this soon vanished into one of the secret pockets in Tancredi's tail coat.

Her fiancé had already taught Angelica to be impassive, that fundamental of distinction ("You can be expansive and noisy only with me, my dear; with all others you must be the future Princess of Falconeri, superior to many, equal to all"). And so she greeted her hostess with a totally unspontaneous but highly successful mixture of virginal modesty, neo-aristocratic hauteur, and youthful grace.

The people of Palermo are Italians after all, and so particularly responsive to the appeal of beauty and the prestige of money; apart from which Tancredi, however attractive, being also notoriously penniless, was considered an undesirable match (mistakenly, as was seen afterward when too late); and so he was appreciated more by married women than by marriageable girls. This merging of merits and demerits now had the effect of Angelica's being received with unexpected warmth. One or two young men might well have regretted not having dug up for themselves so lovely an amphora brimming with coin; but Donnafugata was a fief of Don Fabrizio's, and if he had found that treasure there and then passed it to his beloved Tancredi, one could no more be envious of that than of his finding a sulphur mine on his land; it was his property, there was nothing to be said.

But even this transient resentment melted before the rays of those eyes. At one moment there was a press of young men wanting to be introduced and to ask for a dance; to each one of them Angelica dispensed a smile from her strawberry lips, to each she showed her card in which every polka, mazurka, and waltz was followed by the possessive signature: Falconeri. There was also a general attempt by young ladies to get on familiar terms; and after an hour Angelica found herself quite at her ease among people who had not the slightest idea of her mother's crudity or her father's rascality.

Her bearing did not contradict itself for an instant: never was she seen wandering about alone with head in the clouds, never did her arms move from her body, never was her voice raised above the murmur (quite high, anyway) of the other ladies. For Tancredi had told her the day before, "You see, darling, we (and so you now) are more attached to our houses and furniture than we are to anything else, and nothing offends us more than indifference about those; so look at everything and praise everything— anyway, Palazzo Ponteleone is worth it; but as you're not just a girl from the provinces whom everything surprises, always put a little reserve into your praise; admire, but always compare with some archetype seen before and known to be outstanding." The long visits to the palace at Donnafugata had taught Angelica a great deal, so that evening she admired every tapestry, but said that the ones in Palazzo Pitti had finer borders; she praised a Madonna by Dolci but remembered that the Grand Duke's had a more expressive melancholy; even of the slice of tart brought her by an attentive young gentleman she said that it was excellent, almost as good as that of "Monsú Gaston," the Salina chef. And as Monsú Gaston was positively the Raphael of cooks, and the tapestries of Palazzo Pitti the Monsú Gaston of hangings, no one could complain, in fact everyone was flattered by the comparison; and so from that very evening she began to acquire the reputation of a polite but inflexible art expert which was to accompany her quite unwarrantably throughout her life.

While Angelica was reaping laurels, Maria Stella sat gossiping on a sofa with two old friends, and Concetta and Carolina were freezing with their shyness the politest partners, Don Fabrizio was wandering around the rooms; he

kissed the hands of ladies he met, clapped on the shoulder
men he wanted to greet, but he could feel ill-humor creep-
ing slowly over him. First of all, he didn't like the house;
the Ponteleones hadn't done it up for seventy years and it
was still the same as in the time of Queen Maria Carolina,
and he, who considered himself to have modern tastes, was
indignant. "Good God, with Diego's income it wouldn't
take long to sweep away all these consoles, all these over-
decorated mirrors! Then order some decent rosewood and
plush furniture, and so live in comfort himself and not
make his guests wander around catacombs like these. I'll end
up by telling him so." But he never told Diego, for these
opinions only stemmed from his mood and his tendency to
contradiction; they were soon forgotten, and he himself
never changed a thing either at San Lorenzo or at Donnafugata. Meanwhile, however, they served to increase his
disquiet.

The women at the ball did not please him either. Two
or three among the older ones had been his mistresses, and,
seeing them now grown heavy with years and childbearing,
it was an effort to imagine them as they were twenty years
before, and he was annoyed at the thought of having
thrown away his best years in chasing (and catching) such
slatterns. The younger women weren't up to much either,
except for one or two: the youthful Duchess of Palma,
whose gray eyes and gentle reserve he admired, Tutú
Làscari also, with whom, had he been younger, he might
well have found himself in unique and exquisite harmony.
But the others . . . it was a good thing that Angelica had

emerged from the shades of Donnafugata to show these Palermitans what a really lovely woman was like.

There was a good deal to be said for his strictures; in recent years the consequences of the frequent marriages between cousins due to sexual lethargy and territorial calculations, of the dearth of proteins and overabundance of starch in the food, of the total lack of fresh air and movement, had filled the drawing rooms with a mob of girls incredibly short, unsuitably dark, unbearably giggly. They were sitting around in huddles, letting out an occasional hoot at an alarmed young man, and destined, apparently, to act only as background to three or four lovely creatures such as fair-haired Maria Palma, the exquisite Eleonora Giardinelli, who glided by like swans over a frog-filled pool.

The more of them he saw the more he felt put out; his mind, conditioned by long periods of solitude and abstract thought, eventually, as he was passing through a long gallery where a numerous colony of these creatures had gathered on the central pouf, produced a kind of hallucination; he felt like a keeper in a zoo set to looking after a hundred female monkeys; he expected at any moment to see them clamber up the chandeliers and hang there by their tails, swinging to and fro, showing off their behinds and loosing a stream of nuts, shrieks, and grins at pacific visitors below.

Curiously enough, it was religion that drew him from this zoologic vision, for from the group of crinolined monkeys there rose a monotonous, continuous sacred invocation. "Maria! Maria!" the poor girls were perpetually exclaiming. "Maria, what a lovely house!" "Maria, what a handsome man Colonel Pallavicino is!" "Maria, how my feet are hurting." "Maria, I'm so hungry, when does the supper room open?" The name of the Virgin, invoked by that virginal choir, filled the gallery and changed the monkeys back into women, since the *wistiti* of the Brazilian forests had not yet, so far as he knew, been converted to Catholicism.

Slightly nauseated, the Prince passed into the next room, where were encamped the rival and hostile tribe of men; the younger were off dancing and those now there were only the older ones, all his friends. He sat down a little among them; there, instead of the name of the Queen of Heaven being taken in vain, the air was turgid with commonplaces. Among these men Don Fabrizio was considered an "eccentric"; his interest in mathematics was judged almost a sinful perversion, and had he not been actually Prince of Salina and known as an excellent horseman, indefatigable shot, and tireless skirt chaser, his parallaxes and telescopes might have exposed him to the risk of being outlawed. But he was not talked to much, for his cold blue eyes, glimpsed under their heavy lids, put questioners off, and he often found himself isolated, not, as he thought, from respect, but from fear.

He got up; his melancholy had now changed to black gloom. He had been wrong to come to this ball; Stella, Angelica, his daughters, could easily have coped with it alone, and he at this moment would have been happily ensconced in his study next to the terrace in Via Salina, listening to the tinkling of the fountain and trying to catch comets by their tails. "Anyway, I'm here now; it would be rude to leave. Let's have a look at the dancing."

The ballroom was all golden: smooth on the cornices, uneven on the door frames, in a pale, almost silvery design against a darker background on the door panels and on the shutters annulling the windows, thus conferring on the room the look of some superb jewel case shut off from an unworthy world. It was not the flashy gilding which decorators slap on nowadays, but a faded gold, pale as the hair of Nordic children, determinedly hiding its value under a muted use of precious material intended to let beauty be seen and cost forgotten. Here and there on the panels were knots of rococo flowers in a color so faint as to seem just an ephemeral pink reflected from the chandeliers.

That solar hue, that variegation of gleam and shade, made Don Fabrizio's heart ache as he stood black and stiff in a doorway: this eminently patrician room reminded him of country things; the chromatic scale was the same as that of the vast wheat fields around Donnafugata, rapt, begging pity from the tyrannous sun; in this room too, as on his estates in mid-August, the harvest had been gathered long before, stacked elsewhere, leaving, as here, a sole reminder in the color of stubble burned and useless now. The notes of the waltz in the warm air seemed to him but a stylization of the incessant winds harping their own sorrows on the parched surfaces, today, yesterday, tomorrow, forever and forever. The crowd of dancers, among whom he could count so many near to him in blood if not in heart, began to seem unreal, made up of that material from which are woven lapsed memories, more elusive even than the stuff of disturbing dreams. From the ceiling the gods, reclining on gilded couches, gazed down smiling and inexorable as a summer sky. They thought themselves eternal; but a bomb manufactured in Pittsburgh, Pennsylvania, was to prove the contrary in 1943.

"Fine, Prince, fine! They don't make things like this nowadays, with gold leaf at its present price!" Sedàra was standing beside him; his quick eyes were moving over the room, insensible to its charm, intent on its monetary value.

Quite suddenly Don Fabrizio felt a loathing for him; it was to the rise of this man and a hundred others like him, to their obscure intrigues and their tenacious greed and avarice, that was due the sense of death which was now, obviously, hanging darkly over these palaces; it was because of him and his colleagues, their rancor and sense of inferiority, that the black clothes of the men dancing reminded Don Fabrizio of crows veering to and fro above lost valleys in search of putrid prey. He felt like giving a sharp reply and telling him to get out of his way. But he couldn't: the man was a guest; he was the father of that dear girl Angelica; and maybe, too, he was as unhappy as others.

"Fine, Don Calogero, fine. But our young couple's the finest of all!" Tancredi and Angelica were passing in front of them at that moment, his gloved right hand on her waist, their outspread arms interlaced, their eyes gazing into each other's. The black of his tail coat, the pink of her dress, combining formed a kind of strange jewel. They were the most moving sight there, two young people in love dancing together, blind to each other's defects, deaf to the warnings of fate, deluding themselves that the whole course of their lives would be as smooth as the ballroom floor, unknowing actors made to play the parts of Juliet and Romeo by a director who had concealed the fact that tomb and poison were already in the script. Neither of them was good, each full of self-interest, swollen with secret aims; yet there was something sweet and touching about them both; those murky but ingenuous ambitions of theirs were obliterated by the words of jesting tenderness he was murmuring in her ear, by the scent of her hair, by the mutual clasp of those bodies of theirs destined to die.

The two young people moved away, other couples passed, less handsome, just as moving, each submerged in their transitory blindness. Don Fabrizio felt his heart thaw; his disgust gave way to compassion for all these ephemeral beings out to enjoy the tiny ray of light granted them between two shades, before the cradle, after the last spasms. How could one inveigh against those sure to die? It would be as vile as those fish-vendors insulting the condemned in the Piazza del Mercato sixty years before. Even the female monkeys on the poufs, even those old baboons of friends were poor wretches, condemned and touching as the cattle lowing through the city streets at night on the way to the slaughterhouse; to the ears of each of them would one day come that tinkle he had heard three hours earlier behind San Domenico. Nothing could be decently hated except eternity.

And then these people filling the rooms, all these faded women, all these stupid men, these two vainglorious sexes were part of his blood, part of himself; only they could really understand him, only with them could he be at his ease. "I may be more intelligent, I'm certainly more cultivated, but I come from the same stock as they, with them I must make common cause."

He noticed Don Calogero talking to Giovanni Finale about a possible rise in the price of cheese and how in the hope of this beatific event his eyes had gone liquid and gentle. Don Fabrizio could slip away without remorse.

Till that moment accumulated irritation had given him energy; now with relaxed nerves he was overcome by tiredness; it was already two o'clock. He looked around for a place where he could sit down quietly, far from men, lovers and brothers, all right in their way, but always tiresome. He soon found it: the library, small, silent, lit, and empty. He sat down, then got up to drink some water which he found on a side table. "Only water is really good," he thought like a true Sicilian; and did not dry the drops left on his lips. He sat down again; he liked the library and soon felt at his ease there; it put up no opposition to him because it was impersonal, as are rooms which are little used; Ponteleone was not a type to waste time in there. He began looking at a picture opposite him, a good copy of

Greuze's *Death of the Just Man;* the old man was expiring on his bed, amid welters of clean linen, surrounded by afflicted grandsons and granddaughters raising arms toward the ceiling. The girls were pretty, provoking, and the disorder of their clothes suggested sex more than sorrow; they, it was obvious at once, were the real subject of the picture. Even so, Don Fabrizio was surprised for a second at Diego always having this melancholy scene before his eyes; then he reassured himself by thinking that the other probably entered that room only once or twice a year.

Immediately afterward he asked himself if his own death would be like that; probably it would, apart from the sheets being less impeccable (he knew that the sheets of those in their death agony are always dirty with spittle, discharges, marks of medicine), and it was to be hoped that Concetta, Carolina, and his other womenfolk would be more decently clad. But the same, more or less. As always, the thought of his own death calmed him as much as that of others disturbed him; was it perhaps because, when all was said and done, his own death would in the first place mean that of the whole world?

From this he went on to think that he must see to repairing the tomb of his ancestors at the Capuchins'. A pity corpses couldn't be hung up by the neck in the crypt and watched slowly mummifying; he'd look magnificent on that wall, tall and big as he was, terrifying girls by the set smile on his sandpaper face, by his long, long white piqué trousers. But no, they'd dress him up in party clothes, perhaps in this very evening coat he was wearing now. . . .

The door opened. "Uncle, you're looking wonderful this evening. Black suits you perfectly. But what are you looking at? Are you courting death?"

Tancredi was arm in arm with Angelica; both of them were still under the sensual influence of the dance, and were tired. Angelica sat down and asked Tancredi for a handkerchief to mop her brow; Don Fabrizio gave her his. The two young people looked at the picture with complete lack of interest. For both of them death was purely an intellectual concept, a fact of knowledge as it were and no more, not an experience which pierced the marrow of their bones. Death, oh yes, it existed of course, but it was something that happened to others. The thought occurred to Don Fabrizio that it was ignorance of this supreme consolation that made the young feel sorrows much more sharply than the old; the latter are nearer the safety exit.

"Prince," said Angelica, "we'd heard you were here; we came to have a little rest, but also to ask you something. I hope you won't refuse it." Her eyes were full of roguish laughter, her hand was resting on Don Fabrizio's sleeve. "I want to ask you to dance the next mazurka with me. Do say yes, now, don't be naughty; we all know you used to be a great dancer." The Prince was very pleased and felt suddenly quite spry. The Capuchins' crypt indeed! His downy cheeks quivered with pleasure. The idea of the mazurka rather alarmed him, though; that military dance, all heel-banging and turns, was not for his joints. To kneel before Angelica would be a pleasure, but what if he found it difficult to get up afterward?

"Thank you, my dear girl; you're making me feel young again. I'll be happy to obey you; but not the mazurka; grant me the first waltz."

"You see, Tancredi, how good Uncle is? No nonsense about him, like you. You know, Prince, he didn't want me to ask you; he's jealous."

Tancredi laughed. "When one has such a smart, good-looking uncle one's quite right to be jealous. Anyway, this time I won't oppose it." They all three smiled, and Don Fabrizio could not make out whether they had thought up this suggestion to please him or to mock him. It didn't matter; they were dear creatures all the same.

As she was going out Angelica slid a finger over the cover of an armchair. "Pretty, these; a good color, but those at your house, Prince . . ." The ship was taking its usual course.

Tancredi intervened. "That's enough, Angelica. We both love you quite apart from your knowledge of furniture. Leave the chairs alone and come and dance."

As he was going into the ballroom, Don Fabrizio saw that Sedàra was still talking to Giovanni Finale. He heard the words *russella, primintio, marzolino:* they were comparing the prices of seed corn. The Prince foresaw an invitation soon to Margarossa, the estate which was ruining Finale by his agricultural experiments.

Angelica and Don Fabrizio made a magnificent couple. The Prince's huge feet moved with surprising delicacy, and never were his partner's satin slippers in danger of being grazed. His great paw held her waist with vigorous firmness, his chin leaned on the black waves of her hair; from Angelica's bust rose a delicate scent of *bouquet à la Maréchale*, and above all an aroma of young smooth skin. A phrase of Tumeo's came back to him: "Her sheets must smell like Paradise." A crude, vulgar phrase, but accurate. Lucky Tancredi. . . .

She talked. Her natural vanity was as appeased as her tenacious ambition. "I'm so happy, Uncle. Everyone's been so kind, so sweet. Tancredi's an angel; and you're an angel, too. I owe all this to you, Uncle; even Tancredi. For if you hadn't agreed, I don't know what would have happened."

"I've nothing to do with it, my dear; all this is due to yourself alone."

It was true; no Tancredi could ever have resisted that beauty united to that income. He would have married her whatever happened. A twinge crossed his heart: the thought of Concetta's haughty yet defeated eyes. But that was a brief little pain; at every twirl a year fell from his shoulders; soon he felt back at the age of twenty, when in that very same ballroom he had danced with Stella before he knew disappointment, boredom, and the rest. For a second, that night, death seemed to him once more "something that happens to others."

So absorbed was he in memories which dovetailed so well with his present feelings that he did not notice how all of a sudden he and Angelica were dancing alone. Instigated, perhaps, by Tancredi, the other couples had stopped and were looking on; the two Ponteleones were there too, looking touched; they were old and perhaps understood. Stella was old too, but she was gazing on dully from beneath a doorway. When the band stopped there was nearly a round of applause; but Fabrizio had too leonine an air for anyone to risk such an impropriety.

When the waltz was over Angelica suggested that Don Fabrizio should come and take supper at her and Tancredi's table. He would have much liked to, but at that moment the memories of his own youth were too vivid for him not to realize how tiresome supper with an old uncle would have been then, with Stella only a yard or so away. Lovers want to be alone, or at least with strangers; never with older people, or worst of all with relatives.

"Thank you, Angelica, but I'm not hungry. I'll take something standing up. Go with Tancredi, don't worry about me."

He waited a moment for the two young people to draw away, then he too went into the supper room. A long, narrow table was set at the end, lit by the famous twelve silver-gilt candelabra given to Diego's grandfather by the Court of Madrid at the end of his embassy in Spain; on tall pedestals of gleaming metal the alternating figures of six athletes and of six women held above their heads silver-gilt shafts crowned by the flames of twelve candles. The sculptor had hinted skillfully at the serene ease of the men and the graceful effort of the girls in upholding the disproportionate weight. Twelve pieces of first-rate quality. "I wonder how much land they're worth," that wretch Sedàra would have said. Don Fabrizio remembered how one day Diego had shown him the case for each of the candelabra, vast green morocco affairs with the tripartite shield of Ponteleone and the entwined initials of the donors stamped on the sides in gold.

Beneath the candelabra, beneath the five tiers bearing toward the distant ceiling pyramids of homemade cakes that were never touched, spread the monotonous opulence of buffets at big balls: coralline lobsters boiled alive, waxy *chaud-froids* of veal, steely-tinted fish immersed in sauce, turkeys gilded by the ovens' heat, rosy *foie gras* under gelatin armor, boned woodcock reclining on amber toast decorated with their own chopped insides, and a dozen other cruel, colored delights. At the end of the table two monumental silver tureens held clear soup the color of burnt amber. To prepare this supper the cooks must have sweated away in the vast kitchens from the night before.

"Dear me, what an amount! Donna Margherita knows how to do things well. But it's not for me!"

Scorning the table of drinks, glittering with crystal and silver on the right, he moved left toward that of the sweetmeats. Huge blond *babas*, *Mont Blancs* snowy with whipped cream, cakes speckled with white almonds and green pistachio nuts, hillocks of chocolate-covered pastry, brown and rich as the topsoil of the Catanian plain from which, in fact, through many a twist and turn they had come, pink ices, champagne ices, coffee ices, all *parfaits*, which fell apart with a squelch as the knife cleft them, melody in major of crystallized cherries, acid notes of yellow pineapple, and those cakes called "triumphs of gluttony" filled with green pistachio paste, and shameless "virgins' cakes" shaped like breasts. Don Fabrizio asked for some of these and, as he held them in his plate, looked like a profane caricature of St. Agatha. "Why ever didn't the Holy Office forbid these cakes when it had the chance? St. Agatha's sliced-off breasts sold by convents, devoured at dances! Well, well!"

Around the room smelling of vanilla, wine, chypre, wandered Don Fabrizio looking for a place. Tancredi saw him from his table and clapped a hand on a chair to show there was room there; next to him was Angelica, peering at the side of a silver dish to see if her hair was in place. Don Fabrizio shook his head in smiling refusal. He went on looking; from a table he heard the satisfied voice of Pallavicino: "The most moving moment of my life." There was an empty place by him. What a bore the man was! Wouldn't it be better, after all, to listen to Angelica's refreshing if forced cordiality, to Tancredi's dry wit? No: better bore oneself than bore others.

With a word of apology he sat down next to the Colonel, who got up as he arrived—a small sop to Salina pride. As he savored the subtle mixture of blancmange, pistachio, and cinnamon in the dessert he had chosen, Don Fabrizio began conversing with Pallavicino and realized that, beyond those sugary phrases meant perhaps only for ladies, the man was anything but a fool. He too was a "gentleman," and the fundamental skepticism of his class, smothered usually by the impetuous Bersaglieri flames on his lapel, came peering out again now that he found himself in surroundings like those into which he was born, away from the inevitable rhetoric of barracks and admirers.

"Now the Left wants to string me up because last August I ordered my men to open fire on Garibaldi. But can you tell me, Prince, what else I could have done in view of the written orders I was carrying? I must confess, though, when at Aspromonte I found myself facing that mob of a hundred men or so, some looking like out-and-out fanatics, others like professional agitators, I was pleased that my instructions coincided so with my own feelings. If I hadn't given orders to fire, those people would have hacked us to pieces, my soldiers and me; that wouldn't have mattered much, of course. But in the end it would have meant French and Austrian intervention, and that would have had endless repercussions, including the collapse of the Italian Kingdom of ours which has got itself put together in some miraculous way, quite how I can't for the life of me understand. And I tell you another thing in confidence: those musket-shots of ours were a particular help to . . . Garibaldi himself! They freed him from the rabble hanging around him, all those creatures like Zambianchi who were making use of him for ends that may have been generous but were certainly inept, with the Tuileries or Palazzo Farnese behind them. Very different types those were to the ones who landed with him at Marsala, people who did believe, the best of them, that Italy could be created by repeating 1848. And he knows that, the General does, for when I was making him the genuflection that has caused so much comment, he shook my hand with a warmth that must surely be unusual toward a man who's just fired a bullet into one's foot a few minutes before. And d'you know what he said to me in a low voice, he who was the one really decent person on the whole wretched mountain-side? 'Thank you, Colonel.' Thank you for what, I ask you? For laming him for life? Obviously not; but for having brought home to him so clearly the bluster, the cowardice, worse maybe, of those followers of his."

"Forgive me for saying so, Colonel, but don't you think all that hand-kissing, cap-doffing, and complimenting went a little far?"

"No, frankly. For they were all genuine acts of respect. You should have seen him, that poor great man, stretched out under a chestnut tree, suffering in body and still more in mind. A sad sight! He showed himself plainly as what he's always been, a child, with beard and wrinkles, but a simple adventurous little boy all the same; it was difficult for me not to feel moved at having had to shoot at him. Why shouldn't I, anyway? Usually I kiss only women's hands; then, Prince, I was kissing a hand for the salvation of the Kingdom, a lady to whom we soldiers owe homage too."

A footman passed; Don Fabrizio told him to bring a slice of *Mont Blanc* and a glass of champagne. "And you, Col onel, aren't you taking anything?"

"Nothing to eat, thank you. Perhaps I'll drink a glass of champagne too."

Then he went on, obviously not able to take his mind off a memory which, consisting as it did of a little shooting and a lot of skill, was exactly the sort that attracts men of his type. "The General's men, as my Bersaglieri disarmed them, were cursing away, and d'you know at whom? At him, the only one of them who'd actually paid in his own person. Foul, but natural, really; they saw that childlike yet great man slipping out of their grasp, the only one capable of covering up their obscure intrigues. And even if my own courtesies were superfluous, I'd be pleased even so at having done them; we in Italy can never go too far with sentiment and hand-kissing; they're the most effective political arguments we have."

He drank the wine brought him, but that seemed to increase his bitterness even more. "Have you been on the mainland since the Kingdom was founded? You're lucky. It's not a pretty sight. Never have we been so disunited as since we've been reunited. Turin doesn't want to cease being a capital, Milan finds our administration inferior to the Austrians', Florence is afraid the works of art there will be carried off, Naples is moaning about the industries she's lost, and here, here in Sicily, some huge irrational disaster is in the making. . . . For the moment, owing partly to your humble servant, no one mentions red shirts any more; but they'll be back again. When they've vanished, others of different colors will come; and then red ones once again.

And how will it end? There's Italy's lucky star, they say. But you know better than I, Prince, that even fixed stars are so only in appearance." Perhaps he was a little tipsy, making such prophecies. But at these disquieting prospects Don Fabrizio felt his heart contract.

The ball went on for a long time, until six in the morning; all were exhausted and wishing they had been in bed for at least three hours; but to leave early was like proclaiming the party a failure and offending the host and hostess who had taken such a lot of trouble, poor dears.

The ladies' faces were livid, their dresses crushed, their breaths heavy. "Maria! How tired I am! Maria! How sleepy!" Above their disordered cravats the faces of the men were yellow and lined, their mouths stained with bitter saliva. Their visits to a disordered little room near the band alcove became more frequent; in it was disposed a row of twenty vast vats, by that time nearly all brimful, some spilling over. Sensing that the dance was nearing its end, the sleepy servants were no longer changing the candles in chandeliers; the short stubs diffused a different, smoky, ill-omened light. In the empty supper room were only dirty plates, glasses with dregs of wine which the servants glancing around would hurriedly drain; through the cracks in the shutters filtered a plebeian light of dawn.

The party was crumbling away, and around Donna Margherita there was already a group saying goodbye. "Heavenly! A dream! Like the old days!" Tancredi was hard put to wake Don Calogero, who, with head flung back, had gone off to sleep on an armchair apart; his trousers were rucked up to his knees and above his silken socks showed the ends of his drawers, most rustic sight. Colonel Pallavicino was yawning too, declaring, though, to whoever wished to listen, that he was not going home and would move straight from Palazzo Ponteleone to his headquarters; such in fact was the iron tradition followed by officers invited to a ball.

When the family had settled into its carriage (the dew had made the cushions damp) Don Fabrizio said that he would walk home; a little fresh air would do him good, he had a slight headache. The truth is that he wanted to draw a little comfort from gazing at the stars. There were still one or two up there, at the zenith. As always, seeing them revived him; they were distant, they were omnipotent, and at the same time they were docile to his calculations; just the contrary to human beings, always too near, so weak and yet so quarrelsome.

There was already a little movement in the streets: a cart or two with rubbish heaped four times the height of the tiny gray donkey dragging it along. A long open wagon came by stacked with bulls killed shortly before at the slaughterhouse, already quartered and exhibiting their intimate mechanism with the shamelessness of death. At intervals a big thick red drop fell onto the pavement.

At a crossroad he glimpsed the sky to the west, above the sea. There was Venus, wrapped in her turban of autumn mist. She was always faithful, always waiting for Don Fabrizio on his early morning outings, at Donnafugata before a shoot, now after a ball.

Don Fabrizio sighed. When would she decide to give him an appointment less ephemeral, far from carcasses and blood, in her own region of perennial certitude?

7

Death of a Prince

DON Fabrizio had always known that sensation. For a dozen years or so he had been feeling as if the vital fluid, the faculty of existing, life itself in fact and perhaps even the will to go on living, were ebbing out of him slowly but steadily, as grains of sand cluster and then line up one by one, unhurried, unceasing, before the narrow neck of an hourglass. In some moments of intense activity or concentration this sense of continual loss would vanish, to reappear impassively in brief instants of silence or introspection; just as a constant buzzing in the ears or the ticking of a pendulum superimposes itself when all else is silent, assuring us of always being there, watchful, even when we do not hear it.

With the slightest effort of attention he would notice at all other times too the rustling of the grains of sand as they slid lightly away, the instants of time escaping from his mind and leaving him for ever. But this sensation was not, at first, linked to any physical discomfort. On the contrary, this imperceptible loss of vitality was itself the proof, the condition so to say, of a sense of living; and for him, accustomed to scrutinizing limitless outer space and to probing vast inner abysses, the sensation was in no way disagreeable; this continuous whittling away of his personality seemed linked to a vague presage of the rebuilding elsewhere of a personality (thanks be to God) less conscious and yet broader. Those tiny grains of sand were not lost; they were vanishing, but accumulating elsewhere to cement some more lasting pile. Though "pile," he had reflected, was not the exact word, for it suggested weight; nor was "grain of sand" either for that matter. They were more like the tiny particles of watery vapor exhaled from a narrow pond, then mounting into the sky to great clouds, light and free.

Sometimes he was surprised that the vital reservoir could still contain anything at all after all those years of loss. "Not even were it big as a pyramid. . . ." On other occasions, more frequent, he had felt a kind of pride at being the only one to notice this continual escape, while no one around him seemed to sense it in the same way; and this had made him feel a certain contempt for others, as an old soldier despises a conscript who deludes himself that whistling bullets are just harmless flies. Such things are never confessed, no one knows why; we leave them for others to sense, and no one around him had ever sensed them at all,

none of his daughters with their dreams of a world beyond
the tomb identical with this life, all complete with judges,
cooks, and convents; not even Stella, who, though devoured by the canker of diabetes, still had clung pitiably to
this vale of tears.

Perhaps only Tancredi had understood for an instant,
when he had said with that subdued irony of his, "Uncle,
you are courting death." Now the courtship was ended; the
lovely lady had said "Yes"; the elopement was decided on,
the compartment on the train reserved.

For this was different now, quite different. Sitting in an
armchair, his long legs wrapped in a blanket, on the balcony of the Hotel Trinacria, he felt life flowing from him
in great pressing waves, with a spiritual roar like that of the
Falls of the Rhine. It was midday on a Monday at the end
of July, and away in front of him spread the sea of Palermo,
compact, oily, inert, improbably motionless, crouching like
a dog trying to make itself invisible at its master's threats;
but up there the static perpendicular sun was straddling it
and lashing at it pitilessly. The silence was absolute. Under
the high, high light Don Fabrizio heard no other sound
than that inner one of life gushing from him.

He had arrived that morning, a few hours before, from
Naples, where he had gone to consult a specialist, Professor
Sémmola. Accompanied by his forty-year-old daughter
Concetta and his grandson Fabrizietto, he had had a dreary
journey, slow as a funeral procession. The bustle of the
port of departure and that of arrival at Naples, the acrid
smell of the cabin, the incessant clamor of that paranoiac

city, had exasperated him with the querulous exasperation which tires and prostrates the very weak while arousing an equivalent exasperation in good folk with years of life ahead. He had insisted on returning by land: a sudden decision which the doctor had tried to oppose; but he had been adamant, and so overwhelming was the shadow of his prestige still that he had had his way.

The result was that he had been forced to spend thirty-six hours cooped up in a scorching-hot box, suffocated by the smoke of tunnels repetitive as feverish dreams, blinded by sun in open patches stark as sad realities, humiliated by the innumerable low services he had to ask of his alarmed grandson. They crossed evil-looking landscapes, accursed mountain ranges, torpid malarial plains, landscapes of Calabria and Basilicata which seemed barbarous to him while they were actually just like those of Sicily. The railway line had not yet been completed; in its last stretches it made a wide detour through lunar deserts that were sarcastically called by the athletic and voluptuous names of Croton and Sybaris. Then, at Messina, after the deceitful smile of the Straits had been given a lie by the parched bald hills, there was another detour, long and cruel as the collection of legal arrears. They had gone down to Catania, clambered up again; the locomotive, as it panted up those fabulous slopes, seemed to be about to die like an overforced horse; then a noisy descent, and they reached Palermo. On the arrival platform were the usual masks of family faces with painted smiles of pleasure at the journey's happy outcome. It was in fact from the would-be consoling smiles of those awaiting him at the station, from their pretense—a bad pretense—at an air of gaiety, that there suddenly came home to him what had been the real diagnosis of Sémmola, who to him had spoken only reassuring phrases; and it was then, after getting down from the train, as he was embracing his daughter-in-law buried in widow's weeds, his children showing their teeth in smiles, Tancredi with anxious eyes, Angelica with silken bodice tight over mature breasts, it was then that he heard the crash of the falls.

Probably he fainted, for he did not remember how he had reached the carriage; he found himself lying in it with his legs drawn up, only Tancredi with him. The carriage had not moved yet, and from outside came voices of his family in confabulation. "It's nothing." "The journey was too long." "Any of us might faint in this heat." "It would be too tiring for him to go up to the villa." He was perfectly lucid again now: he noticed a serious conversation going on between Concetta and Francesco Paolo, then Tancredi's elegance, his brown and beige checked suit, his brown bowler; and he noticed how for once his nephew's smile was not mocking but touched with sad affection; from this he got the bittersweet sensation that his nephew loved him and also knew him to be done for, since that perpetual irony had been brushed away by tenderness. The carriage moved off and turned to the right. "But where are we going, Tancredi?" His own voice surprised him. It seemed to echo that inner booming.

"Uncle, we're going to the Trinacria; you're tired and the villa's a long way off; you can have a night's rest and get home tomorrow. Don't you think so?"

"Then let's go to our place by the sea, that's even nearer."

But that wasn't possible; the house was not in order, as he well knew; it was used only for occasional luncheons by the sea; there wasn't even a bed in it.

"You'll be better at the hotel, Uncle; you'll have every comfort there." They were treating him like a new-born baby; and he had just about a new-born baby's strength.

The first comfort he found at the hotel was a doctor, called in a hurry, perhaps during his black-out. But it was not the one who always treated him, Doctor Cataliotti, with a big white cravat under a smiling face and rich gold spectacles; this was a poor devil, doctor to the slum quarter near by, impotent witness of a thousand wretched death agonies. Above a torn frock coat stretched his long, haggard face stubbled with white hair, the disillusioned face of a famished intellectual; when he took a chainless watch from his pocket, the false gilt showed marks of verdigris. He too was a poor goat-skin flask worn through by the jostle of the mule path and scattering without realizing it its last drops of oil. He felt the pulse, prescribed camphor drops, showed his decayed teeth in a smile meant to be reassuring and pitiable instead, and padded off.

The drops soon arrived from a druggist near by; they did him good; he felt a little less weak, but the impetus of escaping time did not lessen.

Don Fabrizio looked at himself in the wardrobe mirror; he recognized his own suit more than himself: very tall and emaciated, with sunken cheeks and three days' growth of beard; he looked like one of those mad Englishmen who amble around in vignettes from books by Jules Verne which he used to give Fabrizietto as Christmas presents. A Leopard in very bad trim. Why, he wondered, did God not want anyone to die with his own face on? For the same happens to us all: we all die with a mask on our features; even the young; even the blood-daubed soldier, even Paolo when he'd been raised from the cobbles with taut crumpled features as people rushed in the dust after his runaway horse. And if in him, an old man, the crash of escaping life was so powerful, what a tumult there must have been as the still brimming reservoirs emptied out of those poor young bodies in a second.

An absurd rule of enforced camouflage—he would have liked to contravene it as much as he could; but he felt that he was unable, that to hold up a razor would have been like holding up his own desk. "Call a barber, will you?" he said to Francesco Paolo. But at once he thought, "No. It's a rule of the game; hateful but formal. They'll shave me afterward." And he said out loud, "It doesn't matter; we'll think about that later." The idea of the utter abandon of his corpse, with a barber crouched over it, did not disturb him.

A waiter came in with a basin of warm water and a sponge, took off his coat and shirt, and washed his face and hands, as one washes a child, as one washes the dead. Soot

from the day-and-a-half train journey turned the water a
funereal black. The low room was suffocating; the heat
fomented smells, brought out the mustiness of ill-dusted
plush; a medicinal odor came from the marks of dozens of
crushed cockroaches; around the night table clung tenacious memories of old and varied urine. He had the shutters opened; the hotel was in shadow, but a blinding light
was reflected from the metallic sea; better, though, than
that prison stink. He asked for an armchair to be taken onto
the balcony; leaning on someone's arm, he dragged himself
out and sat down after those few steps with the sensation of
relief he used to feel once on sitting down after four hours
of shooting in the mountains. "Tell everyone to leave me
in peace; I feel better; I want to sleep." He did feel
sleepy; but he found that to give way to drowsiness now
would be as absurd as eating a slice of cake immediately
before a longed-for banquet. He smiled. "I've always been
a wise gourmet." And he sat there, immersed in that great
outer silence, in the terrifying inner rumble.

He could turn his head to the left; beside Monte Pellegrino could be seen a cleft in the circle of hills, and, beyond,
two hillocks at whose feet lay his home. Unreachable to
him as this was, it seemed very far away; he thought of
his own observatory, of the telescopes now destined to years
of dust; of poor Father Pirrone, who was dust too; of the
paintings of his estates, of the monkeys on the hangings,
of the big brass bedstead in which his dear Stella had died;
of all those things which now seemed to him humble, however precious, of artfully twisted metalwork, of fabrics and

silken tapestries dyed with colors derived from earth and plant juices, which had been kept alive by him, and which would shortly be plunged, through no fault of their own, into a limbo of abandon and oblivion. His heart tightened, he forgot his own agony thinking of the imminent end of those poor dear things. The inert row of houses behind him, the wall of hills, the sun-scourged distance, prevented him from thinking clearly even of Donnafugata; it seemed like a house in a dream, no longer his; all he had of his own now was this exhausted body, those slate tiles under his feet, that surging of dark water toward the abyss. He was alone, a shipwrecked man adrift on a raft, prey of untamable currents.

There were his sons, of course. The only one who resembled him, Giovanni, was no longer here. Every couple of years he sent greetings from London; he had ceased dealing with coal and moved on to diamonds; just after Stella's death a short letter had come addressed to her and soon after a little parcel with a bracelet. Ah, yes. He too had "courted death"; in fact, by leaving everything he had done his best to get as much of death as he could under control while actually going on living. But the others . . . There were his grandchildren too, of course: Fabrizietto, youngest of the Salinas, so handsome, so lively, so dear. . . .

So odious. With his double dose of Màlvica blood, with his good-time instincts, with his tendency to middle-class *chic*. It was useless to try to avoid the thought, but the last of the Salinas was really he himself, this gaunt giant now dying on a hotel balcony. For the significance of a noble family lies entirely in its traditions, that is in its vital memories; and he was the last to have any unusual memories, anything different from those of other families. Fabrizietto would only have banal ones like his schoolfellows, of snacks, of spiteful little jokes against teachers, horses bought with an eye more to price than to quality; and the meaning of his name would change more and more to empty pomp embittered by the gadfly thought that others could outdo him in outward show. He would go hunting for a rich marriage when that would have become a commonplace routine and no longer a bold predatory adventure like Tancredi's. The tapestries of Donnafugata, the almond groves of Ragattisi, even, who knows, the fountain of Amphitrite, might suffer the grotesque fate of being transmuted into pots of quickly swallowed *foie gras*, into noisy little women as transient as their rouge, from the age-old things of patina that they'd been. And he himself would be merely a memory of a choleric old grandfather who had collapsed one July afternoon just in time to prevent the boy's going off to Livorno for sea bathing. He had said that the Salinas would always remain the Salinas. He had been wrong. The last Salina was himself. That fellow Garibaldi, that bearded Vulcan, had won after all.

From the room next door, open on to the same balcony, Concetta's voice reached him: "We simply must; he's got to be called. I should never forgive myself if he weren't." He understood at once; they were talking of a priest. For a moment he had an idea of refusing, of lying, of starting to shout that he was perfectly well, that he needed nothing. But soon he realized how ridiculous all that would be: he was the Prince of Salina, and as a Prince of Salina he had to die with a priest by his side. Concetta was right. Why should he avoid what was longed for by thousands of other dying people? And he fell silent, waiting to hear the little bell with the Last Sacraments. It soon came; the parish church of the Pietà was almost opposite. The gay silvery tinkle came climbing up the stairs, flowed along the passage, became sharp as the door opened; preceded by the hotel manager, a Swiss, flustered at having a dying man on his hands, in came Father Balsàmo, the parish priest, bearing under humeral veil the Blessed Sacrament in its leather pyx. Tancredi and Fabrizietto raised the armchair, bore it back into the room; the others were kneeling. He signed more than said, "Away, away." He wanted to confess. Things should be done properly or not at all. Everyone went out, but when he was about to speak he realized he had nothing to say; he could remember some definite sins, but they seemed so petty as not to warrant bothering a worthy priest about on a hot day. Not that he felt himself innocent; but his whole life was blameworthy, not this or that single act in it; and now he no longer had time to say so. His eyes must have expressed an uneasiness which the priest took for contrition; as in fact in a sense it was. He was absolved; his chin must have been propped on his chest, for the priest had to kneel down to place the Host between his lips. Then there was a murmur of the immemorial syllables which smooth the way, and the priest withdrew.

The armchair was not pulled back onto the balcony. Fabrizietto and Tancredi sat down next to him and held each of his hands; the boy was staring at him with the natural curiosity of one present at his first death agony and no more; this person dying was not a man, he was a grandfather, which is a very different thing. Tancredi squeezed his hand tightly and talked to him, talked a great deal, talked gaily; he explained projects with which he was associated, commented on political developments; he was a Deputy, had been promised the Legation in Lisbon, knew many a secret and savory story. His nasal voice, his subtle vocabulary, flew like a futile arrow over the ever noisier surging away of the waters of life. The Prince was grateful for the gossip; and he squeezed Tancredi's hand with a great effort though with almost no perceptible result. He was grateful, but he did not listen. He was making up a general balance sheet of his whole life, trying to sort out of the immense ash-heap of liabilities the golden flecks of happy moments. These were: two weeks before his marriage, six weeks after; half an hour when Paolo was born, when he felt proud at having prolonged by a twig the Salina tree (the pride had been misplaced, he knew that now, but there had been some genuine self-respect in it); a few talks with Giovanni before the latter vanished (a few monologues, if the truth were told, during which he had thought to find in the boy a kindred mind); and many hours in the observatory, absorbed in abstract calculations and the pursuit of the unreachable. Could those latter hours be really put down to the credit side of life? Were they not some sort of anticipatory gift of the beatitudes of death? It didn't matter, they had existed.

Below in the street, between the hotel and the sea, a barrel organ stopped and was playing away in the avid hope of touching the hearts of foreigners who at that season were not there. It was grinding out "You who opened your wings to God," from *Lucia di Lammermoor*. What remained of Don Fabrizio thought of all the rancor mingling with all the tortures coming, throughout Italy, at that moment from mechanical music of the kind. Tancredi, intuitive as ever, ran to the balcony, threw down a coin, waved for the barrel organ to stop. The outer silence closed in again, the clamor within grew huge.

Tancredi. Yes, much on the credit side came from Tancredi: that sympathy of his, all the more precious for being ironic; the aesthetic pleasure of watching him maneuver amid the shoals of life, the bantering affection whose touch was so right. Then, the dogs: Fufi, the fat pug of his childhood, the impetuous poodle Tom, confidant and friend, Speedy's gentle eyes, Bendicò's delicious nonsense, the caressing paws of Pop, the pointer at that moment searching for him under bushes and garden chairs and never to see him again; then a horse or two, those already more distant and extraneous. There were the first few hours of returns to Donnafugata, the sense of tradition and the perennial expressed in stone and water, time congealed; a few carefree shoots, a cozy massacre or two of hares and pheasants, a few good laughs with Tumeo, a few minutes of compunction at the convent amid odors of musk and almond cakes. Anything else? Yes, there were other things, but these were only grains of gold mixed with earth: moments of satisfaction when he had made some biting reply to a fool, of content when he had realized that in Concetta's beauty and character was prolonged the true Salina strain; a moment or two of frenzied passion; the surprise of Arago's letter spontaneously congratulating him on the accuracy of his difficult calculations about Huxley's comet. And—why not?—the public thrill of being given a medal at the Sorbonne, the exquisite sensation of one or two fine silk cravats, the smell of morocco leathers, the gay, voluptuous air of a few women passed in the street, of one glimpsed even yesterday at the station of Catania in a brown travelling dress and suède gloves, mingling amid the crowds and seeming to search for his exhausted face through the dirty compartment window. What a noise that crowd was making! "Sandwiches!" "*Il Corriere dell'isola!*" And then the panting of the tired breathless train . . . and that appalling sun as they arrived, those lying faces, the crashing falls. . . .

In the growing dark he tried to count how much time he had really lived. His brain could not cope with the simple calculation any more: three months, three weeks, a total of six months, six by eight, eighty-four . . . forty-eight thousand . . . $\sqrt{840,000}$. He summed up. "I'm seventy-three years old, and all in all I may have lived, really lived, a total of two . . . three at the most." And the pains, the boredom, how long had they been? Useless to try to make himself count those; all of the rest: seventy years.

He felt his hand no longer being squeezed. Tancredi got up hurriedly and went out. . . . Now it was not a river erupting over him but an ocean, tempestuous, all foam and raging white-flecked waves. . . .

He must have had another stroke, for suddenly he realized that he was lying stretched out on the bed. Someone was feeling his pulse; from the window came the blinding implacable reflection of the sea; in the room there was the sound of a faint hiss; it was his own death rattle, but he did not know it. Around him was a little crowd, a group of strangers staring at him with frightened expressions. Gradually he recognized them: Concetta, Francesco Paolo, Carolina, Tancredi, Fabrizietto. The person taking his pulse was Doctor Cataliotti; he tried to smile a greeting at the latter, but no one seemed to notice; all were weeping except Concetta; even Tancredi, who was saying, "Uncle, dearest Uncle mine!"

Suddenly amid the group appeared a young woman, slim, in brown travelling dress and wide bustle, with a straw hat trimmed by a speckled veil which could not hide the sly charm of her face. She slid a little suède-gloved hand between one elbow and another of the weeping kneelers, apologized, drew closer. It was she, the creature forever yearned for, coming to fetch him; strange that one so young should yield to him; the time for the train's departure must be very close. When she was face to face with him she raised her veil, and there, modest, but ready to be possessed, she looked lovelier than she ever had when glimpsed in stellar space.

The crashing of the sea subsided altogether.

8

ANYONE paying a visit to the old Salina ladies would nearly always find at least one priest's hat on the hall chairs. All three were spinsters, and their household had been rent by secret struggles for hegemony, so that each, a strong character in her own way, wanted a separate confessor. It was still the custom in that year, 1910, for confessions to take place at home, and these penitents' scruples meant frequent repetition. Add to this little platoon of confessors the chaplain who came every morning to celebrate Mass in the private chapel, the Jesuit in charge of the general spiritual direction of the household, the monks and priests who came to elicit alms for this or that parish or good work, and it will be readily understood why there was such an incessant coming and going of clerics, and why the antechamber of Villa Salina was often reminiscent of one of those Roman shops around Piazza della Minerva which display in their windows every imaginable ecclesiastical headgear, from flaming crimson for Cardinals to cindery black for country priests.

On that particular afternoon of May, 1910, the parade of hats was quite unprecedented. The presence of the Vicar-General of the Archdiocese of Palermo was announced by his huge hat of fine beaver in a delicate shade of fuchsia, placed on a separate chair, with, next to it, a single glove, the right-hand one, in woven silk of the same delicate hue; his secretary's of gleaming long-haired black plush, the crown circled by a narrow violet cord; those of two Jesuit Fathers, subdued tenebrous felts, symbols of modesty and reserve. The chaplain's headgear lay on an isolated chair, as was proper for a person undergoing inquiry.

The meeting that day was no unimportant matter. In accordance with Papal instructions the Cardinal Archbishop had begun an inspection of the private chapels of his archdiocese, to reassure himself about the merits of those allowed to have services there, the conformity of liturgy and decoration with the canons of the Church, and the authenticity of the relics venerated in them. The Salina chapel was the best known in the city and one of the first which His Eminence proposed to visit. And it was in order to arrange for this event, fixed for next morning, that Monsignor the Vicar-General had called at Villa Salina. Unfortunate rumors about that chapel, seeped through many a filter, had reached the Archiepiscopal Curia: not, of course, anything about the merits of the owners or of their right to carry out their religious duties in their own home; such subjects were beyond discussion. Nor was there any doubt thrown on the regularity or continuity of services held there, for these were as near perfection as may be, except perhaps for an overwhelming and perfectly comprehensible reluctance on the part of the Salina ladies to let anyone who was outside their close family circle be present at the sacred rites. The Cardinal's attention had been drawn to an image venerated in the villa, and to the relics, the dozens of relics, exposed in the chapel. There were the most disturbing rumors about the authenticity of these, and it was desired that their genuineness be proved. The chaplain, an ecclesiastic of some culture and high hopes, had been reprimanded severely for not having kept the old ladies sufficiently on the alert; he had had, as it were, a "dressing-down of the tonsure."

The meeting was taking place in the main drawing room of the villa, the one of the monkeys and cockatoos. On a sofa covered with blue material interwoven with pink, a purchase of thirty years before that clashed with the evanescent tints of the precious wall hangings, sat the Signorina Concetta with Monsignor the Vicar-General on her right; on each side of the sofa in two similar armchairs were the Signorina Carolina and one of the Jesuits, Father Corti, while the Signorina Caterina, whose legs were paralyzed, was in a wheel chair, and the other ecclesiastics had to be content with chairs covered in the same material as the walls, which then seemed far less valuable to everyone than the envied armchairs.

The three sisters were all beyond seventy, and Concetta was not the eldest; but the struggle for power which has been hinted at at the beginning had ended some time ago with the rout of her adversaries, so no one would now have dared contest her functions as mistress of the house.

She still showed the vestiges of past beauty; heavy and imposing in her stiff clothes of black watered silk, she wore her snow-white hair drawn up in a lofty coiffure so as to show her almost unfurrowed brow; this, together with contemptuous eyes and a resentful line above her nose, gave her an air that was authoritarian, almost imperial; so much so that a nephew of hers, having caught sight in some book or other of a picture of a famous Czarina, used to call her in private "Catherine the Great": an unsuitable name made quite innocent by the complete purity of Concetta's life and her nephew's total ignorance of Russian history.

The conversation lasted an hour; coffee had been taken, and it was getting late. Monsignor resumed his arguments: "His Eminence paternally desires that Mass celebrated in private should be in conformity with the purest rites of Holy Mother Church, and that is why in his pastoral care he is visiting your chapel first, for he knows it to be a beacon for the laity of Palermo and he desires that all objects venerated there should bring ever more edification to yourselves and to all devout souls." Concetta was silent, but Carolina, the elder sister, exploded, "Now we're to appear as accused before our friends, are we? This idea of inspecting our chapel, excuse me for saying so, Monsignor, should never have passed through His Eminence's head."

Monsignor laughed, amused. "Signorina, you cannot imagine what pleasure your vehemence gives me; it is the expression of a simple and absolute faith, most acceptable to the Church and certainly to Our Lord Himself; and it is only in order to make this faith flower yet more abundantly and to purify it that the Holy Father has recommended these inspections, which have been taking place for some months throughout the Catholic world."

The reference to the Holy Father was not, actually, very opportune: Carolina was one of those Catholics who consider themselves to be in closer possession of religious truths than the Pope himself; and a few moderate declarations of Pius X, the abolition of some secondary feast days in particular, had already exasperated her. "This Pope would do better to mind his own business." Then she began to wonder if she hadn't gone too far, crossed herself, and muttered a *Gloria Patri.*

Concetta intervened. "Don't let yourself be drawn into saying things you don't think, Carolina. Or what sort of impression will Monsignor here take away with him?"

The latter was actually now smiling more than ever; here in front of him, he was thinking, was a little girl grown old in narrow ideas and arid practices. Benignly he indulged her.

"Monsignor will take away the impression of having been in the company of three saintly ladies," said he.

Father Corti, the Jesuit, tried to relax the tension. "I, Monsignor, am among those who can best confirm your words; Father Pirrone, whose memory is venerated by all who knew him, often used to tell me when I was a novice of the saintly atmosphere in which the ladies grew up: and the name of Salina should be a guarantee for that."

Monsignor wanted to get down to facts. "Well, Signorina Concetta, now that everything's clear I should like, with your permission, to visit the chapel in order to prepare His Eminence for the marvels of faith he will see tomorrow morning."

In Prince Fabrizio's time there had been no chapel in the villa; the whole family used to go out to church on feast days, and even Father Pirrone had had to walk quite a way every morning to say his own Mass. But after the death of Prince Fabrizio, when, as a result of various complications of inheritance which would be boring to narrate, the villa became the exclusive property of the three sisters, they at once thought of setting up their own oratory. They chose an out-of-the-way drawing room, which with its half columns of imitation granite stuck into the walls was vaguely reminiscent of a Roman basilica; they obliterated an unsuitable mythological fresco from the center of the ceiling and set up an altar. And all was ready.

When Monsignor entered, the chapel was lit by the late afternoon sun, which fell full on the picture above the altar so venerated by the Salina ladies. It was a painting in the style of Cremona and represented a slim and very attractive young woman, with eyes turned to heaven and an abundance of brown hair scattered in gracious disorder on half-bare shoulders; in her right hand she was gripping a crumpled letter, with an expression of anxious expectancy not unconnected with a certain sparkle in her glistening eyes; behind her was a green and gentle Lombard landscape. No Holy Child, no crowns, no snakes, no stars, in fact none of those symbols which usually accompany the image of Our Lady; the painter must have relied on the virginal expression as a sufficient mark of recognition. Monsignor drew nearer, went up one of the altar steps and stood there, without crossing himself, looking at the picture for a minute or two, his face all smiling admiration as if he were an art critic. Behind him the sisters made signs of the Cross and murmured a Hail Mary.

Then the prelate came down the steps again and turned around. "A beautiful painting," he said, "very expressive."

"A miraculous image, Monsignor, most miraculous!" explained Caterina, poor ill creature, leaning from her ambulating instrument of torture.

"It has worked so many miracles!" Carolina pressed on. "It represents the Madonna of the Letter. The Virgin is on the point of consigning the holy missive invoking her Divine Son's protection on the people of Messina: a protection which has been gloriously conceded, as is shown by the many miracles during the earthquake of two years ago."

"A fine picture, Signorina; whatever it represents, it's a pretty thing and should be treated carefully." Then he turned to the relics: seventy-four of them, they completely covered the two walls on each side of the altar. Each was enclosed in a frame which also contained a card with information about it and a number referring to the documents of authentication. These documents themselves, often voluminous and hung with seals, were locked in a damask-covered chest in a corner of the chapel. There were frames of worked and smooth silver, frames of bronze and coral, frames of tortoise shell; in filigree, in rare woods, in boxwood, in red and blue velvet; large, tiny, square, octagonal, round, oval; frames worth a fortune and frames bought at the Bocconi stores: all collected by those devoted souls in their religious exaltation as custodians of supernatural treasures.

The real creator of this collection had been Carolina; she had found somewhere a certain Donna Rosa, a great fat old woman, with connections in all the churches, convents, and charitable foundations of Palermo and its surroundings. It had been this Donna Rosa who every few months had brought up to Villa Salina a relic of a saint wrapped up in tissue paper. She had managed, she would say, to get some dilapidated parish church or decayed family to part with it. The name of the seller was not given, merely because of understandable, in fact praiseworthy, discretion; and anyway there were the proofs of authenticity which she brought and always handed over, clear as daylight, written out in Latin or mysterious characters she called Greek or Syriac. Concetta, administrator and bursar, would pay. Then would come a search and adaptation of frames. And once again the impassive Concetta would pay. There was a period, a couple of years ago, when the collecting mania even disturbed Carolina's and Caterina's sleep; in the morning they would recount to each other dreams of miraculous discoveries, with the hope that they would be realized, as indeed sometimes did happen after the dreams had been confided to Donna Rosa. What Concetta dreamed no one knew. Then Donna Rosa died and the influx of relics stopped almost completely; anyway, by then there was a certain satiation.

Monsignor glanced rather hurriedly at one or two of the nearest frames. "Treasures," he said, "treasures! What lovely frames!" Then, congratulating them on the fine décor, and promising to return next day with His Eminence ("Yes, at nine exactly"), he genuflected, crossed himself toward a modest Madonna of Pompeii hung on a side wall, and left the oratory. Soon the seats were bereft of hats, and the ecclesiastics climbed into the three carriages from the Archbishopric with their near-black horses which had awaited them in the courtyard. Monsignor made a point of asking the chaplain, Father Titta, to share his own carriage, much to the latter's solace. The carriages moved off, and Monsignor was silent; they drove by the sumptuous Villa Falconeri, with its flowering bougainvillaeas hanging over the walls of the splendidly kept garden; when they reached the slope down to Palermo amid the orange groves, Monsignor spoke. "And so you, Father Titta, have actually said Mass for years in front of the picture of that girl? Of that girl with a rendezvous waiting for her lover? Now don't tell me you too believed it was a holy image."

"Monsignor, I am to blame, I know. But it's not easy to gainsay the Signorina Carolina. That you can't know."

Monsignor shivered at the memory. "My son, you've put your finger on it; and that will be taken into consideration."

Carolina had gone off to pour out her rage in a letter to Chiara, her married sister in Naples. Caterina, tired by the long and painful conversation, had been put to bed. Concetta went back to her own solitary room. This was one of those rooms (so numerous that one might be tempted to say it of all rooms) which have two faces, one with a mask that they show to ignorant visitors, the other which is revealed only to those in the know, the owner in particular, to whom they are made manifest in all their squalid essence. This particular room was airy and looked over the broad garden; in a corner was a high bed with four pillows (Concetta suffered from heart trouble and had to sleep almost sitting up); no carpets, but a fine white floor divided into squares with intricate yellow lines, a valuable money chest with dozens of little drawers covered with marble inlay and semiprecious stones; the desk, central table, and all the furniture in a breezy local craftsmanship, with figures of huntsmen, dogs, and game in amber color on a dark background: furniture considered by Concetta herself as antiquated and in very bad taste, which, sold at auction after her death, is today the pride of a rich shipping agent when his wife gives cocktails to envious friends. On the walls were portraits, water colors, sacred images. All clean, all ordered. Two things only might have appeared unusual: in the corner opposite the bed towered four enormous wooden cases painted in green, each with a big padlock; and in front of these, on the floor, was a heap of mangy fur. To the lips of an ingenuous visitor the little room might have brought a smile, so suggestive was it of the good nature, the care of an old maid.

To one who knew the facts, to Concetta herself, it was an inferno of mummified memories. The four green cases contained dozens of day and night shirts, dressing gowns, pillowcases, sheets carefully divided into "best" and "second best": the trousseau collected by Concetta herself fifty years before. Now those padlocks were never opened for fear incongruous demons might leap out, and under the ubiquitous Palermo damp the contents grew yellow and decayed, useless for ever and for anyone. The portraits were of dead people no longer loved, the photographs of friends who had hurt her in their lifetime, the only reason they were not forgotten in death; the water colors showed houses and places most of which had been sold, or rather stupidly bartered by spendthrift nephews. Anyone who looked carefully into the heap of moth-eaten fur would have noticed two erect ears, a snout of black wood, and two astonished eyes of yellow glass; it was Bendicò, dead for forty-five years, embalmed for forty-five years, nest now of spiderwebs and of moth, detested by the servants who had been imploring Concetta for dozens of years to have it thrown onto the rubbish heap; but she always refused, reluctant to detach herself from the only memory of her past which aroused no distressing sensations.

But the distressing sensations of today (at a certain age

every day punctually produces its own) all referred to the present. Much less devout than Carolina, much more sensitive than Caterina, Concetta had understood the meaning of the Vicar-General's visit and foreseen the consequences: orders to take away all or nearly all the relics, the changing of the picture above the altar, an eventual reconsecration of the chapel. She had never really believed in the authenticity of those relics, and had paid up with the indifference of a father settling a bill for toys which are of no interest to himself but which help to keep children quiet. To her the removal of those objects was a matter of indifference; what did touch her, the day's real thorn, was the appalling figure the Salina family would now cut with the ecclesiastical authorities, and soon with the entire city. The Church kept its secrets much better than anyone else in Sicily, but that did not mean much yet; all would be spread around in a month or two, as everything is spread in this island which should have as its symbol not the Trinacria but the Ear of Dionysus at Syracuse which makes the lightest sigh resound for fifty yards around. And the Church's esteem meant much to her. The prestige of her name had slowly disappeared; the family fortune, divided and subdivided, was at best equivalent to that of any number of other lesser families and very much smaller than that of some rich industrialists. But in the Church, in their relations with it, the Salinas had maintained their pre-eminence. What a reception His Eminence had given the three sisters when they went to make their Christmas visit! Would that happen now?

A maid entered: "Excellency, the Princess is just arriving. Her motorcar is in the courtyard." Concetta got up, tidied her hair, threw a black lace shawl over her shoulders, resumed her imperial air, and reached the entrance hall just as Angelica was climbing the last steps of the outer staircase. She suffered from varicose veins; her legs, which had always been a little short, scarcely upheld her, and she was climbing up leaning on the arm of her own footman, whose black topcoat swept the stairs. "Concetta darling!" "Angelica dear! It's so long since we've met!" In fact only five days had gone by since her last visit, but the intimacy between the two cousins, an intimacy similar in closeness and feeling to that which was to bind Italians and Austrians in their opposing trenches a few years later, was such that five days really could seem a long time.

Angelica, now nearly seventy, still showed many traces of beauty; the illness which was to transform her into a wretched specter three years later was already active, but as yet secreted deep in her blood; her green eyes were what they had been before, only slightly dulled by the years, and the wrinkles on her neck were hidden by the soft black folds of the hood and veil which she, a widow for the last three years, wore not without a certain nostalgic coquetry. "You see," she said to Concetta as they moved entwined toward a drawing room, "you see, with these imminent celebrations of the fiftieth anniversary of the March of the Thousand there's never a minute's peace. Just imagine, a few days ago they told me I'd been put on the Committee of Honor; a homage to dear Tancredi's memory, of course, but such a lot for me to do! Finding lodgings for veterans coming from all over Italy, arranging invitations for the grandstand without offending anyone; taking care to invite the mayor of every commune in the island. Oh, by the way, dear: the Mayor of Salina is a clerical and has refused to take part in the parade; so I thought at once of your nephew, of Fabrizio; he came to visit me, and I pinned him down there and then. He couldn't refuse; and so at the end of the month we'll see him dressed to the nines parading down Via Libertà in front of a big placard with 'Salina' on it in letters a foot high. Don't you think it's a good idea? A Salina rendering homage to Garibaldi! A fusion of old and new Sicily! I've thought of you too, darling; here's your invitation for the grandstand of honor, right next to the Royal box." And she pulled out of her Paris bag a piece of cardboard in Garibaldi red, the very same color as the strip of silk worn for a time by Tancredi over his collar. "Carolina and Caterina won't be too pleased," she went on in her arbitrary way, "but I only had one place; anyway you have more right to it than they have; you were Tancredi's favorite cousin."

She talked a lot and she talked well: forty years of living with Tancredi, however tempestuous and interrupted, had been more than long enough to rub off the last traces of Donnafugata accent and manners; she had camouflaged herself even to the point of copying that graceful twining

of the fingers which had been one of Tancredi's character-
istics. She read a great deal, and on her table the latest
books by Anatole France and Bourget alternated with
D'Annunzio's and Serao's; and she had the reputation in
the drawing rooms of Palermo of being an expert on the
architecture of the châteaux of the Loire, about which she
would often discourse with somewhat hazy enthusiasm,
contrasting, perhaps unconsciously, their Renaissance serenity with the restless baroque of the palace at Donnafugata, against which she nurtured an aversion inexplicable
to anyone who knew nothing of her humble and ill-cared-
for youth.

"But what a head I have, my dear! I was forgetting to
tell you that Senator Tassoni will soon be coming here;
he's staying with me at Villa Falconeri and wants to meet
you; he was a great friend of poor Tancredi's, a comrade-
in-arms too, and he's heard Tancredi talk of you, it seems.
Our dear Tancredi!" The handkerchief with its narrow
black border came out of her bag, and she dried a tear in
eyes that were still beautiful.

Concetta had been inserting, as always, an occasional
phrase of her own into Angelica's continual flow; but at
the name of Tassoni she was silent. She saw once again a
scene, very distant but quite clear, as if through the other
end of a telescope: the big white table surrounded by all
those people now dead; Tancredi near her, dead too—as
anyway, really, she was herself; his brutal anecdote, Angelica's hysterical laughter, her own no less hysterical tears.

It had been the turning point of her life, that; the road she'd taken then had led her here, to this desert not even inhabited by extinct love or spent rancor.

"Oh, I've heard of the bother you're having with the Curia. What a nuisance they are! But why didn't you tell me before? I could have done something; the Cardinal is always very kind to me. I'm afraid that it's too late now. But I'll pull some strings. Anyway it'll all blow over."

Senator Tassoni, who arrived soon after, was a brisk and spruce old man. His wealth, which was great and growing, had been acquired by competition and hard struggle; instead of making him flabby, it had kept him in a state of continual energy which now seemed to conquer the years and make him almost fiery. From the few months spent with Garibaldi's southern army he had acquired a military bearing destined never to be discarded. Blended with courtesy, it formed a philter which had gained him many successes in the past, and now, joined to the number of his securities, was of great use for getting his own way with the boards of banks and cotton factories; half of Italy and a great part of the Balkan countries sewed on their own buttons with thread made by Tassoni & Co.

"Signorina," he was saying to Concetta as he sat beside her on a low stool suitable for a page, which was just why he had chosen it, "Signorina, a dream of my distant youth is now being realized. How often in those icy nights camping out on the Volturno or around the ramparts of besieged Gaeta, how often our unforgettable Tancredi used to talk of you! I seemed to know you already, to have frequented this house amid whose walls his untamed youth was passed; and I am happy to be able, though with such delay, to lay my homage at the feet of her who was the consolation of one of the purest heroes of our Risorgimento."

Concetta was unused to conversations with people she had not known since infancy; she was also no lover of literature; so she had had no immunity against rhetoric and was in fact open to its fascination. The Senator's words moved her; she forgot that old anecdote of half a century ago, she no longer saw in Tassoni a violator of convents, a jeerer at poor terrified nuns, but an old man, Tancredi's sincere friend, who talked of him with true affection, one who brought to her a shadow, a message from the dead man across the morass of time which the dead can so seldom cross. "And what did my dear cousin tell you about me?" she asked in a low voice, with a shyness that brought to life once more the eighteen-year-old girl from that bundle of black silk and white hair.

"Ah, so many things! He talked of you almost as much as of Donna Angelica! For him, she was love; you were the image of his sweet youth, that youth which for us soldiers passes so soon."

Again an icy hand froze her old heart; but now Tassoni had raised his voice, and turned to Angelica. "D'you remember, Princess, what he said at Vienna ten years ago?" He turned back toward Concetta to explain. "I was there with the Italian Delegation for the Trade Treaty; Tancredi put me up at the Embassy like the warmhearted friend and comrade he was, with that great gentleman's affability of his. Perhaps seeing a comrade-in-arms again in that hostile city had moved him, for he told us so much about his past. In the back of a box at the Opera, between one act and another of *Don Giovanni*, he confessed, in his incomparably ironic way, a sin, an unpardonable sin, which he said he'd committed against you, yes, against you, Signorina." He interrupted himself a second to gain time to set his surprise. "He told us how one evening, during dinner at Donnafugata, he had allowed himself to invent a story and tell it to you; a tale of war connected with the fighting around Palermo; and how you believed it and were offended because the story was rather outspoken for the customs of fifty years ago. You had reproved him. 'She was so sweet,' said he, 'as she fixed me with those angry eyes of hers and as her lips swelled with anger so prettily, like a puppy's; she was so sweet that if I hadn't controlled myself I'd have kissed her there and then in front of twenty people and that terrible old uncle of mine!' You, Signorina, will have forgotten it, but Tancredi remembered it well, he had such delicacy of feeling; he also remembered it because it happened on the very day he met Donna Angelica for the first time." And he sketched toward the Princess one of those gestures of homage, with his right hand dropping away through the air, whose Goldoniesque tradition used to be preserved only among Senators of the Kingdom.

The conversation continued for some time, but it could not be said that Concetta took any great part in it. The sudden revelation penetrated into her mind slowly, and

did not make her suffer much at first. But when the visitors
had said goodbye and left and she was alone, she began
seeing more clearly and so suffering more. The specters
of the past had been exorcised for years, though they were,
of course, to be found hidden in everything, and it was
they that made food taste bitter and company seem boring;
but it was a long time since they had shown their true faces;
now they came leaping out, accompanied by the ghastly
laughter of irreparable disaster. It would, of course, be
absurd to say that Concetta still loved Tancredi; love's
eternity lasts a year or two, not fifty. But as one who has
recovered from smallpox fifty years before still bears its
marks on his face although he may have forgotten the pain
of the disease, so she bore in her own oppressed life now
the wounds of a bitter disappointment that had become
almost part of history, so much a part, in fact, that its
fiftieth anniversary was being celebrated officially.

Until today, on the rare occasions when she thought over
what had happened at Donnafugata that distant summer,
she had felt upheld by a sense of being martyred, being
wronged, of resentment against a father who had neglected
her, of torturing emotion for that other dead man. Now,
however, these second-hand feelings which had formed the
skeleton of her whole mode of thought were also collaps-
ing. There had been no enemies, just one single adversary,
herself; her future had been killed by her own impru-
dence, by the rash Salina pride; and now, just at the moment when her memories had come alive again after so
many years, she found herself even without the solace of

being able to blame her own unhappiness on others, a solace which is the last deceiving philter of the desperate.

If Tassoni had told the truth, then the long hours spent in savoring her hatred before her father's picture, her hiding of every photograph of Tancredi so as not to be forced to hate him too, had been stupidity—worse, cruel injustice; and she suffered now at the memory of Tancredi's warmth and imploring tone as he had begged his uncle to allow him into that convent; they had been words of love toward her, words not understood, put to flight by her pride, which at her harshness had drawn back with their tails between their legs like whipped puppies. From the timeless depth of her being a black pain came welling to spatter her all over at that revelation of the truth.

But was it the truth? Nowhere has truth so short a life as in Sicily; a fact has scarcely happened five minutes before its genuine kernel has vanished, been camouflaged, embellished, disfigured, squashed, annihilated by imagination and self-interest; shame, fear, generosity, malice, opportunism, charity, all the passions, good as well as evil, fling themselves onto the fact and tear it to pieces; very soon it has vanished altogether. And poor Concetta was hoping to find the truth of feelings that had never been expressed but only glimpsed half a century before! The truth no longer existed. Precarious fact, though, had been replaced by irrefutable pain.

Meanwhile Angelica and the Senator were driving the short distance back to Villa Falconeri. Tassoni was worried. "Angelica," he said (they had had a very short affair thirty years before, and kept the intimacy—for which there is no substitute—conferred by a few hours spent between the same pair of sheets), "I'm afraid I disturbed your cousin in some way; did you notice how silent she was toward the end of the visit? I hope I didn't, she's such a dear."

"I should think you have hurt her, Vittorio," said Angelica, exasperated by a double though imaginary jealousy; "she was madly in love with Tancredi; but he never took any notice of her." And so a new layer of soil fell on the tumulus of truth.

The Cardinal of Palermo was a truly holy man; and even now that he has been dead for a long time his charity and his faith are still remembered. While he was alive, though, things were different: he was not a Sicilian, he was not even a Southerner or a Roman, and many years before he had tried to leaven with Northern activity the inert and heavy dough of the island's spiritual life in general and the clergy's in particular. Flanked by two or three secretaries from his own parts, he had deluded himself, those first years, that he could remove abuses and clear the soil of its more obvious stumbling blocks. But soon he had to realize that he was, as it were, firing into cotton wool; the little hole made at the moment was covered after a few seconds by thousands of tiny fibers, and all remained as before, the only additions being cost of powder, ridicule at useless effort, and deterioration of material. Like everyone who, in those days, wanted to change anything in the Sicil-

ian character, he had soon acquired the reputation of being
a fool (which in the circumstances was exact) and had to
content himself with works of charity, which, however, di-
minished his popularity still further if they involved those
benefited in making the slightest effort, such as, for instance,
having to come themselves to the Archiepiscopal palace.

So the aged prelate who set out on the morning of the
fourteenth of May to visit Villa Salina was a good man
but a disillusioned one, who had in the end assumed toward
those in his own diocese an attitude of contemptuous pity
(which was sometimes, after all, unjust). This made him
adopt brusque and cutting ways that dragged him even further into the swamps of unpopularity.

The three Salina sisters were as we know deeply offended
by the inspection of their chapel; but, childish and above all
feminine in mind, they also drew a certain undeniable satisfaction from the thought of receiving in their home a
Prince of the Church, at being able to show him the grandeur of the Salinas which in good faith they thought still
intact, and above all at seeing a kind of sumptuous red bird
moving around their rooms for half an hour, and admiring
the varied and harmonizing hues of its differing purples
and its heavy shot silk. But the poor creatures were destined
to be disappointed even of this last modest hope. When,
having descended the external staircase, they saw His
Eminence get out of his carriage, they realized that he was
in informal dress. Only the tiny purple buttons on the
severe black cassock indicated his high rank; in spite of his
expression of injured goodness, the Cardinal was no more

imposing than the Archpriest of Donnafugata. He was polite but cold, and mingled almost too ably a show of respect for the Salina name and the individual virtues of the ladies themselves with a contempt for their inept and formalist devotions. To the Vicar-General's exclamations about the beauty of the decorations in the rooms through which they passed he did not answer a word; he refused to accept any of the refreshments prepared for him ("Thank you, Signorina, only a little water; today is the eve of my Holy Patron's feast day"), he did not even sit down. He went to the chapel, genuflected a second before the Madonna of Pompeii, made a hurried inspection of the relics. Then he blessed with pastoral benignity the mistresses of the house and the servants kneeling in the entrance hall, and said to Concetta, who bore on her face the signs of a sleepless night, "Signorina, no Divine Service can be held in the chapel for three or four days, but I will see that it is reconsecrated as soon as possible. It seems to me that the picture of the Madonna of Pompeii might well take the place of the one now above the altar, which can join the fine works of art I have admired while passing through your rooms. As for the relics, I am leaving behind Don Pacchiotti, my secretary and a most competent priest; he will examine the documents and tell you the results of his researches; and what he decides will be as if I had decided it myself."

Benignly he let everyone kiss his ring, then got into the heavy carriage together with his small suite.

The carriages had not yet reached the Falconeri turn before Carolina with cheeks taut and darting eyes exclaimed, "This Pope must be a Turk," while Caterina had to be given smelling salts. Meanwhile Concetta was chatting calmly with Don Pacchiotti, who had in the end accepted a cup of coffee and a *baba*.

Then the priest asked for the keys to the case of documents, requested permission, and withdrew into the chapel, after first taking from his bag a small hammer and saw, a screw driver, a magnifying glass, and a couple of pencils. He had been a pupil of the Vatican School of Paleography; also, he was Piedmontese. His labors were long and meticulous; the servants who passed by the chapel door heard the knocks of a hammer, squeaking screws, and sighs. Three hours later he emerged with his cassock full of dust and his hands black, but with a pleased look and a serene expression on his bespectacled face. He apologized for carrying a big wicker basket. "I took the liberty of appropriating this to put in what I'd discarded. May I set it down here?" And he placed his burden in a corner; it was overflowing with torn papers and cards, little boxes containing bits of bone and gristle. "I am happy to say that I have found five relics which are perfectly authentic and worthy of being objects of devotion. The rest are there," he said, pointing at the basket. "Would you tell me, Signorina, where I may brush myself and wash my hands?"

Five minutes later he reappeared and dried his hands on a big towel on the border of which pranced a Leopard in red drawn-thread work. "I forgot to tell you that the frames are all set out on a table in the chapel; some of them

are really lovely." He said goodbye. "Ladies, my respects."
But Caterina refused to kiss his hand.

"And what are we to do with the things in the basket?"

"Just whatever you like, ladies; keep them or throw
them on the rubbish heap; they have no value whatsoever." And when Concetta wanted to order a carriage to
drive him back, he said, "Don't worry about that, Signorina;
I'll have lunch with the Oratorians a few steps away; I
don't need a thing." And putting his instruments back into
his bag, he went off on light feet.

Concetta withdrew into her room; she felt no emotion
whatsoever; she seemed to be living in a world known to
her yet strange, which had already ceded all the impulses
it could give her and now consisted only of pure forms. The
portrait of her father was just a few square inches of can-
vas, the green cases were just a few square yards of wood.
A short while later she was brought a letter. The envelope
had a black seal with a big coronet in relief.

*"Darling Concetta, I've heard of His Eminence's visit
and am so glad a few relics could be saved. I hope to get
the Vicar-General to come and say the first Mass in the
reconsecrated chapel. Senator Tassoni is leaving tomorrow
and recommends himself to your* bon souvenir. *I'll be coming over to visit you soon. Meanwhile, a warm embrace to
you and to Carolina and Caterina too.*

"Yours ever, Angelica."

Still she could feel nothing; the inner emptiness was complete; but she did sense an unpleasant atmosphere emanating from the heap of fur. That was today's distress: even poor Bendicò was hinting at bitter memories. She rang the bell. "Annetta," she said, "this dog has really become too moth-eaten and dusty. Take it out and throw it away."

As the carcass was dragged off, the glass eyes stared at her with the humble reproach of things that are thrown away, that are being annulled. A few minutes later what remained of Bendicò was flung into a corner of the courtyard visited every day by the dustman. During the flight down from the window his form recomposed itself for an instant; in the air one could have seen dancing a quadruped with long whiskers, and its right foreleg seemed to be raised in imprecation. Then all found peace in a heap of livid dust.

The End

Born in Palermo in 1896, Giuseppe di Lampedusa was a cosmopolitan Sicilian prince who married a Baltic noblewoman and had lived in London and Paris, but who nevertheless was tied strongly to the island of his birth. He knew several languages well and had read in the original the best of all European literature. In his palace in Palermo he met regularly with a group of young friends to study French literature, and, to the last, his days were spent in readings and discussions with his wife and friends.

For twenty-five years Lampedusa meditated a novel based on the figure of his paternal great-grandfather and set in Sicily during the Garibaldian era. Yet he was sixty before he finally began to write it, and he completed it only a few months before his death. Shortly before he died in 1957, he was told by an Italian editor that his novel was unpublishable. It was not until many months later that an unsigned copy of his manuscript reached an enthusiastic editor, whose prompt inquiries brought to light the story behind the prince who never published anything in his lifetime, but left a masterpiece after his death.

PANTHEON MODERN WRITERS ORIGINALS

THE VICE-CONSUL

by Marguerite Duras, translated from the French by Eileen Ellenbogen

The first American edition ever of the novel Marguerite Duras considers her best—a tale of passion and desperation set in India and Southeast Asia.

"A masterful novel."—*Chicago Tribune*

      0-394-55898-7 cloth, $10.95   0-394-75026-8 paper, $6.95

MAPS

by Nuruddin Farah

The unforgettable story of one man's coming of age in the turmoil of modern Africa.

"A true and rich work of art. . . . [by] one of the finest contemporary African writers."

      —Salman Rushdie

      0-394-56325-5 cloth, $11.95   0-394-75548-0 paper, $7.95

DREAMING JUNGLES

by Michel Rio, translated from the French by William Carlson

A brilliant, hypnotic novel about an elegant French scientist who sets off to study chimpanzees in turn-of-the-century Africa, and his shattering confrontation with the jungle, passion, and at last, himself.

"Very beautiful and very witty."—Mark Strand

      0-394-55661-5 cloth, $10.95   0-394-75035-7 paper, $6.95

BURNING PATIENCE

by Antonio Skármeta, translated from the Spanish by Katherine Silver

A charming story about the friendship that develops between Pablo Neruda, Latin America's greatest poet, and the postman who stops to receive his advice about love.

"The mix of the fictional and the real is masterful, and . . . gives the book its special appeal and brilliance."   —*Christian Science Monitor*

      0-394-55576-7 cloth, $10.95   0-394-75033-0 paper, $6.95

YOU CAN'T GET LOST IN CAPE TOWN

by Zoë Wicomb

Nine short stories powerfully evoke a young black woman's upbringing in South Africa.

"A superb first collection."—*The New York Times Book Review*

      0-394-56030-2 cloth, $10.95   0-394-75309-7 paper, $6.95

THE LEOPARD

by Giuseppe di Lampedusa, translated from the Italian by Archibald Colquhoun

The world-renowned novel of a Sicilian prince and his world, the turbulent Italy of the 1860s.

"The genius of its author and the thrill it gives the reader are probably for all time."
—*The New York Times Book Review*
0-394-74949-9 paper, $7.95

YOUNG TÖRLESS

by Robert Musil, translated from the German
by Eithne Williams and Ernst Kaiser

A classic novel by the author of *The Man Without Qualities,* about students at an Austrian military academy and their abuse of power—physical, emotional, and sexual.

"An illumination of the dark places of the heart." —*The Washington Post*
0-394-71015-0 paper, $6.95

ADIEUX: A FAREWELL TO SARTRE

by Simone de Beauvoir, translated from the French by Patrick O'Brian

Simone de Beauvoir's moving farewell to Jean-Paul Sartre: "an intimate, personal, and honest portrait of a relationship unlike any other in literary history." —Deirdre Bair
0-394-72898-X paper, $8.95

THE BLOOD OF OTHERS

by Simone de Beauvoir,
translated from the French by Roger Senhouse and Yvonne Moyse

A brilliant existentialist novel about the French resistance, "with a remarkably sustained note of suspense and mounting excitement." —*Saturday Review*
0-394-72411-9 paper, $7.95

A VERY EASY DEATH

by Simone de Beauvoir, translated from the French by Patrick O'Brian

The profoundly moving, day-by-day account of the death of the author's mother.

"A beautiful book, sincere and sensitive."—Pierre-Henri Simon
0-394-72899-8 paper, $4.95

WHEN THINGS OF THE SPIRIT COME FIRST:
FIVE EARLY TALES

by Simone de Beauvoir, translated from the French by Patrick O'Brian

The first paperback edition of the marvelous early fiction of Simone de Beauvoir.

"An event for celebration."—*The New York Times Book Review*
0-394-72235-3 paper, $6.95

THE WOMAN DESTROYED

by Simone de Beauvoir, translated from the French by Patrick O'Brian

Three powerful stories of women in crisis by the legendary novelist and feminist.

"Immensely intelligent stories about the decay of passion."
—*The* [London] *Sunday Times*
0-394-71103-3 paper, $7.95

Ask at your local bookstore for other Pantheon Modern Writers titles